STORMS IN AMETHIR
BOOK 5

STEPHANIE A. CAIN

Also by Stephanie A. Cain

Sow the Wind
Fire Soul

Storms in Amethir

Stormsinger
Stormshadow
Stormseer
The Weather War
Shroudling

Storms in Amethir Holiday Novellas

The Midwinter Royal

Circle City Magic (urban fantasy)

Shades of Circle City
Circle City Psychic

With Other Authors

Equus (Rhonda Parrish's Magical Menageries #5)
E is for Evil
F is for Fairy
G is for Ghost

If you would like to receive updates on new fiction, please join my monthly email newsletter list. I give newsletter subscribers first look at everything I do!

*For Tiffany
because ultimately this book
is in honor of best friends*

Contents

Northshore Keep
Simiri
Darkwell
Sandswamp
Ranarr
Dalasan
The Shield
The Blades
Glanyrafon
Firebend
Shrouded Realm
Stony Lonesome
Estermere
Gehb River
Longdale
Maron
Raven Hill
Jorey
Harkenerth
Glimmerguard
Cragmond
Brinepond
Anderly
Southbury
Steelhallow
Swordfish Island

Chapter One

VYX STOOD ON THE city's tall stone wall and stared out across the rolling foothills, imagining the out-landers amassing there. She didn't yet know how large their army was, but she had scouts ranging out farther than their lookout posts. By dusk, she should have some idea of the enemy's numbers.

The sun hadn't lifted above the horizon, but it was close. Mist shrouded the shadowed hills, and Vyx whispered a plea to the spirits. She had little talent for mist-calling, which was why she was warleader and her brother the high priest, but all of her people had enough affinity with the spirits to request it.

"You don't have to do this," Danae said quietly from behind her.

Vyx didn't turn to look at her queen. They had been through all this, time and again. They both knew it was necessary. They both knew it was inevitable. The peace treaties had been broken. The negotiations had failed. Danae would lead the remnants of their people into the mountains, and Vyx would stay behind to cut off pursuit.

"I will miss you, old friend," Vyx said, letting her lips curl in a small smile. She removed her helmet, tucking it carefully under her arm to avoid crushing the raven feather in its crest. "Watch over my brother and my daughter. Zera isn't happy about being ordered to evacuate."

"She's earned her rank, quite independently of you. It's only reasonable she should wish to be part of the defense of Silverdene." Danae stepped up to stand beside Vyx. The queen, clad in worn leather armor, had braided her hair back away from her face, exposing her valemal, the intricate tattoos across her forehead and cheeks.

Lightly armored warriors would travel more quickly than the outland invaders. It was why Vyx had all of the heavy cavalry under her command.

"It is only reasonable she should take honor in guarding the queen and high priest," Vyx countered, and Danae chuckled. They'd been over all this before, as well. The queen brushed her lips against her warleader's cheek.

"She knows her duty. You raised her well."

Vyx sighed. "The message riders have their orders. They'll carry word between us as long as the way is clear, but even if *you stop receiving our messages, don't turn back. Switch to the ravens."*

"You underestimate my resolve." Danae smiled teasingly, but her deep purple eyes were sad.

Vyx shook her head. "Farewell, my queen." When she would have bowed, Danae pulled her into a tight hug.

"Farewell, my warleader," Danae whispered. "May the goddess strengthen your hand and the spirits fight beside you."

Vyx hugged her, then released her and took a step back. "And may the goddess guide your feet and the spirits speed you."

She didn't leave her position as Danae went down to join her troops. She did turn to watch her go, though, and tried to look as if her heart weren't being pulled out through her clenched teeth. Her best and oldest friend, her brother, her daughter—all the family Vyx had left in this world—were riding out of Silverdene to the deep fastness in the mountains. Her throat burned with the knowledge that she would never see any of them again.

Zera led the queen's vanguard; Vyx recognized her daughter's white-and-gold-edged green cloak even from this distance. Vyx saw the horsemen of the vanguard tighten their formation, sitting straighter in their saddles, as the queen swung up onto the back of her gray. For three long breaths, Vyx feared her daughter wouldn't even bid her farewell. Then the tall, slim figure turned in the saddle and lifted a hand in salute.

Vyx lifted her own arm and held it there, even after her daughter turned away and shouted a command to her troops. As one, they leapt into motion, riding for the gates.

As they passed through it, a large troop of infantry began marching for the gate.

After them came wagons, and behind the wagons were those citizens who could walk. More soldiers waited to guard the column's rear. Vyx heard the complaint of cattle being prodded into motion, the braying of mules, the indiscernible shouts of hundreds of people. She drew in a long, slow breath.

The evacuation of Silverdene had begun.

Chapter Two

Zolin Leite shifted in his seat, trying to mask the motion in case Master Inkeri noticed and reprimanded him for fidgeting. The classroom was warm despite the windows that were flung open to catch any sea breeze. A lazy heat and growing humidity filled the room.

To his right, his best friend, Naia Sedorr, scribbled notes frantically. With her head ducked, she looked studious, but Zolin knew better. Naia disliked Master Inkeri fiercely, and it took all her control to keep it disguised. The Diplomat trainees were here to learn discipline, equanimity, and calm. Whatever turmoil they felt on the inside, by now they should all know how to hide it behind an impassive mask.

"So. With all we have discussed, what is the lesson of Tamnen and Strid's Kalischad Truce?" Master Inkeri stood still at the front of the classroom. She clasped her hands loosely in front of her in a posture of waiting. Her smooth face betrayed none of her thoughts as her gaze went first to one Diplomat trainee and then to the next.

Zolin scraped his tongue lightly against his lower teeth. He hoped Naia wouldn't volunteer an answer. Master Inkeri wouldn't want the sort of answer Naia would give. They were so close to the ceremony where they would petition for menteeship. Naia just needed to hold her tongue a few months more.

"Anyone?" Inkeri was a short, muscular woman. Her brown hair was cropped close around her head, her skin the chalky-gray of a native Ranarri. She encouraged her pupils to interact with their lessons, to draw their own conclusions. She just never seemed to like the conclusions Naia drew.

"Not to lose battles," drawled Evfra from near the back of the room. Zolin bit back a grin. Only Evfra could get away with such a response in Inkeri's class.

If it amused Inkeri, she didn't show it. "Certainly the superficial mind would assume so," she said. Her voice was flat, even pleasant, but it was a reprimand.

Zolin looked down at his own notes, groping for something to volunteer. If he spoke up, perhaps Naia wouldn't feel the need to. He felt his best friend's gaze on his face, but he flipped back one page in his notebook, ignoring her.

The silence stretched thick as a blanket over the room. Beyond the open windows, gulls cried and westerly wind whistled but didn't reach the classroom. They would have rough weather tonight, if the wind told true.

"Trainee Sedorr." Inkeri's voice broke into Zolin's reverie. Her voice was almost gentle, which made the hair on Zolin's neck prickle. He didn't like the way Naia disrespected Inkeri, but he also didn't like it when Inkeri seemed to bully Naia. "What do you conclude to be the deeper lesson of the Kalischad Truce?"

Zolin's gaze flickered over to Naia's, heavy with warning. *Only six months until the choosing at Midwinter. Bite your tongue, keep your head down, and don't antagonize Inkeri.*

Too late, he thought of what he should have volunteered aloud. The lesson was that revenge hurt those who took it, as well as those who received it. Or perhaps it was an economic lesson—that Strid had expended so many resources retaking the mines that it was too costly a victory, if not completely pointless. He sucked in a breath, heart pounding as he prepared to interrupt.

Before he could speak, Naia blurted, "That even Diplomats make mistakes."

The words thudded into the silence like arrows into a target. Suddenly the room felt void of air, like the moments before a squall struck. Zolin froze, glaring at Naia. Someone behind them shifted with the faint whisper of cloth.

Inkeri's expression didn't change, though Zolin was certain the master's knuckles whitened for just an instant. But Inkeri only said, "Continue."

Naia straightened in her seat. Zolin wanted to groan at the way it showed her anxiety. "Master Revalis is a highly respected Diplomat, and with good reason," she began.

"He has many successes among the Amethirian expatriates living here in Ranarr, and he has demonstrated a clear understanding of the people of Tamnen. But he underestimated the Strid."

Zolin sucked in a slow breath. Inkeri didn't speak, but she gestured for Naia to continue.

Naia lifted her chin, and Zolin's anxiety bloomed into anger. Why did she *always* have to turn class discussions into confrontations with Inkeri?

"King Harkai was determined to wrest control of the mines away from King Marsede, no matter what the cost. A reasonable ruler would balk at how many of his people died in the fighting. A reasonable ruler would realize the expenditure of gold and food would take a toll on all his people, not just his soldiers. A reasonable ruler would come to the negotiating table willingly—if not before armed conflict began, at least after losing several battles in a row."

Naia cleared her throat and continued, her voice clear, "King Harkai is not a reasonable ruler. Master Revalis forgot that."

Inkeri was studying Naia's face almost openly. Zolin wondered if she had finally reached the end of her incredible patience. She usually held her expression and body language in an iron grip, but even she must slip from time to time.

"A very interesting assessment," Inkeri said at last. She flicked a glance past Naia's face. "Wouldn't you agree, Master Revalis?"

Hot shame flooded through Zolin on behalf of his friend. Had Revalis been there the whole time, listening to her criticism? Of all the Master Diplomats, Revalis was the one everyone wanted to choose them. He was in his forties, the veteran of dozens of negotiations and peace treaties. And Naia had just insulted him.

Zolin closed his eyes slowly, not wanting to witness this.

He heard footsteps as Revalis walked up to stand at the front of the classroom. After a moment, he couldn't resist looking. The master's blue eyes were steady on Naia's face. He was tall and skinny, almost lanky; when he stood still, he resembled a heron hunting in the shallows. But his voice held only pleasant curiosity as he said, "Please elaborate."

Naia cleared her throat again, and Zolin again wanted to smack her. She was as discomposed as a first year! "Master Revalis," Naia said, "it is well known that King Harkai is unstable. If he is not mad, he is at least prone to rages and revels far beyond what is acceptable. His mind is changeable, and even when he has signed his name to an agreement, he doesn't shy away from breaking it. Knowing all that, knowing that he is no stranger to trickery, knowing how much both nations value the Kalischad Mines... Why didn't you anticipate the predawn strike?"

Revalis showed no reaction to her words, damning as they were. Strid's soldiers had attacked the sleeping Tamnese camp before dawn. Hundreds had been killed, not only soldiers but civilian camp workers too. King Marsede had lost a nephew, and the entire peace process had fallen apart.

"What makes you think I didn't anticipate it?" Revalis asked steadily.

Naia faltered only a moment. "Then you had planned for that? Why didn't you warn Marsede?"

Sleeping gods, Naia, shut up. Zolin wished he dared kick her, but any such motion would be clearly visible to everyone in the classroom.

"A Diplomat does not exist to take sides in a disagreement." Revalis spoke slowly but without hesitation. "A Diplomat exists to see all possible outcomes, to review all relevant laws and agreements, and to render a just judgment between two feuding parties."

"So that justifies letting all those people die? Sacrificing them just to be neutral? That's even worse!" Naia burst out.

"Oh, well done," murmured a woman's voice from behind them. Zolin saw Naia twitch minutely, but to her credit, her attention stayed on Master Revalis. Shirin had pitched her comment so it didn't carry beyond her victim's ears.

Still, it would infuriate Naia. She disliked Shirin even more than she disliked Inkeri.

"You interrupt a Master?" Inkeri's voice had chilled. Diplomats were all but forbidden to exhibit any emotion in public, but exerting authority was a vital function of every Diplomat.

"My deepest apologies, Master Revalis," Naia said. "I should not have interrupted."

"You should not have," he agreed mildly. "You should also extend your apologies to Master Inkeri, Trainee. Your behavior has disrupted her lesson."

Naia inclined her torso slightly to Inkeri. "My apologies, Master Inkeri," she said.

Deepest, Zolin thought in despair. *My deepest apologies.* She'd insulted Inkeri by offering her less of an apology than she offered to Revalis.

Inkeri made a dismissive gesture. Her face was impassive again, but her gaze was hard on Naia's face. "You will never get anywhere with lazy reasoning, Naia. No—not *reasoning* at all. *Feeling*." Her voice sent a chill down Zolin's spine. "Your argument is dismissed." She turned away. "Who else—"

"My entire position is dismissed because of emotion?" Naia burst out. "There is reason in emotion. There are reasons *for* emotions."

Zolin closed his eyes again. *Shut up shut up shut up.*

"Have you spent six years in training to ignore the most basic tenets of our practice? Diplomats are impassive. Diplomats are creatures of reason, first and foremost. What part of this do you misunderstand, Trainee Naia?" Inkeri's voice was very cold now.

Gods save him, Zolin was going to lecture her within an inch of her patience once they were in private. What in the deepest hells did she think she would accomplish by arguing with Inkeri like this? Especially with Master Revalis as witness? At this rate, she was going to be thrown out of the training program and condemned to spend her life scaling fish for the kitchens.

Naia's voice shook as she said, "I concede my question was irrational and based on emotion." After a moment, her voice steadied. "But should a Diplomat throw out the day's catch along with the chum? Emotions communicate what people value. Emotions communicate what people fear. Observing and judging a party's emotions can be a useful tool for Diplomats. One fleck of emotion does not taint the whole."

"That 'fleck' of emotion is a flaw," Inkeri snapped. Then she drew herself back in. "That flaw weakens your entire position in the same way a notch in a sword's blade weakens the whole weapon. Would you expect a warrior to fight with a flawed blade? Then as a Diplomat, you should not wield a flawed argument."

Shirin snorted behind them. "Well done, Naia. I'll take your rank yet."

Zolin sucked in a breath, opening his eyes. He avoided looking at Naia, knowing her face would be red even if she'd managed to control her expression. "Perhaps an analytical deconstruction of the emotions involved," he began, but Inkeri clapped her hands once, cutting him off.

"Enough discussion. This conversation is uncontrolled and will not continue. For our next class, you will all copy out the Kalischad Truce with annotations supporting the settlement that was finally reached." She left the classroom, her steps brisk.

Zolin let out a slow, silent sigh. He wasn't sure if his heart would settle down before supper after all this. He knew Shirin would be waiting to deliver a sweetly helpful critique of Naia's performance. Just last year, such a critique would be more helpful than cutting, but this year Shirin spoke as if she drank poison instead of coffee every morning. He wasn't sure what had prompted the change—perhaps it was just that they'd reached their final year of training and Naia was still ranked higher than Shirin—but he couldn't stomach a confrontation between those two after what had just gone on. He took Naia's arm as they prepared to leave the classroom.

Fortunately, Evfra had anticipated the same thing. As Shirin moved to engage with them, Evfra popped out of his seat, much faster than he was wont to move. He was a big man, usually slow to act, with an easy-going mien. But he and Shirin had been close, before this year, and he knew her better than anyone. Besides that, he was the top male trainee, trading class rank with Naia on a regular basis. Shirin wouldn't alienate him without very good reason.

Zolin didn't forget himself so much as to shoot Evfra a grateful look, but he wouldn't forget the gesture. Unfortunately, neither of them could prevent Master Revalis from intercepting Naia.

The older man stood in the doorway, lifting one eyebrow in a summons.

Zolin loosened his grasp on Naia's arm, but kept pace with her as they approached the master. His stomach jumped a little. Hopefully Master Revalis wouldn't think Zolin's actions indicated that he agreed with her assessment of the Kalischad Truce. Though, truth be told, Zolin *did* wonder why Revalis had gone through with it, when it should have been clear to him that it would come to such tragedy.

Revalis' voice was gentle, pitched only for them. "Mind your emotions, Trainee Sedorr." Zolin almost imagined a softening at the corners of his mouth as he looked at her. "You have a fine mind, if you can tame that temper. Your criticisms were well founded, and part of why I nearly annulled the treaty."

He nodded to them and walked away, leaving Zolin gaping after him.

Naia almost ignored the set of Zolin's shoulders as he led the way to his room. His posture told her without words that he intended for her to follow him. He was so good at managing his body language, somehow hiding his emotions while guiding others to do exactly what he wanted.

He wanted to get her in private so he could scold her for what had just happened, that much was obvious. The irony was that he didn't need to; she was going to be scolding herself for the rest of the night.

And that infuriated her.

Why should she be so upset about speaking her mind? Why should she have to tiptoe around topics in the classes where they were supposed to be *learning* something about being Diplomats? Why should the trainees censor themselves instead of asking open questions and getting honest answers from the masters in response?

Despite the churning in her stomach, she followed, because it wouldn't be worth the argument they would have later if she tried to avoid it now.

As soon as the door to his room was closed behind them, Zolin whirled on her. "What were you thinking?" He glared at Naia for several moments and then stalked over to the window.

Naia folded her arms across her chest and widened her stance a little. She had to stiffen her back to keep from leaning defensively against the door. "I was thinking I should answer the question."

"You didn't have to give an answer that insulted one Diplomat and offended another." Zolin leaned his forearms on the windowsill, gazing out to sea.

"You think I should have lied?" Naia's stomach was still churning, and now her heart was beating hard. It was one thing to disappoint or infuriate the masters. It was something else entirely to argue with her best friend.

"I think you could have been more politic! Isn't that what we're supposed to be learning?" Zolin broke off and drew in a long, slow breath through his nose. He would have closed his eyes, as well. It was a calming technique, and for just a second Naia hated him, because she knew it would work.

When he turned to face her again, his brown eyes seemed clearer. "You know I admire honesty, Naia," he said, his voice level. "But a Diplomat must occasionally twist the truth, or even employ half-truths. And you know that."

It was why Zolin was a better Diplomat trainee than she was, Naia thought miserably. She set her jaw and glared back at him, but her anger felt foolish in the face of his tranquil expression.

"At least I'm brave enough to tell the truth," she muttered.

"Bravery and stupidity often look very much alike," Zolin snapped. Perversely, that made Naia feel just a little better. He hadn't completely dismissed his anger; he'd just masked it.

After a moment he sighed. "Oh, sit down. I'll brew some tea. We could both use it, I daresay." Zolin went to his spirit burner and fiddled with it. "I would have talked about the economic ramifications, if Master Inkeri had called on me. I didn't even think of how the Diplomats should have anticipated the predawn strike."

"Inkeri's going to have me expelled," Naia blurted, dropping onto a stool.

"Don't be ridiculous." Zolin measured an astringent-smelling tea mixture into two cups, eyed Naia's posture, and added another spoon to one cup. "We're almost through our training. You know the coursework. You're a genius with maps, you're miles better at strategy and tactics than Jousia, and you've got as thorough an understanding of all the major powers as Evfra. Besides, Master Revalis *did* say your criticisms were sound."

A wash of fondness went through Naia. It didn't matter how strongly they disagreed, she could never stay angry with Zolin for long. He wasn't just a good Diplomat, he was a good person.

As they waited for the water to heat, Zolin fidgeted, brushed his hair out of his eyes, and then shrugged his shoulders a couple of times. "I hate the days we don't have weapons training. Especially if there's been unpleasantness. By the end of the day, I feel like ants are crawling down my back."

"Ick." Naia flicked her nail against his arm. "Don't talk about creepy crawlies, you know I hate them as much as you hate fish." She tilted her head. "Kind of funny, you living on an island and being scared of fish."

"They feel gross." Zolin lifted his small kettle off the burner and poured lukewarm water into their cups to brew it at the customary tepid temperature. "They don't taste gross, though," he added in satisfaction. "Mm, fish rolls and seedcakes."

"But doesn't it bother you, knowing they're slimy and scaly before they get sliced up?" Naia asked innocently.

Zolin rolled his eyes. "Now you're just being rude on purpose," he said.

"I think I'm funny. What is this tea, anyway, Zo? It's nice, but it has sort of a musty taste at the back of it."

Zolin lifted his chin. "Sootheroot, queen's healer, and hawthorne." He looked sideways at her. "It's a calming blend."

It was Naia's turn to roll her eyes. "Just wait until you find fish scales in your satchel some day when you're least expecting it," she threatened, but her words were idle. Zolin was good at blending herbs and spices together; it wasn't magic—Diplomats didn't *do* magic, they just studied its political uses—but it might as well be, in her opinion.

Zolin relaxed when Naia took out her embroidery and began picking at it with her needle. It wasn't a mere pastime, but a means of sending coded communications to other Diplomats. After watching her for a while, admiring the intent way she bent her dark head to her work, Zolin reached for his sketchbook. He would do an ink portrait of her as part of his communications and recording portfolio.

"What happens if you wash out?" Zolin had wanted to be a Diplomat as long as he could remember. As a child, he had been fascinated by the simple brown and tan robes, deep cowls, wide sashes, and general air of serenity worn by

Diplomatic Corps members. As he grew older and learned how important Diplomats were, he yearned to find a place with them.

Now, nearly twenty, Zolin was in what he hoped would be his final year of trainee status. He planned to petition for a menteeship at Midwinter. But he had been feeling woefully unprepared to make his declaration at the Autumn Evener ahead of that. If only he were better at paying attention to details.

"If you wash out, you become a beggar greeting traders on the Ranarr docks." Naia's voice was even and somewhat abstract as she delivered the statement. It was a game the trainees often played, hurling appalling insults and horrible hypothetical situations at each other while simultaneously suppressing their reactions. It had been designed as a training exercise, of course, but it was also just fun.

"Such an ignominious fall," he replied. "Are you certain I might not fetch up against barkeep or fish-monger on the way down?" He kept his tone as dry as possible, but he couldn't tell if his amusement was creeping into it.

"You'll be fortunate not to plummet completely into the mud-flats as a drunken trash-picker."

Zolin clenched his lips together against a chuckle. He envied the serenity on her face, the steadiness of her gaze on her thread. She was younger than he by an entire year. How was she so good at the stoic banter when he still struggled with it?

"Better that than working a stall in the market," he countered, and then realized his mistake as her gaze lifted to his. Her dark eyes flashed with forbidden anger, despite the calm of her expression. Zolin clicked his tongue in apology. "Point to you," he conceded. He'd made a personal attack, and he ought to know better. Naia's parents had been killed in a dockside accident when she was very young. Her father's brother had taken her in, and she had grown up working in his market stall. She had joined the Diplomat training to escape that life.

Diplomats were expected to take note of every weak spot and exploit as much as was necessary, but they were not expected to sink to ad hominem attacks. That was beneath them. Besides, ad hominem attacks never settled true disagreements, and might create deeper tension where none had existed before.

Naia sniffed and turned her gaze back to her needlework. Her fingers darted through complicated knots, switching colors effortlessly with several needles in play. She was probably stitching an appalling insult in retaliation, though he might not be able to read it. Naia's needlework was more advanced than his.

Then again, much of his academic work was ahead of hers, except for geography. Maps conveyed little to Zolin, who had never traveled beyond the shores of the White Stone. But Naia could spend hours poring over the little, hand-colored book of maps that had been her parents' last gift to her.

As the silence stretched between them, Zolin began to wonder if he had mis-stepped more seriously than he realized. Naia had scored the last point; tradition held that she be allowed the opening salvo of the next barrage. But she only plied her needle without speaking, and he could tell she was nibbling at the inside of her lip. He could claim a point for provoking a physical tell, but he was still ashamed of the market stall dig. He trimmed his pen, dipped it in his ink, and drew the long, slow stroke of her cheekbone down to her jaw.

It felt like a very long time before Naia finally said, "What would you want to do? If you couldn't be a Diplomat, I mean." She kept her head down, eyes tightly focused on her work.

Zolin took in a slow breath, trying to keep from making a sound. After six years of friendship, Naia knew him better than anyone. It suddenly struck him as odd that they'd never had this discussion before. Perhaps neither of them wanted to consider a future without each other. Their friendship had been immediate and easy from the moment they met. They might quarrel at times, but they always supported each other.

He took his time before answering, adding shading beneath the portrait's jaw. "I don't know," he admitted finally. He'd never wanted to marry, though Diplomats could. He definitely didn't want to father children. He knew he would be welcome back in his fisher family, but would he be happy there?

"Perhaps I should open a stall in the market," he said finally. He held up the sketch for her inspection, allowing a faint grin. "I could sell portraits."

Naia glanced at the portrait, raised a single eyebrow in acknowledgment, and looked back at her needlework. Her lips curved faintly.

"And you'd be a cartographer, I suppose," Zolin went on. "You could travel to all those places you've read about in books and correct all the mistakes in your book of maps. Maybe you'd even explore places no one else has been." His grin widened. "Maybe you'll find where the Shroudlings came from when they attacked Amethir last time. Or find

an undiscovered island somewhere, full of mythical creatures."

He saw her hands slow at her work as she thought over
his words. Then one hand lifted to tuck her hair behind
her ear, and Zolin felt a pang of guilt. It was another one
of her tells, one she was working hard to eliminate, and it
meant his words had struck deeper than he'd meant. Did
she really think she would wash out? She worked harder
than anyone he knew, harder even than Zolin himself. It
was true that she struggled with emotional control, but she
was a sound strategist and knew their academic material
well. No one could argue she wasn't dedicated. If she could
only control her temper!

"Perhaps I should join the Shadow Diplomats," Zolin
suggested in a low voice. "Then I could be your bodyguard
while you traveled."

She tucked in the corners of her mouth, but it was too
late; he'd seen her smile. Satisfied, he turned his attention back to his sketch. He would work hard to capture a
serene, thoughtful expression on her face, and give her the
portrait as a peace offering.

"But it doesn't matter," he said after a while. "We're both
going to pass our declaration at the Autumn Evener, and
then we'll have mentors lining up to take us on."

Naia didn't reply, but Zolin was watching her closely
enough to detect that her shoulders relaxed. They worked
in silence for the rest of the evening, but it was an easy,
comfortable silence.

Chapter Three

The pre-dawn sky had silvered just at the edge of where the sea met the sky. Arama Dzornaea, soaked and shaking, chilled to her soul, closed her eyes for a moment. They'd lived through the night without being eaten or drowning. But the sirensong had grown more powerful over the few hours since she'd come to.

"What's the point?" Zek whispered. They were the first words anyone had spoken in a long time.

Arama looked over at him, alarmed at the lethargy in his voice.

"Is he injured? Yar! Check him. Is he bleeding any-where?" Her voice wasn't as sharp or authoritative as she would have liked. The night of sirensong and cold had left her shaken along with the ragged remnants of her crew.

"I—I can't quite reach him. I don't see any blood." Yar's words were muffled. "Hey—hold on, Zek!"

She heard a splash, followed by a shout from Yar. Swearing, Arama struggled against the lines that lashed her to the life-buoy. She couldn't get herself untangled, so she could only watch as Yar fell off the bit of flotsam that had kept him afloat. Only then did she realize he was going after Zek. Her first mate must have let himself slip into the water. It was one of the many dangers of sirensong—one Arama still had nightmares about from her first encounter with it.

Kinnet hadn't heard what they said, and it was obvi-ously too dark for her to read lips yet. "What happened?" she demanded loudly. "Don't let go! Qiaru and his folk are coming. They're fighting the seadragons. They'll res-cue us."

After a moment, Zek and Yar both surfaced, splutter-ing and choking. "You damn fool!" Zek shouted. "What did you grab me for?"

"You went in on your own," Yar said. His voice held none of the anger Arama would have felt. "It's something about those sirens. They make you want to give up."

Arama could hear Zek's teeth chattering from several feet away. It was the height of summer, and they could be grateful for that—they might not die of exposure, this time of year. Then again, that just meant they were likely to die being eaten by sirens or seadragons.

"Get back out of the water, both of you," she said. "Kinnet says Qiaru is still trying to reach us."

"Stormsingers don't eat sirens, though," Zek mumbled.

"Come on, Mister Zek. Get yourself out of the water. Yar doesn't know how to swim." Arama forced steel into her voice. To her relief, she saw Zek respond to that. He straightened his shoulders and began shoving Yar up onto the piece of driftwood he'd been balanced on.

"How do you know I can't swim?" Yar demanded.

"You grew up in the desert," Zek said. He sounded clearer, as if he'd shaken off some of the siren-induced somnolence. "Where would you learn to swim?"

"We had canals in Meekin." Yar sounded defensive as he sprawled his gangly, teenage body across the driftwood.

A chittering, hissing shriek rose in the air around them. Arama jerked, unable to hide her reaction from the others. *Sleeping gods damn them,* she thought. *I still have my siren's tooth knife. I'll take as many down with me as I can.*

The siren's tooth knife had been a gift from Lozarr Algot. One of the few men who'd ever tried to see Arama for who she was instead of who he wanted her to be, he'd also shared himself with her until she was unable to resist loving him. Arama touched the hilt of the knife. She couldn't give up now. Lozarr would never forgive her.

A low, throbbing growl, almost a groan, joined in with the shriek. The sirens were getting closer.

"What is that vibration?" Kinnet asked. "Is it normal in this ocean?"

Arama scowled and then realized the light of morning had grown strong enough Kinnet would be able to see her response. She turned to face the stormwitch. "Sirens. They're singing. I'd lay gold that's what you feel. This is one time you're lucky you can't hear." She wondered if a stormwitch would be able to call forth some sort of current in the ocean to drive the sirens away. She'd refused to have a stormwitch on board *Dawn Star* for so many years she didn't remember what all of their skills were.

But then, Kinnet had destroyed all of her seaglass reserves and used up all of her strength just trying to keep *Dawn Star* enough ahead of the storm to keep them from going down. It hadn't worked, just as Kinnet's wife Lijka had been unable to save *Bounder* fifteen years ago. The difference was, this time, Arama had a better understanding of just how hard Kinnet had tried—and just what odds she had been up against.

"I won't make the same mistake twice," she muttered. She licked salt-crusted lips.

"Qiaru!" Kinnet howled. The sudden noise made the others all jump. "No! Stop!"

"What?" Arama tried to propel herself closer to the stormwitch.

"They're killing him!" Kinnet was thrashing her head as if she were in pain. For all that Arama knew, she might be. The bond Kinnet and Qiaru had formed four years ago had always been mysterious.

A screeching went up around them. Something brushed Arama's bare foot under the surface. She jerked in an automatic kick. "The sirens are here!" she shouted, drawing her knife.

"Why bother fighting?" Zek asked. "Let them eat us. It'll be faster than drowning."

"It'll hurt more, too!" Arama snapped.

"Qiaru!" Kinnet howled again. She wasn't looking at Arama, nor was she within arm's reach. Arama couldn't warn her. At least Kinnet's makeshift raft was large enough she didn't have any parts trailing in the water. Maybe the sirens would focus on Arama and Zek long enough for Qiaru to save Kinnet and Yar, at least.

A noise like the creaking of a rusty gate filled the air. The thing that brushed Arama's ankle this time was sharp. She slashed out with her knife, wishing they hadn't tied her to the life-buoy. If she could get free, she could maneuver better and maybe defend the others.

"Don't let go, Zek." Yar's voice was calm but clear in the chaos. "They make you want to give up. But they can't win if you refuse to give up."

Arama, scanning the brightening surface of the water for any threat, flicked a glance at them. Yar had an arm around Zek's neck and chest from behind. The knuckles of his hand were white on Zek's wrist. She'd already known the boy was stronger than he looked.

"Help is coming," Yar said.

Zek slumped back in Yar's hold, sobbing openly. "They'll take everything. They'll eat us all and then the waters will creep ashore and drown everything we've built. We'll be forgotten."

To Arama's shock, Kinnet let out a sob as well. Was she being affected by the sirensong she couldn't even hear? But no—when Arama looked over at her, Kinnet's lips were forming, "Qiaru," over and over.

"Damn this!" Arama shouted. "Come fight me, you coward beasties!"

The sirensong throbbed and swelled, almost as if they understand and were laughing at her. She'd never known just how intelligent sirens were. When *Bounder* went down fifteen years ago, she thought the siren's tooth knife had saved her life. It had almost been as if having that tooth had marked her as a tougher predator than a siren. She had thought there was some respect there. But these sirens didn't seem to care about anything but tormenting her and her friends before they killed them.

She hated this. Give her something to fight. Give her something to *do*. She couldn't *stand* being helpless. Tightening her grip on her siren's tooth knife, she slashed through the lines holding her to the life-buoy. If they wouldn't attack her, she would go under and attack them.

"YES!" Yar's voice was full-throated joy. "Look! Look there!" He was staring to the east.

"What the—" Arama began, but Yar started shouting again.

"Xellax! Xellax! Here!" He was still clinging to Zek with one arm, but the other was waving wildly as if to get someone's attention.

And then, before Arama could turn, the sirensong was drowned out by an ear-splitting roar. Arama clapped her hands to her ears, ducking instinctively. Then she realized what a foolish reaction that was. Xellax—that was the name of Yar's dragon, wasn't it? Had she flown all the way here from Tamnen?

"She flew over the seadragons," Yar babbled. "Qiaru doesn't have to fight. Kinnet, tell Qiaru he doesn't have to fight." He looked over at Kinnet, saw that she had her face buried in her hand, and said, "Oh."

Arama shook Kinnet's shoulder. When Kinnet's gaze found her face, Arama said, "Tell Qiaru not to keep fighting. We're safe now."

She saw the moment Kinnet looked past her and saw the dragon. The stormwitch's olive skin drained of color, her gray eyes going wide. She opened her mouth in a huge "O" of surprise. Then her face fell. "It may be too late," she said, her gaze turning inward.

Arama almost didn't want to turn around. She'd seen stormsingers and sirens and seadragons, but somehow actual dragons still seemed beyond belief.

"Arama, I want you to meet my bondmate, Xellax." Yar's voice was gentle. She wondered if he realized how overwhelming it was for a regular person, someone who wasn't Voice of Dragons, to encounter a mythical creature like this. Arama met his gaze for a moment, then forced herself to turn.

A serpentine neck stretched far over Arama's head. Leathery wings the color of new grass spread out, nearly as wide as the *Dawn Star* was long. Swirling silvery eyes gazed down at her through the dawn. The dragon was apparently...treading water. "Dragons can swim?" Arama blurted. Then she felt her face get hot. "I beg your pardon, great lady," she added, dropping her gaze. "I am honored to meet someone so beloved of Yarrax."

She felt a booming pressure in her head, then the dragon's head lowered to peer at her. At the same time, Yar was giggling, the sound as carefree as anything Arama had heard from him. "Xellax says yes, dragons can swim. They don't really like water this cold, though. They prefer hot baths."

Arama found herself smiling. "And will your bondmate protect us from the sirens? For that matter, have they fled from her?" The song had ceased when Xellax roared.

"She'll *eat* the sirens," Yar promised.

As they talked, Zek's despair seemed to have spent itself. He gazed up at the dragon, silent except for the chattering of his teeth and the shivering of his breath. Arama looked at Kinnet, whose tear-streaked face had relaxed.

"They said something drove the seadragons away," Kinnet said. Her voice was hoarse. "The stormsingers were able to swim through the gap. They'll join us soon. Qiaru thinks he is not mortal hurt."

"I truly hope he is not," Arama said. "Xellax is going to feast on sirens. Maybe she's who drove off the seadragons."

"She saw them as she flew over," Yar agreed. "She was too worried about me to stop, but she swooped low over the ocean, commanding them to leave." He frowned as Xellax rose into the air with a few powerful beats of her wings. "She isn't sure how long they'll stay gone, though. The Twisted—uh, *that* one—may have control over them."

Arama shivered. One didn't speak aloud the name of the Twisted God. She watched the green dragon soar and then swoop down in a dive. The great creature slid into the sea with a huge spray of water. When she surfaced a minute later, her jaws were crunching the long, eel-like body of a siren. Arama couldn't help cheering. Xellax had only eaten two more when the sirens decided they had been overpowered.

When Xellax rejoined them, Yar was already speaking for her. "She'll take us to Crescent Island, but she's worn out. She flew hard all night, and the sirens managed to injure her some. She wants us all to rest and plan once we reach the shore."

"She couldn't just take us all to Ranarr?" Zek's voice was thin with exhaustion.

"She would terrify the people there," Yar said. "And they might attack."

"Not the Ranarri," Arama said. "They're a neutral power, remember, and abhor violence. But no matter. We can signal a ship from the island once we've had time to dry out and warm up."

"Xellax can't carry us all at once," Yar said. "She's strong, but she's tired."

"I'm just grateful she can carry us at all," Arama assured him. "Ask her to take Zek first. Then Kinnet, and then you. We'll need your Voice, or I'd send you first."

Yar conveyed this to Xellax, who seemed to acquiesce. Within a quarter glass, they were huddled on the shore above the tide line. Xellax had ignited a pile of driftwood with her breath and, through Yar, invited the chilled survivors to huddle against her flank for more warmth.

"I thought Darixu didn't want you all to intervene," Yar murmured. His eyes were half-closed with what looked like contentment. Then he nodded. "Oh."

"What?" Arama asked.

"Xellax says Darixu may determine that dragonkind will not interfere in Amethir's war. But he *cannot* tell her to let her bondling be eaten by sirens."

Arama grinned. "I like how you think, great lady," she said, fighting sleep. The last thing she was aware of was another deep, thrumming pulse of amusement from the dragon.

CHAPTER FOUR

O UTSIDE, DAWN HAD BROKEN over the city-state of
Ranarr. But inside the training ground of the Shadow Diplomats, only a single ray of light pierced through
the quiet coolness. A dozen candidates sat in silent rows,
legs crossed, hands resting on their knees. Each one of
them was meant to be striving toward the god of peace,
extending their desire to him and offering up their will.

Zolin had never been good at this part.

It was too hard to quiet his mind, which always had so
many sharp thoughts poking at it from all directions. He
was hungry, despite the quick breakfast he'd eaten on his

way below-stone. His lower back hurt where he'd strained something during his exercises yesterday. His ankles were sore from the hard stone of the floor. He hadn't finished his rhetoric work. And he was still thinking about Naia's strange discouragement from the day before.

A thin switch whistled through the air next to him, cracking hard against the stone.

"You are distracted, Candidate Leite." Master Bekir's voice was low, but Zolin knew it would carry to his fellow candidates.

He cleared his throat. "Yes, Master Bekir," he whispered. "I will refocus."

He kept his eyes closed, but he felt Master Bekir's hovering presence as Zolin shifted from a cross-legged position to one on his knees. The change in position was meant to bring attention back to the body, to refocus before allowing all thought to drift away again, leaving the mind and spirit open to the god of peace.

Usually, all it did for Zolin was make his knees hurt instead of his ankles.

Despair washed over him. He would fail to become a Diplomat. What if he tried for Shadow and failed to be chosen for that, too? Either vocation would be satisfactory—they both served Ranarr in respected ways. But if he were judged unfit for either, what would he do?

For that matter, what actually happened to those judged unfit? He knew it happened, even as late in the training as he was. Early on, it might not matter. If you'd done a year or less, you might find a new apprenticeship or go back to your family, and no shame to you. But each extra year into the training, every selective course of study you did, made you less suited to other trades.

He knew the group ahead of his had lost two, but no one in his group had heard anything from Luard or Katrina since the Spring Evener.

Most days Zolin might dwell on this despair, but he had just refocused. He drew in a long, deep breath and forced himself to release the pain of the thought. He would fail or he wouldn't, but the god of peace demanded only his submission at this moment.

He could do that. He surrendered to the silence, shutting his mind to all outside stimuli. He would do his best for the god of peace.

When the morning practice session was over, Master Bekir touched Zolin's elbow when he would have walked past on the way to the refectory. "Stay a moment."

Zolin went still, watching the master. Had he noticed how distracted Zolin always was? Had he realized just how sharp and jabby it felt to be inside Zolin's mind? Zolin must have given himself away somehow. He often fidgeted without realizing he was moving. He had to pinch his thumb and forefinger together to keep them from rubbing compulsively. And just as his body was rarely still, neither was his mind. Swallowing his anxiety, Zolin waited.

As Shirin left, she darted a narrow-eyed glance back at him, and he knew the others would hear about this.

Bekir was tall. He gazed down at Zolin, his light gray eyes keen and compassionate. "I would speak with you on a matter of great import." He clasped his hands in front of him. "You are advanced in many skills, despite the stillness you lack in your meditation. I know you are aware of the various paths Diplomats may take, from a life dedicated to active service to a brief active service followed by a life of teaching, or even the path of the Shadow Diplomat."

He paused, his gaze shrewd on Zolin's face. "I think it is the path of the Shadow Diplomat you have felt drawn to."

Zolin ducked his head. "I had thought I might be better suited to it," he confessed.

"And yet you cannot be still," Bekir pointed out gently. "Stillness is a skill paramount to Shadow Diplomacy. You have many talents that would serve you well as a Shadow, but you lack that which is most important."

It was true. The Shadows were assassins, sometimes waiting in stillness for hours before striking their targets. Zolin tried to swallow, but his throat felt tight, as if a hand gripped it. So this was it. His fears were coming true.

"Do not despair," Bekir said, and to Zolin's surprise, he rested a hand on Zolin's shoulder. "I have a different path in mind for you. One we do not speak of to our younger trainees. But I have been observing you, and I see your heart and your potential. I wonder if all would be best served by channeling your energy into service to the Deep."

Zolin couldn't breathe. There was still hope for him, then? He'd never heard of this path, but it sounded as if that was by design. He would give nearly anything to not fail after so many years dedicated to his training. Zolin kept his gaze steady on Bekir's, refusing even to blink. "What is the Deep, Master Bekir?"

To his astonishment, Bekir gave him a slow, secret smile. "Come into the Sanctum, Zolin, and I will show you. I do not think you will be disappointed."

He squeezed Zolin's shoulder briefly and then, without a further word, he turned and went to a small door in one corner of the room. Zolin had never seen this door unlocked, but Bekir took a chain from around his neck and opened it with a key hung there. He glanced over his shoulder at Zolin, then ducked through the door into the darkness beyond.

Zolin didn't spare even a moment to think before plunging after him.

The steps wound down, down into the Stone as Zolin followed Master Bekir. Bekir carried a steady lamp, but the rest of the stairway was so dark Zolin couldn't see how far it stretched. His thoughts were racing, but he closed his teeth on his tongue to keep from voicing any of his questions. A virtue of a Diplomat was patience; even serving the Deep, impatience would be frowned on.

The air felt close, their footsteps muffled. How many people served the Deep? How many people ever came down these stairs? Where did they lead? He knew there were many chambers carved deep below-Stone—storage chambers, butteries, apothecaries, infirmaries, dormitories, even the lower refectories. But the chambers Master Bekir was leading him to must be secret from most inhabitants of Ranarr, or surely Zolin would have heard about them.

He was thinking so hard that he failed to realize they were approaching a landing until Master Bekir stopped and spun toward him. Metal glinted in Bekir's hand.

Zolin stumbled backwards, automatically reaching for his dagger. Was Bekir attacking him? Why would he do such a thing?

One step up, two, and Zolin clutched his dagger. He managed to raise it to protect his face only because of the clumsy way he'd reeled back—but it was effective.

Bekir's dagger clanged against his, knuckles rapping painfully against Zolin's own.

"What—" Zolin bit back the rest of his yelp. He knew a Shadow Diplomat wouldn't bother asking. *What* was obvious—Bekir *was* attacking him. Whether he truly intended to maim or kill Zolin remained to be discovered, but without a doubt, Zolin must defend himself.

After his initial surprise, he quickly fell back on the training he'd had from the Shadows. He turned his body to the side to provide a smaller target. He shifted his weight to the balls of his feet and bent his knees, readying himself to take action.

At the same time, Zolin raised his left arm to smack Bekir's dagger away. The leather bracers he wore were not as useful as a shield, but they provided protection.

Bekir struck again, and this time Zolin caught it on his bracer. Still Bekir came on in grim silence. Zolin couldn't read his expression, couldn't see any anger or disapproval in the master's eyes. He was fast, too. Faster than Zolin. That meant if Zolin didn't take the offensive quickly, he would lose the fight.

Zolin leaned on his back leg. His front leg shot out and hooked around Bekir's. At the same time, Zolin struck with his dagger, forcing Bekir to dodge. Now Bekir should be off balance. Zolin thrust out his left hand, palm open to shove.

Bekir's reaction was impossibly fast. Silver flashed and Zolin's palm stung. He faltered half a beat and then shoved anyway, grateful to feel Bekir's weight against the leg still hooked by Zolin's. The master had to pivot on his free foot to disengage, and that gave Zolin time to scramble back another three steps.

Zolin half crouched, his gaze locked on Bekir's. First blood had gone to the master, which might mean the fight was over. But if Bekir intended to kill him, he wouldn't stop now. Similarly, if Bekir was testing him, he might prolong the fight to draw out Zolin's forms.

His heart thudded in his chest for several beats before Bekir lowered his blade and grinned at him. That expression sent a shock through Zolin's stomach. He'd never realized how mobile the master's face was; Bekir had always been grave in previous training.

"Well done," Bekir said, and his voice was warm. "I caught you by surprise, but you recovered well and didn't bother with foolish questions. Not only that, but you were able to counter me and push me off balance."

Zolin held up his stinging hand ruefully. "But you still drew first blood." He didn't relax his guard, despite the almost affectionate look on the master's face. Perhaps this was a ploy to make him lower his defenses. It certainly had taken him aback, but he mustn't let it cost him another touch.

"True, but I've at least two decades of training and practice on you, young Zolin. You'll only improve with time, if you work at it—and now I can see that you've the dedication to keep at it, or else you wouldn't be this good." Bekir wiped his blade on his trousers and sheathed the dagger. "Come, then. You've paid your blood tithe to the Sanctuary Deep, and now you shall gain entry."

Zolin gulped. His heart was suddenly pounding for another reason entirely. What was the Sanctuary Deep? Why was there a blood tithe? What would happen next?

Only one way to find out, he told himself. "I have so many questions," he admitted, hoping it wasn't a misstep.

"No doubt you do." Bekir flashed another grin at him. "And I have answers to all of them, though I shan't be able to share some of them until you agree to join us." He shook his head. "But come! Let me show you what I can."

He went back to the landing, where a dark blue door waited, sconces burning on either side, reflecting off the runes picked out in silver tracery. They were no script Zolin recognized, and he felt a thrill of curiosity. Oh, there was so much to learn already! He had to bite his tongue against blurting out agreement to join the Deep right away.

Bekir led him through the door and into a large chamber that echoed with voices—and, to Zolin's surprise, the croaking of ravens. When his eyes adjusted, he realized there was outside light coming from somewhere. So as deep as they must be, they were close to the outside of the Stone, at least. At that thought, Zolin's chest loosened a little, his breath coming easier.

"This is the Sanctuary Deep, Trainee Zolin," Bekir said, his tone taking on a hint of formality. "This is the Seat of the Deep, where we meet and do much of our work. If you join us, you will find sanctuary here. You will also find fellowship and instruction. Deep's Servants have our own archive, kept separate from the University library. We have our own dormitories and refectory, our own infirmary and apothecary, though we may make use of the common ones as well. But the Sanctuary Deep is meant to be a place of retreat, and at times, the Deep's servants may spend several weeks here without leaving."

Zolin followed him past bookcases and sitting areas. He couldn't see anyone besides them, though he could hear several voices in quiet discussion. There must be smaller chambers surrounding this one.

They went down a short hall decorated with murals in vivid colors. He saw ships and swords, figures of warriors and Diplomats, and interspersed throughout them several birds that must be ravens. Zolin wanted to stop and inspect them, but Bekir kept walking. Zolin trotted to keep up as they moved into a room that was obviously the sanctuary refectory.

This was where the voices originated. Three men and two women shared a long, stone table. They were bent over papers and two had pens in hand, but there were several food dishes between them, and each had a drink. Their conversation paused as heads turned to look at Bekir and Zolin, but they asked no questions. One of the women met Zolin's gaze and nodded, and then they all turned back to their conversation.

"Come with me to my suite of rooms, and I will tell you more about joining the service of the Deep," Bekir said, and turned down a hall to the left side of the room. He glanced over his shoulder. "And we will bandage your hand before you drip all over the deep."

Zolin looked down and realized he was cupping a palmful of blood. He lifted his hand higher, trying to keep it steady so it wouldn't drip. He had a feeling before the night was over, he would be sent to follow his own trail of blood in reverse to clean it up.

The library was crowded tonight, but it was quiet. Naia kept on past the tables where the youngest trainees bent together over homework. She walked on with only a wave for a few of the older trainees she knew. She only saw one Diplomat, one of the training masters who was hunched over a study carrel and didn't look up. He had a stack of books taller than his head and was scribbling away on his notes.

The shelves towered over her as she slipped between them, each individual shelf mostly full. The University library had been collecting books from Tamnen, Strid, Amethir, and the Long Coast, and probably other nations and civilizations long gone, for nearly a thousand years. Naia didn't know if they ever got rid of any books, but she knew the library crawled deep into the limestone chambers inside the White Stone.

For all her fondness for the library, Naia had never been all the way through it. All the same, she *had* discovered some very comfortable hidden corners beyond the most popular sections of the library.

She thought about her final project as she pressed on, slipping past the stacks that held the most often used resources and moved via a complicated system of rails and hand-cranks. Master Penhemmon had approved her topic before she began work on it—an examination of the Derakel Treaty. She'd had to delve deep already, looking for primary sources and scholarly criticisms of both sides. Her argument was strong, she was certain of that.

But Naia knew she needed to haul an extra net for every one she was assigned between now and Midwinter. At the very least she could prove herself academically qualified, and if she did that, perhaps one of the Diplomats would agree that she could still be trained further in emotional control. There would be no second chance; it was Midwinter or failure.

Then, too, she had to consider what would await them *after Midwinter*. After their period as a mentee, each one who achieved full Diplomat rank would be posted for at least another year before being allowed to return home to Ranarr.

She slipped down a curving stairway and found her favorite study spot unoccupied, as usual. An oversized, overstuffed chair was tucked into the curve underneath the stairs, a small table next to it to hold her books. She reached her ankle under the chair and hooked her foot around a low footstool secreted there.

She settled into the chair, kicking off her shoes and curling her legs up underneath her. The plump arm of the chair was just the right height to prop her elbow on the arm and her chin in her hand. It was a perfect place to sit and think.

The Derakel Treaty was tangentially connected to the conflict between Strid and Tamnen, since one of the terms of the treaty was the ransom of two Tamnese nobles captured at the Battle of Salishok. Perhaps she could delve into the reasons those nobles were ransomed, even though the Long Coast cities had been the signatories to the treaty, rather than Tamnen. There might be state secrets involved, and that would certainly add a shine to her project.

For that matter…she sat up straight, gazing blankly at a faded tapestry hanging on the wall opposite her. For that matter, perhaps there were secrets *better* than state secrets. Perhaps there were dirty personal secrets, hidden back room politicking that led to their ransoms. If she were truly fortunate, she might find something that had gone unnoticed by everyone outside the original negotiating table.

She settled back into her chair, smiling faintly. She ought to see if there were maps of the library. She knew there were directory listings, but there was much more to the library than she—or possibly any trainee—had ever seen.

What she sought wouldn't be found in the popular stacks. She would have to go deeper down and deeper in. And she would have to search for it without letting the rest of her work quality slip. Not to mention all her duties in the refectory and her club activities… What if she worked herself to illness? What if she exhausted herself? What if—

Naia jerked her thoughts back to the present again. No sense letting her worries take control.

Finally she took in a long, deep breath and held it until she felt her racing heart begin to slow. She exhaled slowly, allowing her eyes to fall closed. She had to find calm, and the first step was being mindful of her body and breath. If she did that, the god of peace would grant her calm.

Her worries would keep for tomorrow. For tonight, she would simply breathe.

It was long after midnight when Zolin stumbled into his bedchamber, head spinning partly from exhaustion and partly from the way his entire world had been toppled onto its side. His hand was throbbing despite the healing paste an apothecary had bound under his bandage.

His stomach growled sharply. He must have missed at least two meals. Or was it more? Perhaps he and Master Bekir had been below-Stone for more than a single day. Zolin had lost all sense of time passing as Bekir showed him the ancient murals painted on the walls of Sanctuary Deep and the alluring shelves of the Deep Archive.

The murals...he wanted to go back to those, and soon. Zolin's lack in Diplomat training had never been in curiosity or intellect. It had been in his inability to be still.

And now that Master Bekir hinted the Deep could cure him of that...

Zolin shook himself. Time enough to think about that later. For now, if he didn't eat and sleep, he'd be unable to rise for morning session. If he missed morning session, or even if he was too sleepy to perform well, his friends would have questions. And, although Bekir hadn't specifically stated Zolin should keep all this to himself, the entire thing felt very private. It was an offer that had been made to him alone, and it wasn't a decision anyone else could make for him. Not even Naia.

Thunder growled overhead, startling him. It had been a long summer for storms. He'd heard grumbles about the

Amethirians getting out of hand with their weather magic, mostly from traders and merchants in the market.

He didn't know if there was any substance to the accusations, but Amethir had been unsettled for some four years, and the Ranarri Diplomats held some responsibility for that. For all Zolin knew, there might have been concessions granted after the Amethirian prince was nearly assassinated within the very walls of the Diplomats' University.

Zolin was Ranarri born and bred, a son of the sea and stone. He loved the sea in all her glory, calm and wild alike. The Amethirians might pride themselves on controlling the weather, but they rarely did so outside their own waters. The Ranarri were used to storms, and rode them out like the residents of any other seacoast city.

His stomach growled again and Zolin turned from the window to rummage in the cabinet over his desk. He would have biscuits and a handful of nuts, and then he would let the storm soothe him to sleep. All too soon it would be a new day.

CHAPTER FIVE

THE LATE AFTERNOON SLANTED low across the mountains as Warleader Vyx paced the top of Silverdene's walls. It had been three days since the evacuation of the city, and they had yet to catch even a glimpse of the Crelin invaders. Her scouts were guarding the width of the valley to be sure the outlanders didn't slip around the fortress to pursue the vulnerable civilians. The stronghold was closed as tightly as it could be while preserving lines of communication with the scouts. There had been no trouble.

The calm made Vyx uneasy. The evacuation of thousands of civilians and hundreds of warriors—not to mention the livestock—couldn't be accomplished quietly; the outlanders must know they were retreating. Yet they didn't approach, didn't skirt around, didn't even hit them with test skirmishes.

What were they up to?

A commotion rose behind her, pounding hoofbeats and shouts. As faint as it was, she could tell something irregular had happened. Vyx turned, shielding her eyes against the glare of the setting sun. Several soldiers were clumped together in the courtyard, surrounding a mounted soldier. Someone had come through the picket line, but the reaction wasn't chaotic enough for it to be someone hostile.

A messenger from Danae, then? Vyx found the nearest stairs and began making her way down to the ground level. Word from the queen would be welcome. There had been no messenger since dusk the day after the evacuation, and the time between messages would only grow longer as the queen's party traveled further away and they had to rely on the ravens to carry them.

Vyx was only halfway to the courtyard when a junior officer dashed up to her and stopped so quickly he nearly stumbled. He tapped his fist against his chest in a sloppy salute and panted, "Warleader, word from the queen! But it's—" he gulped. "It's Captain Zera, ma'am."

She'll be the death of me, *Vyx thought.* "Captain Zera," she repeated, her voice chilly. "Show her to my office, then."

The officer did his best not to gawp at her and almost succeeded. Then he saluted again. "Yes, ma'am!" And he dashed away again.

"Zera," Vyx muttered, following more slowly. "May the gods keep my temper."

She had been relying on Zera's sense of duty to keep her obedient to her orders. At thirty-seven, Zera was a skilled fighter, and she also had a firm command of her magic. Vyx had done nothing to influence Danae's decision, but she had been unsurprised when the queen chose Zera as her vanguard captain.

The vanguard captain's role was to stay by the queen at all times, protecting her. That she was here, in Silverdene, rather than wherever Danae was, made Vyx's stomach curdle.

She gave the junior officer plenty of time to collect her daughter and escort her to the warleader's office. She loved her daughter, but Zera would receive the same treatment as any wayward officer. Vyx paced the hall several times before finally turning on her heel and sweeping into her office.

She didn't wait for Zera to speak. She tossed her gloves on her desk and bit out, "I gave you explicit instructions as well as official orders. What part of them was unclear?"

She heard Zera's soft intake of breath, but Vyx kept her back to her daughter. She didn't trust herself not to slap Zera, and that wouldn't be right or fair. When the silence stretched another moment, Vyx barked, "Well?"

"Mother..." Zera whispered, and in her voice Vyx heard both that she was sorry and that she was injured.

Vyx turned, narrowing her eyes as she studied her daughter's bloodied face. A smear of dirt crossed her forehead, obscuring the green tracery of her valemal tattoos, and an abrasion on her jaw still oozed blood. "How badly are you hurt?" she asked, and heard her voice soften.

Zera shook her head. "Cuts and bruises, mostly. I was lucky. I'm here on the queen's orders, Mother. We underestimated the outlanders."

Vyx's stomach dropped. "Tell me everything," she ordered, crossing to her washbasin.

"It was mid-morning, just a little after we'd sent our second messenger back to you. One of my sergeants realized we hadn't had a report from the left flank in a while. She was worried. She sent scouts, but before they found the outriders, they saw a column of smoke rising through the sky."

As Zera spoke, Vyx dampened a cloth and began blotting the worst of the blood and mud away from her face. How could this weathered and weary warrior be her little child? "What happened?" she asked softly.

"The outlanders burned Cragmond." Zera's voice was small and tight. "They put everyone to the sword and burned the town."

Vyx closed her eyes, cupping Zera's cheek in one hand. Zera's father's people hailed from Cragmond. It was a large town with a well-established garrison, but it was the seat of the appeasement faction. And look at where that got them, she thought fiercely.

"I am sorry to hear it," she said after a while. Her partnership with Zera's father had been flagging even before the arrival of the outlanders, but she had been as grieved as her daughter when he chose appeasement. She looked at her daughter again and saw the rage etched there behind the grief. That, she recognized. "Did the queen turn aside?"

Zera swallowed. "No. I wanted to—Prince Morsen and I both tried to convince her. But she said there were expectations on her, just as there were on you, and she would not break faith with you."

Vyx huffed. "If we'd seen the smoke here, I'd have been tempted to ride out in force myself," she admitted. "Gods save us. What did the queen do?"

"She sent two scouts for a full report, but we kept marching west along the north bank of the Gehb. She wanted to keep the river between us and Cragmond, in case the outlanders were still there."

"And you had seen nothing from behind you? We've had no evidence that they slipped around us."

Zera tensed and looked away. Her jaw worked for a moment before she said, "They didn't slip around you, Mother. We believe they came by sea, landing at Sothrefen and marching north. There was...There was another column of smoke further to the south."

Vyx swore. "I need eyes out there," she growled. "They won't come through Silverdene; they'll try to swing wide around the stronghold, and we haven't enough warriors to prevent it." She drew in a quick breath. "Sergeant!" she called, and the young officer came in from the hall. "Rapid scouts to Glanyrafon, and make sure they have mistwalkers with them."

The officer saluted and vanished.

"You think they'll burn Glanyrafon, too?"

Vyx looked more carefully at her daughter. Zera was slumped in her chair, her shoulders bowed. They had been straight, her chin defiant, when she left the queen's vanguard out of Silverdene. Had she finally realized just how dire their situation was? Vyx reached out a hand to stroke the graceful tattoos that swirled down Zera's cheek.

"I think they mean to have this land of us, my daughter. At any cost. And I think those who tried to marry and trade with them have just paid in blood for their foolishness."

CHAPTER SIX

NAIA SHOULDN'T GO OUT on a weeknight when she had so much research left to do for her final project. But she'd allowed herself to be lured by the promise of the new Amethirian bard everyone had been raving about. Besides, when Shirin suggested they have dinner at the Chatty Raven, there had been a dare in her dark eyes, and Naia's pride wouldn't let her refuse. Shirin already thought herself better than the rest of them, just because her family was wealthy. If Naia didn't go, Shirin would say it was because she was a poor orphan who didn't really belong at the university.

So they'd gathered in the main concourse of the university, each trainee trying to pretend they weren't concerned about the thunder rumbling in the distance. Everyone knew the stormwitches were fighting amongst themselves. Perhaps that could affect the weather even at the island nation of Ranarr.

She glanced around for Zolin, wondering what had distracted him this time. He had been acting strange all week, even begging off an evening meditation session last night without giving her a reason. His inability to be still bothered him, but she kept trying to tell him that the only way to get better at it was practice. What could be so important that he skipped it?

Shirin huffed, drawing Naia's attention outward. "I'm not going to wait on Zolin. He's always running late" She pushed her long, heavy braids over her shoulder. For such a beautiful woman, she had an ugly heart. Naia couldn't understand why the others liked her so much. "Let's go."

"I promised we'd wait," Evfra said, imperturbable, and Naia had to fight a grin. Evfra was the only person Shirin didn't dare bully or argue with. She'd seen the way Shirin watched Evfra. He *was* nice to look at, with his broad shoulders and a slight cleft in his chin. Not that Naia would ever do anything except look; she couldn't understand why so many people needed kisses and cuddles to tie others to them.

"He'll be along," Naia said, deliberately looking away from the other woman. *You're not worth paying attention to,* she was telling Shirin. It was cheeky, but Naia was ahead of Shirin in their studies. The only thing Shirin did better than Naia was hide her emotions—and, all right, it was a pretty important thing, since Ranarri Diplomats were meant to be impartial, unemotional arbiters, respected by dozens of nations. But the dedication ceremony wasn't until Midwinter. Naia was certain she'd be able to finish taming her emotions by then.

She hoped.

"There he is," Talaria said.

"Finally," Shirin muttered, and began walking without looking around at any of the rest of them. Naia wondered sometimes if Shirin had been placed in their cohort just to test them all, to provoke emotional outbursts from her fellow trainees. The Diplomats were secretive about some aspects of the choosing. She wouldn't put it past them.

Zolin caught up with them, and it was hard to ignore that he was flustered and out of breath. He had so much trouble being anywhere on time, she could almost understand Shirin's impatience. But Zolin was so good-natured it was hard to hold it against him.

"Don't tell me, you got lost in the armory," Naia murmured, and Zolin grunted.

"Thought I had time to smooth out that nick in my dagger. I notched it in practice, and I didn't want to put it away and forget until next practice."

Naia pressed her lips together to keep from giggling. "My stomach is faithful in reminding me when it's mealtime," she said, her voice prim. It wasn't nice of her to tease him, but she knew he also forgot to eat as often as he got lost in some task.

Zolin slanted a glare at her as they passed under the arch separating the University from the rest of the city.

"Now, children," Evfra said, his voice lazy, and they all three laughed.

Naia took a deep breath, shaking her tension away. Trainees weren't required to wear their uniform robes or hide their emotions once they were away from the University, but she usually tried to hold out longer than the others. She knew she needed the practice. But it felt good to be shirking her duties for once.

They had nearly reached the upper plaza, where they could turn right for the markets or left for taverns and restaurants, when a deafening roar split the air over them. Zolin ducked instantly, one hand going to his dagger. Naia and Evfra exchanged a wide-eyed look and stopped walking.

The scream tore again through the noise of the crowd around them. Naia was aware that many of the others were hiding under or behind things, and more than one face was turned up to the sky. She took two careful steps to place herself under a covered doorway. A moment later Zolin joined her.

"What is it?" she asked him.

A third scream came from almost directly overhead. Unable to resist, Naia peered out from her shelter, and all attempts to control her emotion died. She swayed and leaned against the wall, staring in open-mouthed shock.

A huge green dragon had landed on the city wall. It caught her eye and preened its flank. And was that a wink?

"Silent One preserve," Naia whispered.

She stared for several thudding heartbeats.

The dragon gathered itself and launched back into the sky, shrieking as it did so. It disappeared beyond the rooftops with a single flap of its huge, leathery wings.

Into the sudden silence came a babble of voices, frightened, angry, and confused. Naia blinked and turned slowly to look at Zolin.

He stared back at her. "Ranarr doesn't have dragons."

Somewhere in the back of her mind she was pleased that he was as thrown as she. She swallowed. "I think perhaps it does now."

CHAPTER SEVEN

Z OLIN'S HEART HADN'T STOPPED racing since they saw the dragon. Abandoning their plan for a night at the Chatty Raven, the trainees had unanimously decided to return to the University. If the dragons weren't a threat, well and good. But if they *were* a threat, surely the University would be the safest place.

"And besides," Talaria said, "if anyone will know what's going on, it's the masters."

"Let's hope so, anyway," Evfra muttered.

As they approached the University gates, Naia groaned. Zolin glanced over at her.

"I'm starting to see sparkles around things," Naia murmured. "I'm going back to my room. You can fill me in if you learn anything."

"Do you need help?" Seeing sparkles was the first indicator that she was about to be ambushed by a migraine. "I can walk with you."

"No, I still have the tea you mixed for me," Naia said. "Perhaps if I catch it in time, I can work on my analysis for Master Inkeri," Naia said. "It won't be *much* more pleasant than listening to Shirin, but..." She trailed off as Zolin snorted and kicked at her heel.

"Behave," he said, and added, "I'll come as soon as I can."

Evfra, Jousia, Shirin, and Talaria had outpaced them. Zolin hurried to catch up.

"I don't imagine anyone will tell us anything," Talaria was saying.

"Perhaps they won't tell *you*," Shirin said. Her voice often had a bite to it these days, but now the edge was sharp enough to draw blood. "But Master Inkeri will tell *me*." She did a fancy step that made her robes flare at the hem like she thought she was a heroine in a tale. Zolin forced himself not to roll his eyes. Sometimes he thought Naia had a point about Shirin's inflated sense of self.

"I think they'll tell us something," Evfra rumbled, lifting his chin to point ahead of them.

Master Diplomat Revalis Ingen was standing near the entrance fountain, watching them approach. Zolin wasn't sure Evfra was right, but when Revalis saw them, he lifted his head in acknowledgment and then waited as they walked up to him.

"Good evening, trainees," Revalis said, tilting his head slightly in greeting. Zolin thought he looked extremely suave, with a long, purple-brown braid and high cheekbones. His skin was as chalky-gray as the rest of theirs, but there was a hint of brown underneath it. He wondered if he was Ranarri-born or if his family came from away. Zolin wondered if he himself would ever have as elegant an appearance as Master Revalis.

Zolin joined the others in making the correct bow from trainee to master—a shallow bend at the waist, gaze straight forward without meeting the master's eyes.

"It is good you have returned to the University." Revalis's voice was smooth, with a rich undertone, and entirely emotionless. "We have unanticipated guests, and I seek two senior trainees to perform table service." He let his gaze brush each of them in turn. "Zolin," he said, and Zolin's heart leaped in anticipation. Then Revalis added, "And Shirin." Zolin felt his heart sink.

Of all the bad luck, to be forced to work with Shirin! Zolin had served the masters' table many times, and always accredited himself well, but he'd never been paired with Shirin. He would have to be extra attentive to make certain she didn't have to pick up any slack for him. She would do it, he was certain, but she would do it in a way that made herself look very good, and wouldn't care about covering for him.

He didn't allow any of this to show on his face, of course. He merely folded his hands in front of him and bowed again. From the corner of his eye, he saw Shirin bow, as well, and to his surprise, she seemed as sober as he felt.

Revalis nodded in dismissal to the other trainees, turned on his heel, and walked away. It was obvious he expected Zolin and Shirin to follow. Zolin cast a glance over his shoulder at Talaria, who wore a sympathetic expression for just an instant.

As he turned to follow, he caught another glance of Shirin and realized the master had chosen them both because they were two of the only three dressed in trainee robes. And Jousia's robe was hanging strangely, as if she had a heavy book in one pocket, which she probably did. Not to mention the messy bun her hair was scraped into. Clearly, Revalis wanted his trainees to be presentable.

It was a bit odd Shirin was in uniform, come to that. She usually dressed her finest if they were leaving University grounds. Jousia, Marek, and Talaria had a running bet that Shirin was trying to catch the eye of recently-widowed Councilman Peligrin. He wasn't yet thirty and had a great deal of money and influence. Zolin hadn't bought into the bet, but he thought there was a good chance it was true. Shirin excelled at her studies, but she always seemed to be looking further than the horizon of their menteeship. It was as if she wanted more.

Master Revalis led them up a wide set of stairs, along an open colonnade, and up yet another set of stairs. Zolin couldn't help glancing over at Shirin, only to find her glancing back at him. There was no expression on her face, but he could almost see his own question reflected in her gaze. Was Revalis taking them to the council chambers?

The stairs opened out into a wide, airy hallway with immense double doors at the other end. There were two much smaller doors on either side of the hall. Revalis led them to the one on the left.

The room inside was luxurious and bright, the windows all open to catch a pleasant breeze. It was also empty. Zolin glanced at Shirin again, but this time she studiously kept her gaze on Revalis.

"Our guests will be here shortly," the Diplomat said. He gestured to an unobtrusive door on the wall adjacent to where they had entered. "Through that door is a small pantry. The kitchen staff will be bringing refreshments. You will wait there until you are summoned. You, Zolin, will serve the young man. Shirin will serve the woman."

He straightened to his full height, which was considerable. "I will not bind you to the Diplomat's Oath of Confidence, but I do expect discretion from both of you."

With that, he turned his back on them both, an obvious dismissal. Zolin went to the pantry door ahead of Shirin, wondering if she would be willing to speculate with him afterward about the nature of their visitors.

Walking up a familiar set of stairs in the University of Ranarr, Arama was still cursing herself for letting Yarrax and Xellax talk her into this. A captain didn't maroon her crew, even when she knew they were perfectly safe and a small sloop was heading around the northern end of Crescent Island to rescue them. Not to mention the fact that a captain, whether pirate or privateer, shouldn't be the one to carry messages around for gods and dragons.

"That's what you have me for," Yarrax had assured her, and Arama knew the pressure in her head indicated his dragon's amusement, and against her better judgment, she'd given in. Damn the boy for being so winsome, anyway.

"You're angry with me," he said now. He was taller than she was, but he was having to trot to keep up with her. She huffed out a breath and deliberately slowed her pace just a little.

"I'm not angry *with you*," she growled. "I'm just angry."

"Oh, that's all right, then. There's plenty to be angry about, as long as you're not angry with me." His mouth was quirked in a funny half-grin when she glared at him. His silver eyes unsettled her even more now that she'd met the dragon and seen that their eyes matched.

Arama lowered her voice. "Did Xellax tell you where she was going?"

"No, but she says it's cool and airy, and there are ravens, which is always good."

"It is?" She gave him a confused look.

"Ravens and dragons get along. Ravens are very clever, you know. Not as clever as dragons, but certainly as clever as people." He gave a skip and then settled back in at her side.

Arama rolled her eyes and focused on the top of the stairs. She couldn't understand what he was talking about half the time, but she supposed a prophet ought to be a little obscure, or what would be the point of prophecy? "Damn that storm, anyway," she muttered. "And damn the whole bloody war. And damn Vistaren, for that matter."

Tight fingers clutched at her elbow. "You don't mean that part," Yar said, startling her with his urgency.

"Of course not," she said, trying to make her expression less like a thundercloud. Sometimes he seemed so wise that she forgot he was still a teenager, and a sheltered one, at that. "I'm just angry."

"Damn the stormweapon," Yar suggested, and Arama snorted.

"I can get behind that," she agreed. "Damn the stormweapon."

She paused at the top of the stairs. The person who had given her the message—and whether that person was a Diplomat or a servant, Arama still didn't know—had told her to wait in the room on the left. At least the door on the left was smaller and less obtrusive than the double doors at the end of the hall. Arama glowered at them. She'd been here once before, several years ago, when Prince Vistaren and Princess Azmei had first entered into their betrothal treaty. She hadn't liked it any better that time, but at least then she'd had Lozarr at her side.

Now it was just Arama and Yarrax.

And somewhere, a dragon that was talking into Yar's mind.

At least they didn't have long to wait. She and Yar had barely settled into their chairs when the door opened and they stood again. A tall man with black hair came into the room. He was perhaps ten years older than Arama, and she had a sudden strong sense of recognition, though she knew beyond a shadow of a doubt that she had never met this man.

"Storm Petrel," the man said affably, and shocked her by grinning. "I've long wanted to meet you."

She stared at him. "Well, *you're* no Diplomat, thank the gods," she blurted, and that made him laugh.

"My name is Dennath Bekir," he said. "Master Ingan thought you'd be more comfortable meeting with me."

"Perceptive of him." Arama found herself fiddling with the hilt of her sirentooth knife and forced herself to stop.

"You made rather an...impressive...entrance earlier today." Bekir went to stand by one of the empty chairs and paused, glancing at her in a question. Arama nodded, and then joined him when he sat. "I daresay Ranarr hasn't seen so much excitement since...well." He grinned again. "Since the last time you visited. I am sorry I missed that."

Arama made a face at him. "Don't be. It was a mess."

He shrugged. "Handled well by you and yours, though. Better than by us, I think." He leaned forward and met her gaze with a direct, silver-gray gaze of his own. "And now you return to us, carried by a dragon and accompanied by a...messenger, I think Revalis said?"

"Voice," Yar put in. Arama blinked. She hadn't thought he was paying attention.

"Voice, yes." Bekir stroked his chin. "Am I to take it that you are this age's Voice of Dragons?"

Yar straightened in his seat and gaped at the man for a heartbeat. Then he bobbed to his feet and said, "I *am* Yarrax, Voice of Dragons, bonded of Xellax, who brought us here."

Bekir nodded. "Welcome, then, Voice of Dragons. I am no less honored to meet you than to meet the Storm Petrel, for all that I've known about her much longer."

Arama snorted, and the man flicked her an amused glance that shot another jolt of recognition through her. *Why* did he seem so familiar?

"You might feel a little less honored when you learn why we're here," she told him.

"I suspect it involves the civil war the Amethirians are waging among themselves," he said. "It has come to us that Prince Vistaren has raised his banner against his father, though reports vary as to his motivation, Nevertheless, I am aware of your ties to the prince and his companions. I am certain you must be here representing him."

His shrewd guess put her on the wrong foot. "I'm here because my damned ship sank," she snapped, and then bit her tongue.

Bekir breathed out slowly and sat back in his chair. "Now that, I did not anticipate," he admitted.

As soon as Zolin and Shirin were dismissed, he took the most direct path to Naia's door. He tapped softly and then, finding the door unlocked, let himself in.

"They kept you late," Naia mumbled.

A lantern burned low in the sconce by the door. Zolin turned the wick higher and slipped out of his boots. Naia was sitting in a chair by the window, which was propped open a few inches for fresh air. She had shrugged out of the robes that marked her as a trainee, but they were draped sloppily over the other chair.

He sighed and lit her spirit burner. Obviously the tea she'd brewed earlier hadn't helped as much as she'd hoped, but he would brew some more anyway. He stepped up beside her and saw her eyes were closed, her head tilted back.

"You're heating water," she murmured. She didn't open her eyes.

Without asking, Zolin moved behind her, his fingers slipping gently into her hair to work the muscles at the base of her skull.

"I thought it prudent."

He heard her breath catch at the sharp discomfort his fingers woke. He was so good at catching and releasing her pain that she used to tease him to study healing. They'd only realized as they got older that she was the only one it worked on.

It isn't magic, he would say, his gaze flat. *I just know you.*

"So what is it?" Naia kept her voice low and warm.

"The dragon brought people from Amethir." His conscience kicked at him when he said it, remembering Master Revalis's confidence. But Zolin and Naia told each other everything.

"Amethir. About the war?" She slurred just a little, leaning into his touch. He walked his fingers up along her skull under her ears.

"I'm not sure. I didn't hear much, I had to keep jostling with Shirin for a good position to eavesdrop."

"Shirin?" Naia's voice sharpened a little and he felt her tense.

"Master Revalis chose us because we were the only two wearing trainee grays." Zolin lifted his free hand to pet her hair once, softly. "It's too bad your migraine hit when it did, or he might have chosen you in her stead."

Naia grunted. "She was probably better at it then I was."

Zolin ignored that. "I know the woman was Arama Dzornaea. Master Bekir called the boy Voice."

"Does Amethir want intervention, then?"

"I didn't get the impression they were here on purpose, exactly," Zolin said, thinking back about the tense way the sea captain had sat in her chair. She'd been snappish, which was no surprise, from the stories he'd heard about her, but she'd also almost deferred to the boy. Which was especially strange since the boy definitely wasn't Prince Vistaren and had to be younger than Zolin.

"It sounds very suspicious. I wonder if they'll tell us anything about it, or keep us wrapped in cotton wool until the Autumn Evener. Ouch, that bit there."

He worked his fingertips further into her hair, just below her skull bone, where he knew she collected the worst of her tension.

"So what's really bothering you?" she asked, her voice quiet enough he was tempted to pretend he hadn't heard.

He might as well pretend. He certainly didn't have an answer.

What part of everything troubled him most? Was it the dragon? The sudden appearance of the Storm Petrel and her mysterious companion? Was it thought of Autumn Evener's rapid approach? Was it fear of failure? The fear that he and Naia would be separated if one or the other washed out? Or even if they didn't, that they were posted at far ends of the world from each other? Was it just fear of the unknown?

Was it the niggling, chest-tightening sensation he got at times, lately, when the others looked at him and Naia? He knew they thought he and Naia were a couple, but that was never going to happen. Naia had walked out with young men from town a time or two, but she'd confessed she didn't understand why people enjoyed it so much. Zolin sympathized. He couldn't stand the thought of sex, himself. Even thinking clinically about it made his skin crawly.

Then again, perhaps he felt odd because of the weather, which was too hot and sticky. Perhaps it was the fish curry he'd eaten for lunch, which had been much spicier than he'd expected. It might even be the thunderstorm brewing over the bay.

"Go on, you can tell me." She still had her eyes closed, and the lighting in the room was dim. Her migraine was already incipient, so he couldn't make it worse. It was perhaps the best time for him to bring up the strange tangle of emotion he'd been wrestling with since Midwinter.

They were allowed to relax their emotional behavior in private, but Zolin wasn't sure there was any point. He didn't himself understand what was troubling him, so what was the point of speaking?

I still don't even know what it is! he protested silently.

Naia didn't speak. She must feel him arguing with himself, but she didn't prod.

"I'm still not sure," he said finally.

"All right."

Her voice was serene, but Zolin still felt a hot jolt of shame. They talked about everything! They had for years. Hadn't she shown herself trustworthy again and again? Hadn't she trusted him in turn? He was taking the coward's way, putting off this conversation.

The spirit burner hissed and spat, the water finally hot enough to brew his headache tea. He pulled away to prepare the tisane, feeling guilty about the relief that interruption brought him.

"You have to let it cool all the way," he reminded her as she finally opened her eyes and twisted to look up at him.

"Of course. A burned mouth is no better than a migraine," she said, but she curled her fingers around the cup when he held it out. Her gaze was steady on his. "Whenever you *are* ready to talk about what's bothering you, I'm here."

Zolin nodded, rested a hand briefly on her shoulder, and let himself out of the room.

Chapter Eight

*T*HE LAMP GUTTERED AND *flickered, sending shadows careening across the warleader's office. Vyx leaned
over the lamp, adjusting the wick until the flame steadied
again. "We are running low on oil."*

*Zera looked across the table at her mother, seeing the ex-
haustion in the warleader's face. Her mother wasn't so old,
just over threescore years, and in times of peace she could
expect at least another century. But the arrival of the outlanders had shattered any hope of peace.*

*Zera had been training as a mistwalker when the ragged
Crelin fleet made landfall in the far northwest of their king-*

dom. The Srelang had taken pity on the refugees at first, not seeing them as a threat. Zera remembered the arguments that had raged in the halls of the palace as her parents and uncle and the queen and her consort had tried to determine what to do when the outlanders kept arriving.

What had originally been four ships soon became ten, and then a dozen, and then a score. And the outlander settlement around Northshore Keep kept growing, and the outlanders built more ships, and then had come the surprise attack from the north. The Crelin outlanders had made a secret pact with the Vedick islanders, and the two armies combined had swept the Srelang south to Dalasan.

That had been when Zera shifted her training from mist-walker to mistwarrior. Her duty to queen and country had seemed clear. And now, five years later, her training had led her here, to die fighting alongside her mother to give their people one final chance at survival.

"You look grim," Vyx said. Her violet eyes were studying Zera's face. She had one hand curled around a mug of hot tea.

"I have not told you what Danae intends to do," Zera said. "Prince Morsen was not in agreement with her, but he acquiesced. I am not certain the Exemplars will be so compliant."

"They will have little choice but to be compliant with their queen's wishes," Vyx said. She sat forward. "What does the queen intend?"

Zera wiped a hand over her face, wincing as her rough palms caught at the abrasion on her jaw. "She has been in consultation with Duergo and the priestly conclave. They believe we have angered the gods somehow, and that we must plead with the spirits to intercede on our behalf."

"*Well enough.*" *Vyx shrugged.* "*Why would the prince argue with that?*"

"*That isn't what he spoke against.*" *Zera sighed.* "*He spoke in opposition to the…solution…my uncle proposed.*"

When she rode out at the queen's side two weeks ago, she had not expected to see her mother again. Somehow it had seemed easier to accept before she'd seen the burned villages and towns the Crelin left behind them. Once they'd seen Cragmond's smoking ashes, Zera began waking from dreams of her mother burning alive.

"*She means to close the mountains,*" *she said finally.* "*The priestesses have determined that a large enough sacrifice will win the spirits' approval, and that if our mistwalkers work strongly enough, in enough harmony with one another, that they will raise a wall of mist around the mountain fastnesses.*"

Vyx set down her mug and straightened her shoulders. "*And we are that sacrifice.*"

Zera nodded, her gaze never leaving her mother's face. Her mother's thin lips, marked with lines of sun and laughter, tightened. She had never looked so beautiful to Zera before. Or so fragile.

The silence between them was interrupted as the war drums boomed out across the night. The enemy had been spotted.

In an instant, mother and daughter had shed their weariness, coming to their feet and moving to the door as one. As the drums beat on, they hastened to the battlements.

"*The scouts are coming,*" *one of the sentries reported.* "*But it looks like half the outland army is marching on their heels.*"

Zera looked out, squinting through the gathering darkness. She could see two riders approaching, their horses running flat out. There was a raggedness to their gait. Those horses were on their last legs.

"They won't make the walls," Vyx said. She leaned on the stone wall, peering intently at them. Her back was curved tensely, as if she were trying to urge them faster with only her will.

"We could send out a troop to meet them," the sentry offered.

Vyx shook her head. "Not without cover."

"I can help with that," Zera said suddenly. Just because she had shifted from the peaceful ways of the mistwalker to that of the warrior didn't mean that she had forgotten everything she had learned before. "Get me a bowl."

She could tell her mother read her intent. Moments later a copper bowl half full of water was placed in front of her. Zera cupped her hands over the surface of the water, sending out a plea to the spirits.

Half of the strength to call up mist came from the mistwalker, but the other half had to come from the willingness of the spirits. Pride would serve the mistwalker ill.

Please aid us, *she thought.* Look on our desperate position and grant us enough mist to shroud our enemies' eyes. Bring our scouts safely through the mist to us. I don't ask you to fight on our behalf. I only beg you to hide us.

The sentry exclaimed, "A mist! A mist is rising!"

Zera didn't allow herself to smile, but she couldn't quell the satisfaction that rose inside her. Her pleas had been heard.

"Good. You've bought us all time." Her mother smiled at her, resting one hand on her shoulder. "Let us pray it holds long enough for all we must do."

"I raised it to give our scouts a chance to get in," Zera said, studying her mother's expression. *What did she intend?*

Vyx nodded. "And it will. It will also give you a chance to get out."

"I'm not leaving you, Mother!" It had been difficult enough to ride away as commander of the queen's vanguard. Now, knowing that the Srelang nation was sacrificing their warleader and warriors, knowing that her mother was going to die, Zera couldn't imagine leaving her again.

"You must." Vyx gripped Zera's hand with strong, callused fingers. "I will not gainsay the queen's decision, but I will make a decision of my own to amend it. You must ride out. The other nations must know what has happened here."

"It's too late for anyone to help us," Zera protested.

"To help us, yes. But it is not too late to bear witness. It is never too late to bear witness."

Zera didn't know what to say to that. Together she and her mother leaned over the battlements, peering through the ever-thickening mist. Zera didn't know if she would be able to tell when the scouts got close to the keep. She hadn't asked the spirits for any special knowledge.

"Come. We cannot waste any more time." Vyx led the way down the stairs.

Zera followed obediently, her stomach sinking. Some part of her knew that her mother was right. Danae meant to seal the Srelang Kingdom against any outside interference, and that was her decision to make. But the warleader wanted the story told to the outside nations, and that was an order Zera must carry out.

When they were back in Vyx's office, the warleader gathered several scroll cases and a bag of coins. Zera didn't see everything she put in the pack she was filling, but she did see bandages, herbs, and what looked like a thick bundle of letters or documents. No food, but they would go through the kitchens on the way out.

"It would be better if we'd never welcomed these Crelin to our shores," Vyx said. "But we cannot die with our story untold. I bind you, as the death order of your commander: Go to Ranarr. Tell the high king what has happened. Tell them the treaties they witnessed are all broken. Let the Crelin not win uncursed by our allies."

Zera swallowed and then swallowed again, trying to relieve the tightness in her throat. "I don't understand why they turned on us," she whispered. "Why couldn't we all live together in peace?"

"Because there would never be enough, in their minds. We know this land, we know how to ask the spirits and the gods for blessings. We know how much bounty is open to us. But the outlanders never listened to us. They never understood how to ask humbly for things, instead of just taking." Her words were bitter, but her tone was only sad.

Vyx stuffed a few last things into the pack and cinched it closed. "Come, Zera. It is time."

Chapter Nine

W HEN ZOLIN WOKE IT was still so dark he didn't think the morning bells could have gone yet. But there were footsteps in the hall outside his door, and voices raised in morning greeting.

He sat up, rubbing a hand over his jaw. There was a day's growth of stubble there, and it would never do to arrive at lessons unshaven. He pushed the shutter on his window wider open, surprised at how low and ominous the clouds hung outside. It also must be later than he thought; he would have to hurry.

He shaved so quickly he scraped a line of soreness along the bottom right of his jaw. It wasn't bleeding, but it would hurt all day, he knew. Splashing cool water across his face stung. He ran wet fingers through his hair, attempting to tame it somewhat.

After jerking on a clean tunic and shrugging into his gray robes, Zolin joined the ranks of trainees making their way to the refectory for breakfast. He didn't want to take the time, but his stomach was reminding him sharply about yesterday's missed meals.

Besides, if he didn't have at least one cup of coffee, he might as well just resign from the trainee program here and now, regardless of the decision that lay before him.

You might have to cure yourself of that, he thought, *if you're to serve the Deep.*

But if the Deep's servants could cure the hither-and-yon flight of his thoughts, perhaps it could also cure him of the need for coffee. Master Bekir had spoken ominously of trade-offs, and had made it very clear there was sacrifice involved. To Zolin, no sacrifice seemed too dear if it meant the quietening of his mind. He was so exhausted by spending day after day inside his own thoughts.

His parents had meant the best for him, he knew, when they dedicated him to the Diplomats. His frenetic energy had earned him constant detention in his regular lessons, and his lack of attention to the nets had meant more than one lost catch, which they could ill afford. The Diplomats were famous for their mental discipline, so if anyone could make anything of Zolin, surely it would be the Diplomats. And so his parents had resigned themselves to the loss of their firstborn son and approached the admissions officer on his behalf. Zolin had been accepted, sight unseen, and just like that, he was a Diplomat trainee and his younger brother Ronir was their father's apprentice on the ship.

And for the first few years, it had seemed to work. Certainly the mental training had helped, and Zolin had begun to retain the things he studied. He became deeply interested in coastal cultures in general and the Long Coast in particular. He dreamed of visiting the allied city-states of the Long Coast and seeing in person how they were different and similar to Ranarr, an island nation.

But with his approaching age of candidacy, Zolin knew deep in his gut that he was not meant to be a Diplomat. He certainly wasn't meant to be the sort of Diplomat who brokered treaties between nations. He probably wasn't even meant to be the sort of Diplomat who maintained records in a dusty office, sorting through the minutiae of each draft of a treaty to record the changes in wording.

He'd always been good at the oar and good at the tiller, and once he became a Diplomat trainee he became good at the bow and dagger. He'd hoped that, if worse came to worst, he could join the Shadow Diplomats, making peace in the dark rather than the light.

But now...

His feet slowed and someone bumped his shoulder from behind, tossing an absent apology. Zolin stepped to the side, his eyes going unfocused.

Now he learned there was a third option, one that would bring all his skills together, one that would put him outside everything that was familiar—but one that would compensate for his deficiencies and ensure he could be a good servant to Ranarr.

And if nothing else, this would be on my terms, Zolin thought with sudden fierceness. *This would be my choosing.*

They couldn't all be Evfra or Naia or Talaria. The trainee program was considered elite for good reason. Zolin was smart and a good fighter, and he knew it. Those just weren't the only qualities necessary to become a good Diplomat.

Besides, if Zolin swore to the Deep, perhaps Master Bekir would explain more about what happened last night in that meeting he had with the Amethirians. It had been a shock to see Bekir when Zolin entered the room carrying a tray, but Zolin had controlled his expression, and he even thought Bekir had been pleased with him. Perhaps, if he did well, Zolin could even be part of whatever was happening.

Zolin closed his mouth, gave a single nod, and changed course. His decision was made.

Master Bekir didn't look up when Zolin hesitated in the doorway to his office. His quill kept moving across his paper and he lifted his free hand in a gesture to wait. Zolin clasped his hands loosely in front of him and shifted his weight back to his heels to wait.

Bekir wrote several more sentences, from what Zolin could tell, before he looked up. He gave Zolin a brief smile that warmed Zolin to his toes.

One of the best things about the Deep Order, from what he could tell so far, was that they were not expected to remain expressionless. They were part of the Diplomatic Corps, they served the god of peace, but they were somehow outside many of the strictures that ruled even the Shadow Diplomats, who had so many other freedoms.

No matter what concessions they demanded of him, Zolin thought it would be worth it to feel no shame when he allowed emotion across his face.

"You have made your decision, I take it?" Bekir said.

Zolin shifted back onto the balls of his feet, coming to attention. "Yes, Master Bekir."

Bekir steepled his fingers in front of his face. "And is it, as I hope, that you will become one of the Deep Order?"

Zolin swallowed hard. He was proud that his voice betrayed no hesitation when he repeated, "Yes, Master Bekir."

"Excellent." Bekir slid the papers he had been writing across his desk, turning them so Zolin could read them.

The first was a contract. Zolin's eyes skipped first to, "I, Zolin Leite, do pledge myself to the Deep." Below that, "I, Dennath Bekir, accept as my mentee this new Servant of the Deep." Underneath that were lines for them to sign and date the pledge.

The second page was even more surprising.

Rules of the Deep Order

1. Those of the Deep must never speak their true mission outside of Sanctuary Deep.

2. Those of the Deep may use any means to achieve their true mission objectives.

3. Those of the Deep will receive such powers as they will need to accomplish their mission.

4. Those of the Deep shall not be bound by the Diplomatic Code.

5. Those of the Deep agree that when they have fulfilled the requirements of their mission, they will make their final return to the Deep.

Zolin stared at the brief list and then licked his lips and read them again. *Such powers as they will need*, that must mean the gifts of a still mind and body that Bekir had mentioned. But not having to swear to the Diplomatic Code? And what did that mean, *their final return to the Deep?*

For that matter, the way the whole thing was worded made it sound like each person sworn to the Deep only ever had one mission. Most Diplomats served on many missions over the course of their lives, which could stretch many decades long. Was that not the case with the Deep? Was one of the tradeoffs Bekir had mentioned in years of his life?

What are you getting yourself into, Zolin?

"What makes you hesitate?" Bekir asked. His voice was gentle, his gaze understanding as he looked at Zolin. "Speak."

"I...I thought being sworn to the Deep was for life." Zolin chose his words carefully. "I did not look upon the Deep as a punishment, but as a truly worthy alternate path."

"So it is," Bekir said. "For life, and a worthy path, both." He stroked one hand over his white-streaked brown beard. "I have been sworn to the Deep for nearly thirty years now."

"Then...making the final return to the Deep..." Zolin faltered, unsure how to ask.

"The Sanctuary Deep is a physical place, which you have seen," Bekir said. "It is also a final joining with the god of peace in a metaphysical way." He leaned back slightly in his chair. "There are aspects of this life I cannot speak of until you are my sworn mentee. But I will tell you what I may."

He gestured at a chair that stood against the wall. It was stacked with books, but Zolin set them carefully on the floor and carried the chair over to join Bekir. When he settled into it, Bekir was in the act of pouring two cups of tea. The fragrance of cardamom and nutmeg tickled Zolin's nostrils.

"I prefer mine hot, rather than tepid," Bekir warned, and it was true; Zolin saw steam curling up from the cup.

"I have never tried hot tea," he said, reaching out for it. He needed to prove he could have an open mind, even if he didn't understand everything.

"The heat eases some of the bite of the trynen." Bekir's lips curled faintly. He was silent for several heartbeats, and when he spoke again, his voice was fond. "You have been here long enough that you have, perhaps, heard of my friend, Tanvel."

Zolin's heart leapt. So this *was* about Amethir! "The Master Shadow who took Prin—ahh, Trainee Aevver as his student?" Zolin caught himself only just in time; they were careful to never admit Tanvel's student Aevver was truly Princess Azmei of Tamnen in disguise after the failed assassination attempt several years ago. It was common knowledge, but it would not do to be so indiscreet.

"The very same," Bekir agreed. He blew softly across the surface of his tea and then sipped it. "He was my dearest friend in the world. We were in the same trainee year and studied together every night. We petitioned at the same Midwinter. He chose Shadow Diplomacy, and I thought to do the same. We believed our lives were twined together for always."

Twined together for always. Zolin thought of Naia with a pang, though he suspected Tanvel had been more than 'just' a friend. Taking Bekir's example, Zolin blew across his tea before sipping as well. The tea scalded him anyway, and he sucked in a breath, curling his injured tongue.

"But when I would have chosen Shadow Diplomacy, the Deep spoke for me," Bekir said. "Just as the Deep has spoken for you."

Zolin frowned. "So you were parted?"

"For a time." Bekir's gray eyes were distant as he looked at his teacup. "Fundamentally, our bond did not change. But there was so much I couldn't confide in him. It was a deep ache between us for many years." He closed his eyes.

Zolin felt a pang of sorrow for Master Bekir. He'd never thought of any of the masters as people with outside lives, he realized. But Bekir had loved and dreamed, and Zolin knew how Tanvel's story had ended.

"Just before sailing on his final voyage to Tamnen, Tanvel came to me." Bekir kept his eyes closed as he spoke. "He introduced me to his student, close as a daughter to him. We spoke of the dreams we had fulfilled and those that never came to be." He sighed softly. "And at our parting, he told me that he was embarking upon his true mission. He bid me farewell and said that the Deep had spoken for him, as well, so we had been joined even in that, despite not knowing. It had been part of Tanvel's mission to carry that burden, to keep it even from me."

Bekir opened his eyes and sought Zolin's gaze. "Then he went to Tamnen. He executed his mission and, so doing, died. And in the moment of his death, I felt him rejoin the Sanctuary Deep in spirit, and I finally understood in a way I never had before."

Zolin looked down, pretending he hadn't noticed the glimmer of a tear on Bekir's cheek. He swirled his tea cup gently, watching how the liquid moved.

Somehow the Deep was even more appealing after he knew that story. Not only would he have a mission for his life, but he would have purpose in addition to that mission, as Master Tanvel had. Perhaps he would even take a mentee as Tanvel had. As Bekir had offered for him. And perhaps if he must be parted from Naia, it would at least be for a great and noble purpose.

He lifted his gaze to study Bekir's face, this time not flinching from the two wet tracks down Bekir's cheeks. Despite the tears, the gray eyes held no sorrow, but contentment and affection. The lines at the corners of Bekir's eyes and lips spoke of laughter as well as care, unlike the unlined faces of so many Master Diplomats Zolin knew.

How long had it been, he thought suddenly, since he'd seen someone weep? How did people outside their training respond to tears? Would he be able to relax his own guards again someday? Or was it only allowed in private, between those called by the Deep?

I want this, Zolin thought. *Whatever the cost.*

He took a sip of his tea, trying not to show how odd the hot liquid felt. If the heat dulled the bite of the trynen, he couldn't tell. It seemed bitter enough to him. But even that was something new and interesting. "I will sign your contract, Master," he said quietly. "I wish to pursue this life you have led. I wish to be your mentee."

Bekir nodded, his expression warming. "I am glad, Zolin. I wish to be your mentor."

Zolin reached for the pen. "Is it signing the contract that makes it official?" he asked, dipping the nib and tapping it carefully against the inkwell so he wouldn't blot the ink. "Or is there more at Autumn Evener?"

"There is more at Autumn Evener, certainly," Bekir said. "The joining rites and the announcements don't happen until then. But it will be official, nonetheless. I look forward to teaching you."

Zolin found himself suddenly unable to repress a grin. "Master Bekir," he said, scrawling his name on the line, "I look forward to learning from you."

Naia left her room early, when the stone walkways were still wet from the previous night's storm. She always slept poorly when she had a migraine, and last night had been worse than usual. Zolin was troubled about something, and for the first time she could remember, he hadn't confided in her about it. When she'd woken from her last troubled dream of swooping, shrieking dragons and seen the thin line of dawn at her window, she'd decided she might as well rise.

She resented the migraine that had forced her to take to her bed. She was grateful Zolin had been able to work some of his magic—*not magic,* he always protested, but he didn't know the depth of relief he brought her. And on top of the migraine and final projects, now there were dragons! It was almost enough to make her go back to bed to hide from it all.

A breeze lifted her hair from her forehead and she looked up. Breakfast wouldn't be served for another hour, but she could sneak a pastry or two from the refectory, and then she'd have two entire hours to spend in the library before class. Far better to bury herself in research than go back to bed for more nightmares.

She made her way to the tall, double doors of the library's main entrance. The wood gleamed gently in the soft light, seeming to issue a welcome. Naia had always felt at home in the library, whether she was browsing the stacks or studying at one of the front tables. She'd felt even more at home when she discovered her secret study spot.

She wondered suddenly if there were Diplomats whose sole positions were to perform research in the library. Even as the thought occurred to her, though, she smiled and pushed it away. Research and comfort were all well and good, but she wanted to see the world.

The library was nearly empty, perhaps because of the early hour. Naia hiked her leather satchel more securely on her shoulder before wandering further back, past the tables and into the stacks.

She pressed on, slipping past the most popular stacks, filled with frequently-accessed reference materials as well as the tomes that were most often assigned by the masters.

"Deeper down and deeper in," she whispered to herself. There must be texts that hadn't been added to the general library catalogs.

What she sought might not even be in book form, she realized. She might have to delve into the original documents and scrolls of the archives.

The next several chambers housed solid, immovable shelves built for thick tomes and document boxes. Then Naia came to a doorway she had to duck to get through. One the other side, the ceiling was much lower and the shelves were carved directly into the stone. One white stone wall was honeycombed with niches of various sizes, and Naia's feet slowed as she peered at the treasures stored within—scrolls, yes, but also pendants, chunks of seaglass, even weapons in some of them.

Weapons. What were weapons doing in the *library*?

She shook her head and went through the next door, where she was presented with a choice. Left or right? She frowned. Perhaps she should have consulted the library catalogs before traveling this far. But what she was looking for wouldn't be on a list anywhere, or else people would already know about it. Naia wouldn't need it, because if people knew about it, it wouldn't matter anymore.

She sighed and turned left, climbing down several steps into a chamber lit with only two small lamps. Despite her anxiety, the library was beginning to have an effect on her mood. She couldn't help but be filled with wonder any time she found a part she'd never explored. As she realized she had found just that, she *also* realized the far end of the chamber was shrouded in mist.

"Weather? Inside the library?" she whispered, and the sound of her own voice made her flesh prickle. When had it grown so cold in here? How deep had she traveled? Would she even hear the bells marking time this far into the library?

Maybe she should have turned right back there instead of left.

She crept forward, peering through the mist with narrowed eyes. As she passed one of the lamps, she took it from its bracket and carried it with her. The heat of it was welcome, but the contrast made her shiver.

She almost dropped the lamp when she realized there was something inside the mist. Whatever it was, it was tall and thin. Not a bookshelf, nor a reading lectern, nor any other piece of furniture likely to be in a library. And then the something moved, and Naia did drop the lamp.

It landed with a brassy clang, rolled away from her, and went dark. Naia sucked in a breath, wanting urgently to back up, but unable to move her feet. Behind her, the other lamp flickered as if in sympathy with its fallen companion.

As the something moved closer, Naia realized it was a person-shaped figure. It wasn't looking at her, though. It was looking down at one of the shelves. Then it crouched and cupped its hands, and a soft, silvery-purple light pooled in its palms.

Naia sucked in a breath. The soft light illuminated the figure's face perfectly. The violet, pupil-less eyes, the blade-thin nose, and the tattooed swirls on its face and arms would have been enough, but the magic made her certain.

She'd seen sketches that looked like this in history texts.

"Shroudling," she whispered.

The Shroudling tilted its head to one side, pinning her with its weird gaze. Then it took a step backwards, away from her, and vanished into the mist.

Heart pounding, Naia edged forward, straining to see it. But the mist was retreating, trickling down like water through cracks in the stone floor, slipping into crevices in the wall. The second lamp flared back into life, once more hanging in its bracket.

The Shroudling was gone.

CHAPTER TEN

NAIA BACKED INTO THE corner opposite where the Shroudling had stood. She sank onto her heels and fumbled in her satchel, hoping her water flask wasn't empty. Her mouth was suddenly dry,

She could leave for more water, but her heart was pounding too hard to even think about turning her back on a mythical, magical being. Besides, what if she left and then never found her way back here again? No, she couldn't just walk away.

No one had seen Shroudlings in twenty years or better, however long it had been since the Amethirians' war with the Shroudlings. A good Diplomat would have those dates memorized, she chided herself. But no one knew exactly when—or even why—the Shroudling War had ended.

The Ranarri had made attempt after attempt to bring the Shroudlings to the table. The Amethirians, who had lost nearly an entire generation of soldiers in the war, had been more than happy to negotiate.

The Shroudlings, however, made no demands, issued no threats; they just struck silently, without warning, and slipped back into their magical mist. Then, after so much slaughter, they simply vanished, drawing a thick shroud of cloaking fog around their mountain fastnesses. No matter how much the Amethirians might wish to conquer the Shroudlings, they were forced to accept that there simply were no more Shroudlings to be conquered.

So what was a Shroudling doing here? There couldn't be ill-will against the Ranarri. They'd been trying to end the war peacefully! And while Ranarr did have a small population of Amethirians living on the island—those whose trade or craft brought them to the White Stone, or those who studied at the University—Naia wouldn't expect them to be of much import to the Shroudlings.

She frowned at the bookshelf across the room. What had the Shroudling been looking for? Becoming aware of the tension in her forehead, she wiped her fingertips across it, pushing the frown away. With Midwinter as a deadline, she should work on concealing her emotions even when she was alone.

She took a quick breath and stood. It took two attempts, but she forced herself across the room and crouched in front of the shelf. It held boxes of various sizes, stacked neatly on top of one another. Naia leaned in and sniffed.

Cedar boxes, from the fragrance. She lifted down one of the boxes and removed the lid.

The box was filled with letters. Some bore seals that had been broken, while others were rolled and tied with ribbon. The paper didn't seem ancient, and when she unfolded one of the letters, it was supple in her fingers.

To her surprise, she could read the documents. She had studied several languages, of course, but she didn't even have to draw on her studies. Some of the letters were in Ranarri, and most were written in what she clearly recognized as an archaic dialect of Amethirian.

"But there must be hundreds of them," she murmured, looking at the other boxes on the shelf. Were they all full of letters? Ten minutes of quick inspection told her that yes, most of them were full of letters. One had what appeared to be a woman's jewelry set in it, while another had a tiny shoe, hand embroidered and well scuffed on the bottom. The child it had been made for couldn't have been older than three or four.

Icy air wafted against the back of Naia's neck. She froze, watching wide-eyed as a tendril of fog slipped across her sight and curled under her chin. "What?" she breathed, or tried to breathe. But the mist was thickening quickly, her heartbeat speeding to match it, her chest growing tight. She swallowed and slammed the lid down on the box she'd been inspecting. Then she whirled to confront the Shroudling.

When she turned, the Shroudling disappeared. One moment it had been there, looking solid and terrifying, and the next, it was gone. As Naia sucked in a few panicked breaths, it flickered back into her vision, but well out of reach.

Was it truly a Shroudling? Or... her flesh prickled... or was it a ghost?

That pupil-less violet gaze seemed to pull her in. The Shroudling was focused on her face, and as they gazed at one another, Naia was overwhelmed with a wave of anguish and grief that wasn't her own. The terror, yes, that was hers. But the deep, gut-wrenching sorrow was not of her own experience. She felt tears well up in her eyes, though she hadn't cried in the ten years since her parents had died in that dockside accident. Her throat tightened and she choked out a sob, followed by another, and another, until she was all but keening in heartbreak and loss.

How would her parents have felt if it had been Naia instead of them who fell victim to the runaway cart and collapsing dock winch? How awful would it be to sacrifice everything to save your child, only to have that child fail, in the end? Naia choked, trying to stop herself, and then wailed her sorrow.

Then the Shroudling vanished again, and the cold and mist and emotion vanished with it. Naia pressed a hand against her chest, trying to force her heartbeat to slow, her lungs to expand. Her tears itched on her cheeks and, embarrassed even though there was no one to see, she scrubbed her face against the sleeve of her tunic.

Without warning, the Shroudling reappeared. The grief slammed into her as if she were pinned between a ship and the dock. But this time the Shroudling made a gesture, and the grief eased. When Naia looked, she saw that the Shroudling was looking at the boxes.

"Do you want me to leave them alone?" Naia whispered. She licked her lips. Was she willing to leave them alone, if that was what the Shroudling wanted? Her pulse fluttered with the excitement of discovery as well as fear.

The Shroudling made no motion. It pointed its eerie gaze at Naia's face. With no pupils, how could she tell if it were really looking at her, though? She trailed her fingertips against the lid of the box that held the child's shoe. The Shroudling's gaze seemed to follow the movement.

"Do you want me to take them?" Naia wasn't sure she should—but then, she had asked the archives to give her something that would prove her worthy. Whether these boxes contained that or not, her fingertips almost throbbed with the desire to open them and comb through their contents.

The Shroudling's gaze came back to Naia's face. "You want me to take them," Naia repeated, and a sudden surge of approval told her she was right.

This time, when the Shroudling faded from view, it didn't return.

Naia lost track of how long she stood staring at the empty spot where the Shroudling had been. Her mind was whirling with everything she remembered about the Shroudling War, about Amethir's politics and culture, and what she had been taught about the events that occurred the year before she was born.

Twenty years ago, the Shroudlings had attacked several Amethirian villages without any warning or provocation. Several of the attacks had occurred on the same day, so it was obvious they had been coordinated. But the Shroudlings had never given any reason for their hostility.

As far as Naia was aware, no one had ever discovered their motivations. After they retreated behind their mists, other conflicts had taken precedence. The Diplomats had probably made a note to pursue Shroudling lore in their free time. But humans seemed to love war so much that Diplomats rarely had any free time.

She sighed and began gathering the boxes. She made certain the ones with physical objects were among those in her stack. Then she want to find an empty trunk to load them in. She wouldn't be able to move them far without a cart, but most chambers of the library had one tucked away somewhere. She would take the boxes to her study alcove.

She would explore these boxes, these artifacts of a life lived long ago—or had it been so long? The Shroudlings had been in the world as recently as twenty years ago. That wasn't a lifetime. Well, it *was* Naia's lifetime, but it wasn't so long. If her Shroudling wasn't a spirit, if it were, instead, some magical being, she might even yet find it.

The question was, did she want to?

What secrets might she uncover? And did she have time to pursue these secrets when there were so very many boxes of documents she might have to comb through? The thought of Midwinter loomed in her mind again, and she shivered.

But then she remembered what Zolin had suggested just a last week. If she did wash out of the Diplomat Corps, perhaps she could become a cartographer. Perhaps she would be the one to travel to Amethir, into the Shroudling Mountains, and rediscover this lost people.

Better to do it as a full Diplomat, she thought. But she shook off her concerns and began pushing the cart back the way she had come. Twice she had to backtrack to avoid flights of steps too long to wrestle the cart up them. Fortunately the library had been built with the carts in mind, so there were always alternate ramps, even if they took a little searching out.

When she reached her study alcove with her cart of archival treasure, she could hear the bells ringing. She sucked in a breath. Was that—it couldn't be midday already, could it? She'd missed all her morning classes!

She rolled the cart behind the chair, hiding it in the shadows under the stairs. Then for good measure she scribbled a "do not move" note on a stray piece of paper. Generally the librarians and scholars alike respected that sort of note. There was one study carrel on the second floor that had stacks of books rumored not to have been moved for eight years.

Stepping back and giving her alcove a once-over to be certain it appeared innocuous enough, she looped her satchel over her head and settled it against her side. It wouldn't do to miss her afternoon classes. She would have to spend her lunch break apologizing to her morning masters, as it was. She would swing past the refectory and ask Jousia to save her something she could eat before their afternoon seminar on theories of stormwitchery.

Jousia did save her food, but she also nagged her about missing classes. Naia shrugged it off. This was too important.

The University bell was ringing eight o'clock as she settled into her comfortable chair with the first box at her feet.

She selected the first document at random and unfolded it. The ink had faded to a rusty-black color. To her surprise, it was just a list.

tea
wheat
dried fish
jerky
leather strips
fletching thread
horseshoes
bandages
shoe leather
needles
spirit incense
medicinal herbs
travel bread
water buckets
paper
quills
sealing wax
ink
waxed canvas rolls

It covered both sides of one sheet and half of another. Blinking, Naia set the list aside and reached for another. This one looked more promising. The words were written in deep purple ink, the linen paper creased with age.

Dear Brother,
We are at Raven Hill as I write this, but I expect orders to move inland any hour now. Perhaps we will meet again soon.

I know you have been consulting with the other priests, and I am certain you believe peace is still a possibility. I have seen too much to believe that. These outlanders conduct themselves as rapacious, warmongering conquerors. They push and push their way inward. We grant them land by the coast to settle. They take it and want more. We share our harvest with them. They eat greedily and raid our storehouses. We marry their sons and daughters. They brutalize our women and enslave our men.

There is enough room for us all here, and our peoples could be stronger together. Alas, they seem to believe our existence here is a threat to their own. Nothing we do or say convinces them otherwise.

Danae has chosen Zera to lead her vanguard. I am proud of my daughter for the honor she has earned. And you know she has earned it. Despite the great love between our queen and me, I would not prevail upon that friendship for personal gain. Zera's dedication to her warrior's way has been fierce. Although she felt called to the way of the mistwalker from childhood, the way of the mistwarrior has been good to her.

I fear Zera has not yet seen all that her new duties may oblige her to, however. She and I have fought side by side for so long now that she has become nearly indispensable to me. Yet I must replace her, and I must do so quickly, for I believe our queen will be taking her leave of us soon.

Danae intends to come to you at the temple and take counsel with you. She faces hard choices in the days to come. The prince urges one course, I have urged another, and I am certain you will have yet a third course to suggest. Dark days are ahead of us.

*If we don't meet again soon, know I love and honor you,
and I will conduct myself in a way to make you proud to be
my brother. I pray that we all survive the coming storm.*
Yours,
Vyx

Survive. What a horrible word, Naia thought. Life wasn't meant to be survived. It was meant to be lived. Naia longed for more. She wanted to be sure of her home, sure of her food, sure of her livelihood. She wanted to live without doubt, to feel secure. To be respected.

If she longed for more, Vyx must have, too.

Naia traced her fingers over the letter open before her, bewildered. Who were the 'rapacious, warmongering conquerors,' she wondered. And what was a mistwalker? She couldn't remember coming across that title in any of the histories. Then again, there were no books about the history of the Shroudlings, at least none except what was written about the war twenty years ago. And *those* were all written by Amethirians.

As she considered it, she didn't even know where the Shroudlings had come from originally. Had they always lived in those mountains? Had they come with the Amethirians when they sailed across the sea? Were they invaders from the west or the north?

"I have more questions than when I began," she muttered. She set the first letter in the box lid and reached for another.

It looked like the same handwriting. It struck her that these papers looked much older than twenty years. What if these letters hadn't been written during the Shroudling War? But then, how had they come to the Ranarri archive?

How old were they? How had they survived? And how, ancient dialect or no, could she read them?

She shook her head slightly and smoothed the paper carefully so she could read it.

My queen,

We have fortified a position halfway between Cragmond and Estermere. We can hold here for some time. It is a secure enough location that I can send out my scouts to the surrounding villages and towns, while advancing long-range scouts to the edges of the outlander territory.

I believe Holywell is still ours, but they have been a seat of appeasement. The temple there, as Duergo must have told you, is often in contention with our head temple. He has long tolerated it to spare the peace of the town's citizens, but I know he bears them little good feeling.

Unless I hear otherwise from you, I will remain here at least a fortnight to give my quartermasters time to restock and prepare for another march.

My the spirits protect you and the gods guard you.
Warleader Vyx

Frowning, Naia reached for the next document. Would they all be letters from Vyx?

But no, the next letter was in another handwriting.

Sister,

Greetings from the high temple. Your words reached me borne by a sulky Zera, who informed me that she had not believed herself the queen's messenger when chosen for her vanguard. I had to suppress a laugh, she looked so like the scowling little girl with twin braids who used to tell me that uncles were not supposed to tease.

Queen Danae has tasked me with a secret project that does not sit lightly on my shoulders. I probably defy her to even tell you of it, though I shall put pen to no more details that that. Remember me in your prayers, sister. Your words, and those of my niece and the queen, have convinced me there is no peaceful solution to our conflict with the outlanders. But all other alternatives weigh heavily on my mind.

Zera says she has not heard from her father in months. I know he was with the appeasers when last we spoke. Is there no hope of bringing him around? Your marriage might have run its course long since, but he is still her father. If you think words from you might sway him, I urge you to write to him. Tell him to come inland.

As for you, take care. I may have other sisters, but that does not make me eager to lose you.

I have made offerings to the spirits for your protection, and I will continue to do so.

Be safe.

Duergo

My dear Duergo,

Having resupplied, my army is marching to Silverdene. We expect to rendezvous with Queen Danae there. I am sending outriders to each village and town as we pass by, urging the common folk to bundle their prize possessions and join our march. It makes for slow going, but I don't have the numbers to protect each settlement, so I shall bring the settlements with me.

I don't know what the queen is planning, but I will not leave our farmers and craftsmen undefended. I hope she will have an answer for me when we arrive. Silverdene is a mighty fortress, but it is not designed to hold so many as I expect we will have when we get there.

Last night a courier arrived from Holywell, saying that the priestess in charge of the temple had been injured in a hunting accident. Her wound rotted, and when the courier was sent, she was not expected to live. The priestess is well known for her love of the sport, but the timing seems suspect. I do not know if the city remains loyal to the queen. Not knowing if word has reached you, I felt I should inform you.

I hope we meet again soon.

Love,

Vyx

At the end of the letter, the same hand, writing in haste, had added, *I have just learned the Crelin have reached Longdale. We do not know the fate of the city, but I can see a column of smoke in the southeast. Whatever your plan, I hope it is quick. V.*

The *Crelin* had reached Longdale? Were the Crelin the invaders, then? Wasn't that one of the ethnic groups recognized inside Amethir? Naia frowned and flipped the page over, but there was nothing more.

CHAPTER ELEVEN

Zolin left the Sanctuary Deep late in the afternoon, stomach rumbling. Although he'd drunk copious amounts of trynen tea lately, he seemed to be missing a lot of meals since being called by the Deep. He hoped that was only a temporary inconvenience.

Bekir had taught Zolin a new series of stances and forms, though Zolin couldn't tell yet if they were meant to be fighting poses or meditative poses. He had always done better with the sort of meditation that involved movement, so either way, he thought it a good sign.

Even better, Bekir had praised Zolin's quickness at learning the stances. When he dismissed Zolin for dinner, he told him to attend morning lessons as usual the next day, then return to the Sanctuary Deep after lunch.

Then he had pointed Zolin through a door he hadn't yet taken.

"The way is shorter to your rooms through here," he'd said, a glint in his gray eyes. "Go with grace."

Zolin went through the door and immediately began climbing a set of stone stairs. They were just a little short and shallow, so he had to watch his step. More than once, he stepped a little too far and stumbled forward, catching himself against the wall.

Grace is a key component of this training, Bekir had said as he guided Zolin's hands six inches apart, turned as if they cradled something between them. *You must flow like air, like water.*

Zolin wondered if these steps were another method to teach him about the Deep. He stopped climbing and closed his eyes, exhaling slowly. Reaching out his left hand, he let his fingers just touch the wall. Then he slid his right foot forward until it touched the step in front of him.

"Very well," he whispered. "Grace. Careful movement." He licked his lips. "Patience."

He waited there for several deep breaths. He wasn't sure what he was waiting for, exactly, but it had to mean something that Bekir's last words had been to go with grace.

As his heartbeats passed, Zolin began to feel silly. He hoped no one was climbing the steps behind him, or coming down from...wherever the steps led. Wouldn't it be a fine thing to have a collision with another person called by the Deep?

He shoved the thought away, breathing deep to still his doubts. It didn't work, not really, but as he breathed, measuring *one-two-three in, pause, one-two-three out, pause, one-two three in—*

His fingertips caught fire.

Zolin yelped, jerking his fingers away from the wall. He stared at them, heart thudding with the sudden discomfort. But then he realized two things.

First, that he hadn't actually caught fire.

Second, that a glowing line pulsed gently on the wall he had just been touching.

Leaning closer—but not close enough to burn his face if the line flamed up again—Zolin held his breath. As he watched, the glow began to fade.

"Wait," he muttered, and regulated his breathing once again. Three beats, pause, three beats, pause...and as he established a calm rhythm to his deep breathing, the glow steadied and grew brighter again.

What is this? The glowing line was at just the height a hand rail would be, if the stairs had a hand rail. Was that all it was? Just a guiding light to show people the way? Or was there more to it?

Master Bekir had hinted that powers would come to him. He hadn't indicated what sort of powers they would be, except that they would help him accomplish his mission. Zolin didn't even have any idea if the powers that came to each servant of the Deep were the same, or if they were unique to each person.

And he probably wasn't going to be able to determine that tonight. He took a few more measured breaths, then reached out and brushed his fingertips against the glowing line.

Golden light flared, and this time the heat warmed his fingers but didn't burn them. He felt a matching glow build in his chest. Whatever this was, he would embrace it and follow wherever it led him.

He took a step up, then another and another. His feet found the steps naturally now, without stumbling or stepping too far. He realized suddenly that he was smiling so hard his cheeks hurt.

There is still hope for me, just like Master Bekir thought.

Zolin hadn't yet reached the top of the stairs when the line next to him began to dim. His grin faded a little until he looked further ahead and realized he was approaching a landing. The stairs continued on beyond the landing, but the glow was limning the shape of a door. "I can take a hint," he murmured, and placed his hand on the doorknob.

It wouldn't turn, but Zolin was still riding on that warm glow of magic. Rather than grow impatient and frustrated, he closed his eyes and let his breathing fall back into the three-pattern. It took a while to even out; he had climbed a lot of stairs. But eventually something twinged in his chest and he realized his heart and breath had fallen back into rhythm.

He put his hand on the doorknob again and felt a click as the lock opened under his touch. When he tried the door this time, it stuck just enough to make him throw more force into it. Then the door burst outward and Zolin stumbled forward into soft blackness. He heard someone gasp as he swore and flailed at the blackness. Then the blackness was jerked away and Naia's incredulous voice said, "*Zolin?*"

Naia had nearly fallen asleep in her library chair, gazing blankly with heavy eyelids at the faded tapestry hanging on the wall opposite her. She was thinking about Vyx and Duergo and wondering what she must have felt when she penned those last words in her postscript. Then something clicked audibly in the silence of the library. A moment later the tapestry billowed toward her and footsteps scuffed the stone floor.

Naia's heart jumped in her chest as she jerked upright in her chair. The papers fell from her lap, scattering around her. She bolted to her feet as someone cursed—but in that same instant, relief washed over her in a flash of hot and then cold. She knew that voice.

She tore the tapestry away from the flailing mass and stared at her friend. *"Zolin?"*

Zolin scrambled to his feet, his eyes wide as they met hers. A broad grin was still fading from his handsome face, though it vanished an instant later. Naia's gaze traveled past him to the dark outline of a doorway.

"Good even, Naia." Zolin's voice was admirably close to being level as he brushed himself off. "I do apologize for interrupting your study. The door was stuck."

Naia swallowed against a sudden urge to laugh. "The door to where, please?" she inquired, attempting to sound as cool and unconcerned as she ought to.

He shifted on his feet, stepping to one side in a manner that blocked her from peering through the doorway as he shoved it closed. "To deeper in the Stone," he said pleasantly. He met her gaze with a disarming straightforwardness. Then he let his gaze drop to the papers scattered around her, and Naia just *knew* it was deliberate. "Oh, dear," he said. "I must have startled you."

Naia swallowed again, trying to suppress the giggle bubbling up in her throat. "I was asleep," she said, and she could hear just how shaky her voice was. Blast it, she almost sounded as if he had *frightened* her.

Though to be honest, after the evening she'd had, she supposed she could excuse herself for being afraid. Her half-sleeping mind had more than half believed him the spirit of Vyx or Duergo, whichever one it was haunting the library.

At least it was Zolin who had burst in on her, rather than Shirin. Naia suppressed a shudder as she thought of the other woman prying and hounding her about it. She was likely to sabotage Naia entirely just for the sheer fun of it.

"I'll help you gather your papers." Zolin knelt, suiting his actions to his words, before she could protest. She was surprised to see one of the hands reaching out was wrapped in a bandage, through which the pink of fresh blood flow was beginning to seep.

"You're injured." She knelt next to him, catching at his wrist. Zolin jerked his hand away from her, tucking it behind his back.

Naia settled back onto her heels, her eyes wide as she stared at him. He'd given too much away with that gesture, and they both knew it. This was Zolin—she should ignore it, or else chide him teasingly, either reaction would work. But tonight they'd both shown more reactions than they should have.

A choice then, she told herself, thoughts speeding through her head. *Acknowledge our unDiplomatic reactions, propose an entente or at least a waiting period. Offer secret for secret, trade for trade.*

"Well," Zolin said. He rocked back onto his heels as well, his expression much like hers must be, she thought.

"Well," she agreed.

He would have been analyzing the situation just as rapidly as she had. In a moment he would decide, and she mustn't let him be the first to speak, or she would have lost yet another advantage.

Then again, if she *allowed* him to speak first, she would be deliberately sacrificing an advantage in order to trade on that later. Naia licked her lips and took a slow, slow breath. She felt calm wash through her.

"Sit down, Zolin," she invited.

Zolin held out her documents. She took them without looking down, hoping none of them had torn, and relaxed a little. "Look in the box and read what's in there," she said. "Your Amethirian is better than mine. You shouldn't have any trouble."

He blinked at her for a moment. "I thought you were working on your final project," he said, lifting the lid of the box.

"Not anymore, I don't think." She glanced around them then looked back at him, lower lip caught between her teeth. "What it is...I'm actually not sure yet. But I think I've found something important."

After reading the letters between Vyx and Duergo, Zolin was inclined to agree, but *what* exactly that important thing was, he couldn't begin to say. There were dozens of documents. If they were all correspondence between the siblings, they must cover a long span of time.

Naia had shoved back so far in her chair she felt walled off from him. She was watching him guardedly. Her hands were folded loosely in her lap, but he could tell from the disheveled look of her braid that she'd been tugging it as he read the letters.

"Who are these people?" he asked finally.

"I...I haven't quite figured that out," she said, and his gut twisted. She was lying. Lying. To *him*.

But he couldn't call her a liar to her face. It would offer her insult and it would make a tense situation even worse between them. So he pretended he didn't know and spoke smoothly. "There are lots more letters."

"Yes." She paused for a breath. "I thought you might want to help me read them."

So. She'd figured out who these people were, but she wasn't lying to keep it a secret forever. His jaw relaxed, which was when he realized he'd clenched it. "All right." He was proud that his voice was so level.

She took several letters from the box and handed them over to him, keeping about the same number for herself. "Thank you."

She wanted him to come to his own conclusions. Of course. She was unsure of whatever theory she'd come up with, so she wanted an independent theory. Zolin abruptly felt much better, though he couldn't quite suppress the churning of his stomach. She could have just said that, but she'd chosen to lie instead. Why?

Diplomat trainees weren't forbidden to lie, of course, just as Diplomats weren't sealed to the truth. Diplomacy often called for deception and misleading, though outright lies were avoided whenever possible. Diplomacy was built on trust, after all, even if at its most base level. But Zolin and Naia didn't lie to each other. They just—didn't.

Zolin bent his head to read the next letter.

CHAPTER TWELVE

M OTHER,

I am grateful for your guidance and support, but please do not make any more attempts to change my mind. I have no regrets about leaving the temple behind. I have not spoken to you before of my early fears and doubts, and I have not told you the circumstances of my leaving, but if it will convince you, I will do so now.

Ever since the outlanders appeared on our shores, I have wondered why the gods allowed it. Why the gods destroyed their lands, to make them seek out new lands to occupy. But I allowed myself to be soothed by others. The gods were giving us an opportunity to show generosity, I was told. Perhaps the spirits had guided the outlanders here to be our partners. For a time, I allowed myself to be pacified by such words.

Then came Dalasan.

I was not the only mistwalker whose faith was shaken by the disaster at Dalasan. Nor was I the only one who asked questions that could not be answered. But even so, the priests attempted to answer them. We were being tested. We had displeased the spirits and blasphemed the gods. We deserved punishment.

But punishment has never been one of the tenets of our faith. It was a hard tincture to swallow, and more than one novice, mistwalker, and priest left the temple entirely. Our eldest initiate, nearly ready to take her life vows as a mistwalker, was found dead by her own hand.

When the streaked sickness appeared, I could no longer stomach the way of peace. It burned through the countryside, and we healed the sick as best we could, but our tinctures and spirit-pleas did less than they should have. It killed the elderly and children of entire villages, and we could do no more than keen for the dead and burn incense for the spirits to guide them into eternity. And then it came to our temple.

When I realized I had the sickness, I bundled my things and left the temple. I gave instructions that no one enter my rooms, that no one touch me as I left. I could not even kiss my daughter goodbye. We did not know—we still do not know—how it infects others, but I made offerings to the spirits and begged them to create a barrier around me, and they heeded my pleas.

I walked into the woods, found a small seep by a fallen log that offered shelter, and lay down there to die.

I lost track of the days I spent wracked with pain, riddled with fever. I saw visions of blood and fire, visions that are burned yet into my memory. Our women raped, our children crippled, our elders beaten. I will not scribe the details here.

But I know these visions were true visions. They were a foretelling from the spirits. In the months since, I have heard enough reports to know at least some of them have, indeed, come to pass.

One morning I woke, and I was myself again. My mind was clear. My hands shook, but I could sit up. I washed myself and ate foraged mushrooms and berries. And then I went, not to the temple, but to the barracks.

They tried to turn me away at first. They thought I was an old woman. I didn't understand, but I finally convinced them of my identity and intent. Only when I was assigned a room and sent to the bathhouse to purify myself did I understand.

My hair had gone completely silver, from root to tip. I believe the fever must have burned the color from it. When you meet me again, you will know me by the scar over my left eyebrow. They added the warrior's markings to my facial valemal, though they did them in purple to match my first tattoos.

And you will meet me again, Warleader. Queen Danae has seen my dedication and honored it. When my training is complete, I will be sent to your command.

I pray you will accept me as I now am.
With honor and love,
Zera

My dearling,

I take pen in hand on the eve of the queen's council of war, just in case events do not play out as we hope.

I will not bore you with details of the circumstances or the varying plots each faction puts forth for her analysis. You have chosen the temple, and envious though I am of your surety, I am proud of you. Perhaps I chose ill when I abandoned my own temple path to take up the sword. We cannot know now, of course, what might have been.

In any event, on the chance this is the last letter you ever receive from me, I want to be sure to tell you in no uncertain terms how very much I love you. The years I have spent as your mother have given me great pleasure as I watched you grow and become your own person. I have seen your character shape and form, and I am certain it pleases the gods and the spirits as much as it pleases me.

You are the most honest, forthright person I have ever known. Your unshaken faith and close communion with the spirits from such a young age has been an inspiration to me. I wish that my own faith had remained unshaken as yours has. I would not see your dedication spoiled for anything.

Please know that, whatever comes next for me, I have chosen my path with both eyes open. I have sworn myself to the queen's service, I have taken the vows of a mistwarrior, and I have accepted her appointment as commander of her vanguard. All of this I do, not only for my queen and for my country, but for you. I do this so you will grow to full womanhood in safety and peace.

Cadwyn, little one—yes, I know you rolled your eyes just now, and yes, I am aware that you are several years older than I was when I entered the temple, but you will always be my little one, deep in my heart. So, little one, know that of all my accomplishments, you are the one that will outlast me. You are my link in the chain. Let that chain never be broken.

Your devoted mother,
Zera

Brother,
I send this letter by raven on the eve of what I fear will be my last day.

Silverdene is besieged. You will not be surprised, since it is crucial in your plans. I hope you know the confidence I place in you. You've made the right decision. I go to my death proud of the sacrifice we make for our people.

Zera will need you, if she survives the mission I have sent her on. If she does not...watch over our Cadwyn, brother. Do not let our legacy die.

And our queen will need you. She will second-guess herself. She will suffer from the sacrifice she has ordered us to make. It will be left to you to convince her she has pleased the gods and spirits.

I write as if I know the outcome. Take it as faith rather than arrogance.

Farewell, Duergo.
Your loving sister,
Vyx

Frowning, Naia set aside her last letter. "Have you ever heard of Silverdene? I couldn't find it on any map."

Zolin looked up at her. "No, but if you couldn't find it, the city must truly have been obliterated." He shifted on his stool and Naia realized he was probably uncomfortable. Perhaps they should have taken these letters back to her rooms. But there were spells of protection and preservation over the library, and who knew how old these documents were? She didn't want to risk these ancient documents more than she must.

She breathed a sigh and then caught herself. They were in a place that was only semi-private. She felt a pang of sadness as she tried to erase any trace of emotion from her expression.

What would it be like to not struggle against emotional reactions all the time? she wondered. *To smile and frown whenever you wanted? To show anger when you felt like it? Even if you felt like it all the time?*

It had been so long she couldn't truly remember. She knew intellectually that she had cried when her parents were killed. But by the time her uncle died, she had only wished she could cry. She was so tired of hiding herself.

"You're preoccupied." Zolin's voice was quiet, his gaze steady on her face.

She looked down. "I'm only tired," she said, knowing he would see through it. "All the extra work to prepare for Midwinter, plus our regular duties."

"And you're fretting over this, on top of that," he added. When she looked up, there was a light of affection in his brown eyes. "Whoever these people are, they're long dead, Naia."

"I know." She tilted her chin at the box. "But these letters...someone preserved them for a reason, Zolin. And I think I found them for a reason." *I was* led *to them for a reason.* She pressed her tongue against the roof of her mouth to hold the words in. She wasn't ready to talk about the Shroudling—or the ghost—yet. "I don't understand everything, but I get the sense that there are answers here."

"Answers to what?"

She lifted one shoulder. "Perhaps to questions we don't yet know to ask. Who knows? But we're nearly finished with our training, and neither of us have heard of the Siege of Silverdene."

"Maybe it didn't come to a siege," Zolin suggested.

"Or maybe the invaders slaughtered everyone in the city," Naia countered.

"The winners tend to record the history that gets passed down." Zolin looked back down at the letter in his hand. He smoothed it against his knee. His expression gave nothing away, but Naia knew he was giving her words consideration.

She hadn't seen dates on any of the letters. At least, there was nothing that looked like the dates they used now. If the letter writers had a different way of marking time, she hadn't found a clue to it. All she knew for sure was that many of these papers were old, very old. One of them had flaked a corner into dust before she realized how carefully she had to handle them. The parchment scrolls had fared better, and she thought the bottom of the box was covered in rolls made of some sort of animal skin, though she hadn't delved that far in her reading.

"Have you told anyone else about these?" Zolin's voice broke into her thoughts.

"No. I didn't want to overreact. I wouldn't even have told you, yet, if you hadn't stumbled on me."

Zolin nodded slowly, and Naia bit her tongue in surprise. She had never seen him so expressive as he was tonight—at least, not anywhere but in their rooms, and even then it was rare.

"What do you think of all this?" she demanded, after the silence grew too loud to bear.

"I don't know yet. I think...your instincts are correct; you've found something that matters. But until we know who these people are, when they lived...what nationality they were..." He pressed his lips together for a moment. "I think you should put this out of your mind until our next rest day. We have enough to be getting on with in our courses."

Naia tried to smother a surge of resentment. Of course he would say that. He wanted to be a Diplomat even more than she did, and for the right reasons. He was better Diplomat material than she ever would be. But he wasn't wrong, she knew.

"All right." She held out her hand to take the letters from him. "I'll put it aside. But don't you work on it without me."

"Naia," he said, and she knew she wasn't imagining the reproach in his voice. "I would never do that."

Chapter Thirteen

Z OLIN SIPPED HIS TRYNEN tea and grimaced. "Why do you brew it so much stronger?" he asked. He didn't mind drinking hot tea as much anymore, but it was *so* bitter.

He and Bekir had been sitting in silence for some time. The practice room they occupied was chilly and stuffy at the same time, and the Deep's echoing vastness seemed emptier than usual. Zolin still didn't know much about what occupied the other people he encountered down here, and he couldn't help being curious.

Bekir looked up and set his book aside. "What do you know about the trynen?"

Zolin was beginning to realize any time he asked a question he was just as likely to get a question back in response. He made a wry face, and Bekir chuckled, likely knowing what he was thinking. Zolin felt like he was completely transparent to Bekir most of the time.

"It's just something in the water here," he said. "Ranarr is limestone straight through, and the trynen is some sort of mineral that leaches into the water supply. It's harmless, but it's what gives us our skintone. People who leave Ranarr often end up looking like they're not from here, if they're gone long enough."

Bekir nodded. "True, as far as it goes. Or...mostly true, anyway." He tapped one finger against his own tea cup. "Trynen is harmless for most Ranarri. We of the Deep tend to...mm, overuse it isn't quite the right word, but it will do."

Zolin's heart kicked in his chest. "So for us it isn't harmless."

"Again, most of the time it is. The trynen enhances the abilities we use to reach the Deep. The more we consume, the stronger our abilities—but sometimes the strongest Servants of the Deep fall ill in ways even our peacehealers cannot treat." His gaze was gentle on Zolin's face. "It isn't anything that happens quickly. Many Servants of the Deep will never become afflicted. Most, even."

"How long do Servants of the Deep live?" Zolin's heart was thudding. He tightened his hands around his cup and stared down into the treacherous drink.

"Most live a normal lifespan," Bekir said. "Several of our current masters are well into their seventies or eighties. My own master, Udena, was one hundred and four when he died." He smiled ruefully. "I meant to tell you about this in due course, but I feel I'm going about it poorly. You shouldn't be alarmed."

Zolin licked his lips. "You did say there were tradeoffs."

Bekir chuckled. "Just so. Tell me, would you trade the feeling of the Deep reaching through you to light the trynen traceries in the stairways?"

"Is that why they glow?" Zolin exclaimed. "I wondered. They were too intricate to have come from my thoughts alone."

"Don't underestimate yourself." Bekir leaned back in his chair, contemplating Zolin. "Your mind does not follow the same paths as others, it is true, but that is not a bad thing. You bring a unique perspective to things. Combined with your natural skill with the Deep, I believe that will make you a valuable gift to the world."

Zolin's cheeks heated and he ducked his head, glad the trynen kept blushes from showing easily.

It is not a thing to be ashamed of.

Zolin jerked upright, staring at Bekir. "Did—did you put that thought in my head?" he demanded.

The Deep gives us many gifts. You will learn this one, and I suspect you will discover many that I have never known.

Zolin gulped his tea. It had cooled, and he realized Bekir had been right. As it cooled, the bitterness of the trynen made saliva spring unpleasantly into his mouth.

"I am, perhaps, throwing too much at you at once," Bekir said aloud.

"No!" Zolin straightened, smiling. "No, I want to learn everything! What else will I be able to do?"

"Can a man know until he tries?" Bekir countered, smiling back at him. "Let us try some of the movement disciplines first, and then we will begin practicing mind speech."

Did it let you read someone's mind, Zolin wondered, but he didn't voice the question. He wondered if it would be fair to read someone's mind if you were negotiating a peace. He wondered if he would even *want* to read someone's mind. That could be a dangerous thing.

Bekir stood. "Come. I'll teach you a new sequence of movements."

The next two weeks were a blur to Zolin. He learned how to use the magic of the Deep to influence a person's mood, to make a listener more amenable to his point of view, and even how to provoke someone's temper. Privately, he vowed he would never use *that* ability with Naia, though he wished he could try to calm her temper.

Master Bekir had warned him he was strictly forbidden to practice any of his mood-altering abilities outside of the Deep. Zolin supposed it made sense, but he was curious, until Bekir told him that if it were done clumsily, it could cause someone to fall in love falsely or commit violence. After that, Zolin vowed to stick with his calming tea blends.

Bekir finally gave Zolin a small, cut-glass jar of trynen, along with explicit written instructions on how to brew it, what *not* to mix with it, and what to do if his heart began racing or he felt sick to his stomach after drinking too much of it.

Zolin kept meaning to ask how much information he could share with Naia, but she seemed to have eased up on her obsession with the letters she'd found, becoming more preoccupied with her final project.

He finally settled on telling her that he was doing private study with Master Bekir, and leaving it at that. She'd eyed him shrewdly, and he knew she was aware he had only skimmed the surface of the truth, but to his relief, she let it slide.

"If everyone on Ranarr drinks the trynen, does that mean everyone can touch the Deep?" he asked Bekir late one night, as he balanced his weight all on one foot, maneuvering his arms in patterns that would entice and gather power to him.

Bekir was standing to one side, arms folded, watching him narrowly. "I suppose every Ranarri born has some capacity," he said slowly, "but it is rare to see it in great concentration outside of the Diplomat corps. The peacehealers channel it in a different way to how we use it. I would venture there are some herbal healers who also touch it, though whether they know it or not, I cannot say."

"It seems strange that we keep it a secret." Zolin shifted to his other foot, sweeping his arms in a wide arc. "The Amethirians are so proud of their stormwitches."

"And look where that has got them." Bekir raised an eyebrow. "Do you truly think it would be better if we worked openly with our talents? And do you think the Deep would allow itself to be used so?"

Zolin swallowed. He hadn't thought about it that way. Was stormwitchery a living thing? He could feel that the Deep was, though he couldn't begin to explain how. But he knew it had to be courted and coaxed and treated properly.

"Still, we could do so much good. We could make everyone get along."

"Make everyone?" Bekir snorted. "If we were to compel harmony, how would it be harmony at all? We would simply be oppressors. The Deep is useful, yes, but only to influence, never to force. Remember that."

Zolin wobbled, caught himself, and then had to lower his other foot to keep from falling. His hands tingled, and he realized he'd lost his grip on the power he had been building. "I don't think it liked what I was saying," he confessed, rubbing his palms against his trousers.

"I imagine not. Wouldn't it hurt your feelings if Naia failed to understand something important about you?" Bekir's voice was carefully neutral, but Zolin couldn't tell why.

"Of course it would. It would hurt my feelings if anyone did."

Bekir tilted his head. "Not Naia in particular?"

Zolin's gut twisted as he realized what Bekir was asking. "We're not like that," he said tightly. "She's my best friend. We're not supposed to fraternize with other trainees, anyway."

"That doesn't stop everyone," Bekir said gently.

"It doesn't have to stop us. We're not *like* that," Zolin repeated. "Neither of us. We're friends, that's all." Then he snorted. "That's *all*, as if that isn't everything. I don't know why people have to force things into more than what they are, when what they are is wonderful enough."

Bekir shifted, and only then did Zolin realize his mentor had been uncomfortable in the first place. "I didn't want to ask, but I needed to know," Bekir said.

Why, Zolin wanted to ask, but he supposed there were half a dozen reasons why Bekir might need to know. And at least he'd bothered asking instead of just assuming. "You could ask Naia and she'd tell you the same thing," he said, trying not to sound sullen.

"I am glad to hear it," was all Bekir said. "Now. Let's see if you can perform that sequence more gracefully this time around."

CHAPTER FOURTEEN

IT HADN'T TAKEN ZOLIN long to fall utterly in love with the Sanctuary Deep. Every free moment he got, he slipped away down the stairs that led into the heart of the Stone. It didn't matter if it was full of people—most of whom Zolin hadn't officially met yet—or if he were the only person there, his footsteps echoing amid raven calls through the tall main hall.

He knew he was probably imagining it, but his mind felt calmer in the Deep. Not calm, never that, because even when he was sitting as peacefully as possible on a hard wooden bench in the Deep refectory, he couldn't help thinking about his studies or the mosaics—which Master Bekir had admitted were yet to be translated fully—or even the purpose of the ever-present ravens.

And he still hadn't been introduced to any of the ravens, either, he realized, and then jerked his thoughts back to the present, which was him sitting across a coffee table from Talaria.

"You're twitchier than usual this morning," she observed, and because they were at Meki's Coffee Shop and not in the University proper, she laughed softly.

"My thoughts won't settle. Go over the last declension again."

She was used to him asking her to repeat herself, so she just huffed another laugh and complied. It sounded right to him, but he'd forgotten to study last night. He'd stayed too late in the Deep and stumbled to bed in the wee hours of the morning.

Zolin knew he should at least attempt to behave more normally. His training schedule had always shared each class with at least one of his friends. Now he was hiding the Deep, and there were dragons and Amethirians in Ranarr. And now he had Naia's secret to keep, as well—whatever that secret was. He still wasn't sure what to make of all the documents she'd uncovered, especially since she'd declined to elaborate any further the night she'd shown them to him. He wanted to know the circumstances of her discovery. *Where* had she found them? How could no one else know about them?

And why did the timing of her discovery seem so ominous?

Talaria clicked her fingers in front of his eyes. "Zolin," she said, and her voice was a little sharper than it usually was, even when she was annoyed with him. "You aren't paying attention. Where is your mind wandering?"

Shoving away his guilt, he looked down at his hands. "The Autumn Evener," he murmured. "Well, the Evener, and dragons, actually."

It was only partly a lie, he excused himself.

He could almost feel her gaze soften, and he finally forced himself to meet her eyes. "Are you nervous?"

She swallowed. "Terrified. You?"

"The same." He quirked his lips in what he knew was a terrible attempt at a smile. "There's so much left to do, I don't know where to start. You're miles ahead of me at the languages. I keep mixing up the third and fourth person in Lankish. And I'm only halfway through my politics and treaties project."

And I'm sworn to the Deep now, and I'm still not even sure what that means. His stomach roiled suddenly as it occurred to him that swearing himself to the Deep might only have complicated his life even more, rather than making it easier. After all, he still had all those projects to complete and spoken exams to pass, didn't he?

His breathing quickened as his heart began thudding harder. He felt an incipient ache creeping into his forehead. He struggled to even his breathing out.

Talaria tilted her head, holding his gaze. "Remember your methods," she said. "List everything that needs doing..."

He grunted in barely-hidden impatience because that's how he always reacted. "List everything that needs doing, list the right next step for each thing, assign a priority, and then do the most important right next thing," he parroted.

"You say that as if it didn't work every time you remember to do it." Her tone was fond, warming the cold that had settled in the pit of Zolin's stomach.

It was true. Talaria had helped Zolin come up with these coping mechanisms at the end of their first year. He'd managed to muddle through training despite his noisy, sharp-pointed brain, but he'd done poorly on his end-of-year assessment, and Talaria had stumbled across him before he'd gotten his emotions under control. She'd comforted him, and then she'd set her rigorous genius to helping him find ways to work inside his head, rather than in spite of it. They discovered they enjoyed studying together, and Lankish was one class he didn't share with Naia.

"I'll try," he agreed. "But I think I shouldn't have had so much coffee this morning. It always makes it harder."

She didn't snort or roll her eyes at him—after all, they *were* in public—but he could tell she wanted to. "You'd best get to your morning session, then," she said. "You have weapons first, right? That should burn off some of the energy."

He stood up, resting two fingers lightly on the back of her hand as he did. "You're a gem, Tali. I'll see you at supper." Then he left the coffee shop quickly, before she could question why he wouldn't be at lunch.

Zolin was still whispering his methods under his breath when he reached the University portico. "List everything...list the right next step...assign priority...do the most important right next thing...List everything..." The problem was that there was *so much*. Zolin wasn't even sure how to begin listing everything.

He turned his steps toward one of the unobtrusive doors he'd discovered led down into the Sanctuary Deep. He ought to go to his weapons class. Until recently it had always been his favorite. But he always took more bruises when his thoughts were this full and spinny.

No, far better to claim a spot at one of the Sanctuary refectory tables so he could do as Talaria suggested and follow his method.

"...list the right next step..." he whispered, and clipped his shoulder against someone who didn't quite manage to dodge out of his way.

"Will you never learn to watch where you're going?" Shirin's voice was level, almost pleasant if anyone else heard her, but her tone was pure poison in Zolin's ears.

"My regret, Shirin," he said automatically, pressing his hand to his sternum and inclining his torso in apology.

Shirin straightened to her full height and looked down along her straight nose at him. "Why are you still here, Zolin?" Her words were soft, her dark eyes sparkling intently on his. "Everyone knows you aren't going to make it past the Evener. You might as well withdraw on your own and save face."

Even a month ago, her words would have made him flush and stammer. But terrified as Zolin might be by the prospect of Midwinter, the nature of his fear was changing. He had Master Bekir now. He had the Deep. He had the Sanctuary and all the knowledge and wonder it promised.

He lifted his chin. "One might ask the same of you, Shirin," he observed. "Hasn't Councilman Peligrin spoken for your hand yet?"

As soon as the words were out of his mouth, a cold jolt of regret speared through him. Oh, he shouldn't have fired back. She wouldn't let this go—she never let anything go, but now he'd given her reason to be curious. He should have just responded the way he always had.

Shirin's eyes narrowed. "Where are you off to at this hour of the morning?" she hissed. "You have weapons just like I do."

Might as well lose a boatload of fish as a full net, Zolin thought regretfully, and said, "Then why aren't you going, either?" He made his voice bright and held her gaze with his. Oh, he was bad at this sort of thing; it was why he'd always tried to keep his head down and ignore her jabs. He hated the verbal sparring, which was yet another clue he should have noticed, telling him he wasn't meant to be a Diplomat.

She pressed her lips tightly together. He'd gained her attention for real now, but hopefully he'd also made her angry enough at his back-talk that she wouldn't notice the shabby, medium-blue door several paces behind her. Caught up in his thoughts, he'd been indiscreet; he'd been on a straight line for the door, despite the serene caution Master Bekir was always urging.

"Something has changed with you," Shirin said slowly. She flicked a glance behind him, then back to his face. "I'm surprised to not see Naia with you. Everyone knows you've been sneaking around together."

She was feeling her way now, he realized, and suddenly Zolin had to suppress a surge of glee. She wasn't sure what had changed, but it had shifted the balance of power between them. Shirin had always thought herself above them: more clever than Naia, more beautiful than Talaria, and more ambitious than Evfra. But Zolin wasn't responding to her with the proper deference.

He would have to remember to warn Naia about this. Shirin knew how to be nasty in half a hundred little ways, and she never seemed to get caught in her poison by the masters. Perhaps it was her parents' wealth that kept her out of trouble, for all that the Diplomats were supposed to be egalitarian in nature.

"She has theorycraft this morning; she's probably already at lecture," Zolin said. He took one deliberate step to the side and walked past Shirin without looking back. He shifted his trajectory to make it look as if he were going to stop by the refectory on his way to class. It was the best he could do, but he felt confident it would work. He might have surprised Shirin this morning, but she was still too stuck in her own perception of the world. She wouldn't imagine Zolin had any truly interesting secrets. The most obvious explanation would be the one she settled on.

But now he was going to have to hurry. It wouldn't do to arrive in the weapon yard without coffee, and if he didn't get to the refectory before they had finished clearing away breakfast, he might have to do some fast talking in order to come away with anything.

Blast the woman, anyway, he thought. What had twisted her heart so much that she felt the need to belittle and thwart her classmates so? The rest of them might be rivals, but they helped each other even so. One person's weakness might be another's strength. But Shirin had held her emotions held close since their first year, and this year she'd only grown colder.

Perhaps one day she'll turn into an iceberg and float away, he thought, and permitted himself a brief, tiny smile. They should be so lucky.

Chapter Fifteen

Zolin forced himself to look engaged during classes that day. In reality he was itching to slip away into the Sanctuary Deep. It was a growing need in him, he realized, the peculiar quiet that seeped into his bones when he was in the Sanctuary. Was it just a craving for trynen? Or was it the Deep itself? He wasn't sure. Bekir had instructed him in some things, but others, he said, were for Zolin to discover on his own—or were secrets until after Autumn Evener.

Every time Zolin shifted in his chair or glanced around the room as his mind wandered, Shirin was watching him.

Once he met her gaze and held it, his heart thudding in his chest. Shirin's eyes narrowed, but then Master Inkeri spoke and Shirin jerked her attention back to the Diplomat.

Zolin forced himself to sit still after that; if he couldn't focus his thoughts on the lecture, he would at least try to make himself appear focused. He let his thoughts drift back to the Deep and its hidden corners and alluring passages. He wondered if anyone had ever fully explored the Deep. Had it been built by the Ranarri Diplomats? Or had it merely been discovered by them and occupied? Master Bekir had been frustratingly vague on the matter, and when pressed had finally said Zolin would have to take it up with the archivist after the Autumn Evener.

Nowhere in the Deep was forbidden, as long it wasn't behind a locked door. Bekir had encouraged Zolin to explore, promising there would be more time after the Evener for formal instruction together. It was strange to have so much unstructured time again; Zolin had taken extra classes each year in an attempt to exhaust his mind into obedience.

He ought to enjoy the new free time. Instead, it felt almost oppressive.

Someone kicked his foot. Zolin jerked his attention back to the present and saw that everyone was gathering books and notes, preparing to leave the classroom. Naia, sitting on one side of Zolin, tilted her head slightly and tapped her foot against his again.

"Think I must have dozed off," he murmured, and felt oddly warmed by the glimmer of amusement in her dark eyes.

"Dozed off with your eyes open," she murmured back, and stood. "Will you sit with Evfra and me at dinner? Neither of us has refectory duty."

Evfra bounded to his feet, suppressing a sudden grin. "Better yet, let's go out on the town," he said. "My treat to you both," he added as she shifted in her seat. "And to Jousia, if she'll join us."

"Of course I will," Jousia said from behind him. "We'll take Talaria, too. We should go back to the Chatty Raven. Naia still hasn't heard the Amethirian bard play."

"Nor have I," Zolin reminded her, feeling buoyed. If they managed to slip away without Shirin noticing, he could tell everyone about his encounter with her. Then they would all be forewarned about any trouble—and he'd have several extra eyes watching for it.

The Chatty Raven was constructed of the same white stone as the rest of Ranarr, but it had been painted a deep blue color. The yard was swept clean and the sign, boasting a flying raven, was freshly painted. As they approached the tavern, voices rose in laughter inside. A stringed instrument jangled briefly and then someone began playing a pipe of some sort.

Zolin and Naia exchanged a glance and a furtive grin. Evfra recognized the song and started singing along, and Talaria giggled when he missed a note. *Oh, glory*, Zolin thought. *I love these people so much.*

It was just beginning to sink in that after years of growing up and learning together, they would all be going in different directions in a few short months. *We need to make the most of this time.*

He slung an arm over Jousia's shoulders—she was barely five feet, which subjected her to that sort of treatment often. She gave him a sour look, but when she saw his expression, she relaxed against him, thumping him gently with her elbow.

"I'm glad we ducked Shirin," she confided to him. "But why was she so bent on finding out where you had sneaked off to? She seems to think Naia's been sneaking along with you, but the rest of us know better."

"Eh, she's on a rampage." Zolin shrugged. He didn't like letting anyone think he and Naia might be fraternizing. He didn't want it, and he didn't think it had ever occurred to Naia. "I almost collided with her earlier, and then I didn't grovel the way she thought I should."

Evfra broke off his song. "Oh, so that's why she snapped at me. I dropped my homework before class, and when I bent down to pick it up, she nearly tripped on me. When I stood up again, she snatched it from me, wadded it up, and threw it over the university wall." He snorted.

Zolin blinked. Evfra had always seemed fond of Shirin—they certainly spent a lot of time studying together—but he never gave her more leeway than anyone else. But she'd always seemed to respect and even like Evfra in return. If even he had been the victim of her ire, things must be bad.

"It's probably halfway to the Sandswamp by now," Naia remarked. "Goodness knows she rarely needs an excuse to be horrid."

"I think she's bitter that her parents sailed to Tamnen just after the Spring Evener," Talaria said. "She wanted to go with them, but the masters wouldn't give her leave."

Evfra and Jousia exchanged a glance that made Zolin wonder if they knew more than they were saying, but Naia scoffed, interrupting. "Just like her to think she could get around the rules. But let's not ruin tonight by talking about her."

"Agreed," Talaria said. "She'll sour the mood."

"Just watch her and try to stay clear, that's all," Zolin said. He squeezed Jousia's shoulders gently and let her go through the tavern door ahead of him.

The tavern was crowded for a midweek evening, and he wondered if it was because of the figure who sat on the little raised area by the cold hearth. The bard was slender, with rich brown skin, shaggy black hair, and a mischievous grin playing around their lips. Nimble fingers flew over the strings of their lute, which was clutched tight against the bard's body.

Evfra tapped Zolin's shoulder and pointed. There were a few empty chairs around a table tucked into an odd nook that didn't seem to have a direct view of the bard. Zolin looked around the room, saw no other tables, and shrugged. He'd rather be able to watch, but the music was the point, after all.

They squeezed around the small table and Evfra lifted a hand to flag down a serving girl. She waited out the bard's music and the crash of applause afterwards and then took their orders for food, barley water, and tea. Another server took a wooden stein to the bard, who took two gulps and grinned broadly.

"I must pause for a brief repast, my friends." Their speaking voice was a husky alto that fell like velvet on the ears. Zolin leaned to look past Talaria for a better view.

"But I'll return forthwith, and then we shall have the ballads!"

The lute vanished as if by magic, and suddenly the bard was juggling several brightly-colored orbs. They kept juggling as they wended their way between tables and vanished into the kitchen.

The room broke into a roar of approval and then the swell died down into spirited conversation. Zolin looked around at his friends and caught Naia watching him. He grinned broadly at her and wanted to laugh at the way her expression went very still for a moment. After that brief hesitation, though, she smiled at him. She had a nice smile, and she didn't use it very often. She tried too hard, Zolin thought—but then, he had the luxury of knowing there was no stricture against expressing emotion among those who served the Deep.

"Can you believe it's only three weeks to the Autumn Evener?" Talaria asked.

"Don't let's talk about that, please," Jousia said. "We're here to have fun."

It was a sentiment with which Zolin heartily agreed, at least for tonight. He darted his hand in, beating Jousia to snatch the last fish roll from the shared platter.

"Hey," she protested, but she was laughing.

"I'll pay for another platter," he said, and waved at the server. "How is your dissertation on Portunese matrimonial customs coming?"

It was the easiest way to distract her, as he well knew. Jousia was passionate about her studies; although the skills of a Diplomat didn't come naturally to her, she worked hard. He chewed on his fish roll and settled back in his chair as she began an enthusiastic description of how Portun's Midwinter customs differed from other nations. In Tamnen, Midwinter was the best time to arrange alliances and engagements, but in Portun, apparently, the Eveners were considered more propitious. Midwinter was for revelry and gift-giving once the Longnight vigil had been kept.

Zolin wasn't as interested in far eastern cultures as Jousia, but he'd had several classes about the various eastern nations. He was able to keep up his end of the conversation well enough, but he relaxed when the server brought their next platter. He and Jousia both had their mouths full when a jangling chord announced the bard's return.

"Good even, my friends!" the bard cried, and was answered by a chorus of cheers. Zolin was uncertain of the bard's gender; they were slender as a sapling and wore clothes and a hair style that could reflect male, female, or neither. Although they had performed a few sleight-of-hand tricks, they weren't dressed flashily, which Zolin took to mean their music was the main focus.

Into the mountains, across the sea,
I hope my love still waits for me.
We took ship to sail southerly
Before the mists arose.

My fair young maid of amethyst eye
Plighted troth to wed by and by.
But I needs must sail southerly
A fortune for to grow.

The waves rose high, the winds blew keen
A darkness fell on Silverdene

*My love and I have parted been
Because the mists arose.*

Zolin twitched as the bard's voice soared on the word 'Silverdene,' and his gaze flew to meet Naia's. Yes, she'd heard it, too. She was staring at the bard, but, sensing Zolin's attention, looked over at him. After a moment, she nodded and turned her focus back to the bard.

Zolin straightened in his seat and glanced around, wondering if any other tables had come free. He couldn't see the bard well at all from where he was sitting. But if anything, the tavern was even more crowded than when they had first arrived.

Talaria leaned in, her shoulder pressing against Zolin's. "What's with Naia?" Her voice was low in Zolin's ear. "I thought she was enjoying herself."

"I think she is," Zolin replied, but when he met Talaria's gaze, he realized he hadn't fooled his friend.

"You both jumped when the bard sang that last verse." Talaria narrowed her eyes playfully at Zolin. "Don't tell me you two really *are* carrying on an illicit love affair. I've got gold riding on your pure and pristine friendship."

Irritation flashed through Zolin. The others were *betting* about his private life? He glowered at Talaria. No one was placing bets on which of the servant girls *she* was sweet on. "Not that I appreciate it at all," he said, "but your bet is sound."

Talaria had the good grace to look abashed, but she didn't let the matter drop. "What is it, then? I thought she wanted to hear the Amethirian bard."

Zolin sighed. Talaria could be like a wharf cat with a fish when something piqued her interest. "It's Silverdene."

Talaria looked at him blankly.

"The bard mentioned Silverdene in their song." Zolin drummed his fingertips on the table top. "That name came up in some of Naia's research, and neither one of us have ever heard of it."

"Who's Silverdene?"

"Not who, what," Zolin corrected. "Or, more accurately, *where*. We think it's a city. But we have no idea where it is—was—whatever."

Talaria frowned at the table for a moment, thinking. Then she shrugged. "Doesn't sound familiar to me. At least I can tell you it's nowhere in the Long Coast. Closest city-state there is Surdan, but that's a bastardization of Solordanel, and I've never seen it called anything but Surdan once the Lordanil Accord was reached."

Zolin cast back to his Long Coast history. "And that was, what, five hundred years ago?"

"Nearer six. But yeah. Sorry, Zo, I can't help you with Silverdene."

Well, it had been worth mentioning. At least Zolin could rule out somewhere. Naia would be glad to hear it.

The bard wrapped up a lively instrumental piece, and Zolin could see Naia quivering in her seat. To his surprise, she glanced his way and then relaxed back into her seat.

For the next half glass, the bard reigned. They played sea shanties and war songs, tales of true love and bitter revenge. The group of trainees settled into silence broken only by clapping at the end of each song. It wasn't until the bard strummed a few notes and called for requests that Naia stood.

"Have you any more songs about Silverdene?" she asked.

The bard straightened on their stool and turned to contemplate Naia. "Indeed, I have," they said, not sounding entirely happy about it. "But I'll warn you, it's a sad song, and long."

"Please," Naia said, and to Zolin's astonishment, she flipped a *silver* to the bard.

The bard caught the coin midair with deft fingers and flashed a grin at Naia. "If the lady pays in silver, the lady gets her pleasure," they said, standing and delivering a deep bow. Zolin didn't look at Naia, but he knew she would be blushing. Fortunately the bard only fiddled briefly with the tuning pegs and began picking out a low, slow ballad.

> *It was the fortress Silverdene*
> *Where the last of us made our stand*
> *Our nation rent by our own queen*
> *and blood baptized the land*
>
> *The queen's men stood against the foe*
> *until the order came:*
> *The troops took to the mountain road,*
> *but the warleader remained.*
>
> *Proud she stood atop the wall,*
> *her cloak spun on the wind.*
> *Her silver blade she lifted tall,*
> *Queen's honor to defend.*
>
> *Her daughter she had bade farewell*
> *who rode in the queen's van*
> *and saluted her mother with a yell*
> *as strong as any man.*

The mist rose high around the hold
as scouts brought their reports
Warleader planned her defense bold,
the outlanders to thwart.

"Warleader, see the marching foe—
They come close to our walls!"
She smiled at the trembling boy
"I do not fear death's pall."

"Warleader, what is that dreadful sound?"
Her laugh was quick and free.
"The cries of those for darkness bound,
and the gods hear not their plea!"

"Warleader, why do we not retreat?"
Her scorn cut to the bone.
"Our foe is drunk on their conceit,
We shall prevail alone."

The battle raged against the walls
and no reserves arrived
The warleader stood to save us all,
a sacrifice much prized.

The queen retreated to the vale
and there deep magics wrought.
The priests' offerings could not fail
as the warleader fought.

The lightning flashed over the walls,

> *the thunder roared with glee.*
> *O'er the defenders fell a pall—*
> *They knew they could not flee.*
>
> *They were the last line of defense,*
> *were those of Silverdene.*
> *And when they fell, the nation rent*
> *in two that one had been.*
>
> *And honored was the sacrifice*
> *of many a valiant soul,*
> *as mist arose at a costly price*
> *no honor could console.*
>
> *The spirits wept to see our plight,*
> *the gods moaned for our pain.*
> *The warleader met final night*
> *with the fall of Silverdene.*

As the bard's last note faded, the entire tavern took a collective breath. Zolin swallowed against a tightness in his throat. A glance at his friends told him they were all affected.

"Enough melancholy!" roared a voice, making Zolin jump. The tavern keeper had come out and was waving a bar rag at the bard. "You'll drown us all in our tears! Give us a dance, Seh Bard, and forget this war and gloom."

The room broke into laughter, though at Zolin's table, only Evfra joined in. The bard winked at Naia and flashed her a grin. "My lady's coin is spent," they said, and jumped into a lively jig that bounced and rippled through the room.

Evfra immediately began tapping his fingers against the table. After a few moments he jumped to his feet. He grabbed Talaria's hand and they joined the people already dancing in a hastily-cleared space in front of the bard. Zolin leaned back, looking over at Jousia and Naia.

"I have an early study session tomorrow," Jousia said, and shoved her chair back from the table. "I really should head back."

"We'll walk with you," Naia said. Zolin had a feeling she wanted to discuss the bard's song and go back to look at her boxes of artifacts and documents. He shrugged and stood as well.

"Let me tell Talaria," he said, and waved to catch their friend's eye. When he was satisfied Talaria had seen him, he turned and gave the two women a faint smile. "Ladies, your escort awaits."

Chapter Sixteen

"Just how long do they propose to keep us waiting?" Arama muttered. She was pacing. She'd been pacing a lot over the past week, in between conferences with Bekir and that Diplomat, Revalis. Yar, blast him, was content to sit in a patch of sunshine somewhere, communing mentally with his dragon, or perhaps just meditating. Arama wasn't sure and didn't want to be rude in interrupting.

She shoved the fingers of both hands through her hair, puffed out a breath, and dropped into her desk chair.

There she sat, tapping her fingertips and staring at the blank paper in front of her.

Arama didn't truly have any cause to complain about their treatment by the Ranarri. Bekir had personally seen them settled in a pleasant suite of rooms very similar to the ones the prince's party had occupied several years ago. The food was plentiful and delicious, and a young page of some sort had been placed at their disposal. The girl didn't speak unless spoken to, and her knowledge clearly only stretched to domestic matters like meals, clothes, bathing, and other minutiae.

Finally Arama picked up her pen, dipped it carefully into the inkpot, and began writing. She'd already sent one brief letter, just to let Lozarr know she was alive, but she owed him more.

Dear Lo,

We have been at the Ranarri University for a week now. Yarrax's bonded dragon carried me and Yarrax here. We've been guests of the Diplomats . Apparently they'd had correspondence with you or Vistaren or someone in Maron. Anyway, they knew more than a little about what was going on.

They sent a ship to pick up the rest of the Dawn Star crew. If you see Lijka, let her know Kinnet is safe. She should join us here soon.

It's fortunate I have money on deposit with the banker's guild here. I've been able to replace some of the things we lost in the wreck. Being on Ranarr without you is strange. We went past Forenna's earlier today, when we visited the market. It made me smile, thinking of the evening we spent last time we were here.

I'm going to treat Yarrax to dinner tonight, but I'll take him to the Chatty Raven. I've heard there's a new-come bard from home, and as much as I like Ranarr, I confess I'm feeling a little homesick.

She paused, then added hastily, *I didn't lose my siren-tooth knife.*

Love,

Arama

When the ink was dry and the letter sealed, she waved the little page girl over. "See that this is sent quickly, please," she said. She slipped a small sack of heartfruit candy into the girl's hand along with the letter. The Ranarri viewed tips as bribery, but small gifts were perfectly acceptable.

The girl gave her a shy smile and left their rooms.

Feeling better, Arama stood, clapping her hands together. "Yar!" she called through the open door between their rooms. "Get ready to go. We're dining at the Chatty Raven tonight!"

The tavern was crowded, but the two of them were able to squeeze into a tight corner near the back. Arama breathed in deeply through her nose. It smelled like home. There would be seedcakes, of course, but they would be spiced with cardamom and flail rather than nutmeg and glisterwort. The last time she'd been here, the innkeeper kept a good store of Amethirian wine. He'd become a favored tradesman since Prince Vistaren held a meeting with the Amethirian expatriate faction here some years ago. She had high expectations.

Yar wasn't talkative, but he looked everywhere with keen interest, and he seemed more present than he had all day.

When he caught Arama looking at him, he gave her a wry grin that almost looked sheepish.

"I'm hungrier than I thought," he admitted.

Arama hummed in amusement. "Lost track of time and forgot to eat lunch, didn't you?" She shook her head teasingly. "I can tell we're going to have to get you a body servant. You're too skinny."

He looked down at himself. "I've always been this skinny."

"Doesn't mean you're supposed to be," she countered. "There's no need to deprive yourself these days, my lad. I want you to order plenty of food tonight. We've got coin to cover it."

He opened his mouth, whether to protest or agree, she never found out, because the serving girl came up to them just then. When Arama asked what was on offer, the girl spouted off a list that made Yar's eyes widen. If he *had* planned to argue, that list changed his mind. He ordered fish rolls and fried onions and cheese bread. Arama added her own order, and had just asked for two pints of Amethirian ale when a hush spread over the room.

The serving girl vanished as the bard struck the first golden notes of a song Arama had grown up singing.

Everything she'd heard about the bard had been justified. Nimble brown fingers flew over the strings of their lute and lush lips curved with emotion as they sang. After the first two songs, they slowed the pace, drawing out one of the old ballads of Rona and Fann. Arama didn't think she was imagining the tiny grin on their face as they sang the verse of Rona's marriage to Aevvar and Fann's oath in return. It reminded her of the way Vistaren had always loved those hero tales. With a pang of regret, she realized she missed not just Lozarr, but the prince and Azmei as well.

At the end of the song, she found herself on her feet, applauding. The bard shook back shaggy black hair and winked at Arama, then jumped into a sea shanty sung on every Amethirian ship for the past three hundred years. With a roar of approval, the whole crowd broke out into song.

As she belted out the words of the chorus, Arama noticed a group of younglings dressed in the gray robes of trainee Diplomats. They were clapping along with the beat, though only one of them was singing. It made her grin. At least they weren't all as solemn and impassive as their elders.

The ballad of Silverdene the bard produced for one of the requests left Arama feeling strangely melancholy, and when she glanced over at Yar, he was nodding over his second mug of ale. She nudged him awake and settled their bill. As they exchanged the stuffy air of the tavern for the humid but fresh air of the courtyard, Arama realized the trainee Diplomats were also leaving.

Arama approached, meeting the eyes of the taller woman in the group. "You look as though you must be heading back to the University, yes?" Arama said. "We are staying there. Would you mind if we walk with you?"

"You're Captain Dzornaea," the young man blurted, and when she looked curiously at him, he blushed.

"I remember you," she said, and grinned. "You've a deft hand at serving refreshments. I'm Dzornaea, and this is Yarrax."

"I'm Naia," said the taller woman, "He's Zolin, and this is Jousia. We would be pleased to have you walk with us. You're from Amethir, aren't you?"

"I'm not," Yarrax said. "I'm from the dragons."

When Naia looked curiously at him, Arama hastily said, "But I'm from Amethir, yes. Have you ever been there?"

"I've never left Ranarr." Naia tilted her head as they began walking. "But I'd like to see Amethir. I love maps, and I've studied your languages. I hope to be posted there someday."

"I confess to being a bit homesick just now," Arama said, smiling at her. "The food, the music... I'd been here before, a few years ago. I'm glad to see it hasn't changed."

"Have you ever heard of Silverdene?" Naia asked. Then she glanced at Zolin, though Arama hadn't heard the young man say anything.

"Can't say I have. I didn't know either of those songs the bard sang about it. If it's in Amethir, it must be inland. I know the coast better, for obvious reasons." She grinned.

Naia shook her head. "The bard is the first person I've found who even knows it existed. But I've been working on a research project, and I came across the name. It seems to be a city, or maybe a fortress. I'm not quite sure which."

Arama shook her head, puzzled. "There are only two really big cities in Amethir, and they're Maron and Dalasan. Simiri's a small city, but I've never been there. Maybe it's got a Silverdene Castle or something." She shrugged. "Or maybe it used to exist and doesn't anymore. The bards love old songs, and the older the better, sometimes."

Zolin said, "Can you tell us more about the situation in Amethir?"

Arama glanced sharply at him; it was an obvious attempt to change the subject. "I can tell you what it was before I sailed, near a month ago. A lot could have changed since then, but when I left, I sailed under my own flag as admiral of Prince Vistaren's navy." Such as it was, and now she'd lost the single ship that had made up that navy. She pressed her lips together to keep from glowering.

"Why did the prince rebel against his father?" the third woman asked. She was actually a bit shorter than Arama, and from the way she moved, she was as used to being underestimated for her height as Arama had been. She might be taken more seriously if her vest weren't buttoned crookedly, Arama thought wryly.

"It's a complicated situation, and I'm not sure a pirate is the best person to explain it," Arama said, "but it comes down to this—there's something odd going on with their stormwitchery, and the prince and the king disagree on both the problem and the solution."

Jousia looked startled for an instant. "Something wrong with the stormwitchery?"

"I said 'odd,'" Arama pointed out, though privately she thought 'wrong' was much more accurate. "The stormwitches at the Academy aren't having much luck in identifying what it is. But we've started seeing seadragons on the ocean, and one even attacked a lighthouse at Maron Harbor. Something weird is definitely happening."

The act of laying it all out for them made her twitchy again, impatient to be somewhere she could actually do something to help Vistaren. Not that it seemed likely she could help, since her ship was at the bottom of the ocean. Her heart thumped uncomfortably at that thought.

"Do you think they'll call on us to mediate?" Zolin asked.

Arama glanced at him. He seemed a little on edge, which was odd for a Diplomat. Then again, he was only a trainee. Perhaps he'd grow out of it, or whatever the Diplomats did to erase any emotion from their chosen negotiators. "I hope so. I know they've had a letter from someone. I would guess Vistaren or Azmei, honestly, because I don't see the king requesting it. But so far that Master Bekir hasn't said so, and Diplomat Revalis might as well have his lips sewn shut for all he tells me."

Zolin snorted, then coughed and smoothed his expression out. "Master Bekir and Master Revalis are two very different sorts of Diplomat," was his only comment.

Arama blinked. Then Bekir *was* a Diplomat? She certainly hadn't gotten that impression from him...but then again, perhaps that had been his intention. Set her at her ease, gain her trust, and then turn the shining Diplomat personality on her. She frowned. She liked Bekir. It would be a shame if that had all been a ploy.

Their arrival at the gates of the University grounds saved her from having to respond, though. Jousia bid them farewell, saying she was headed for the library. Zolin and Naia went in the direction of the trainee housing. Arama and Yar were left to make their way back to their assigned quarters. Neither of them spoke as they walked. When they finally parted to go to their own rooms, Arama wasn't sure if the evening had been a good one or not.

Chapter Seventeen

Naia unlocked the door to her room, gesturing for Zolin to go in ahead of her. Her skin itched from not showing her agitation. As soon as the door was shut and locked behind them, she spun to face her best friend.

"Did you hear that? Silverdene! That bard *must* know where it is!"

To her irritation, Zolin merely nodded, his expression blank. "Do you think they'll tell you without more silver changing hands?"

She glared at him, trying to hide her embarrassment. "If you're going to be like that—"

"Like what? Observant? I've never seen you spend that kind of money so impulsively." Zolin's eyebrows drew together. "Naia, you're really starting to worry me."

"Worry you? Why?" she snapped. "Because I spend my money on the song I want to hear instead of buying an extra plate of fish rolls?"

Zolin sighed. "Because I'm starting to think you're obsessed. Pestering Captain Dzornaea about it, even!"

Naia scowled at him. "I'm not *obsessed*, I'm just trying to figure out where the boxes of letters came from. If I can do that, it'll prove what a good researcher I am. They'll have to pay attention to whatever I uncover." She paced to the window and back. "It won't matter that I criticized Master Revalis and contradicted Master Inkeri."

Zolin folded his arms. "That's not really what this is about."

"It can't hurt!"

"Actually," he said, drawing the word out as if thinking. "I think it could. Didn't you already register your final project with the masters? Do you think they'll be pleased if you change it with only a few weeks to go?" He shook his head. "I thought you'd put the letters aside to focus on your project."

"This isn't about changing my project." Naia flopped down on her bed. "It's about making a discovery that could change our understanding of—of—of history!"

"Or it might be nothing of import," he countered. "Have you thought that maybe the masters already know about all this? There are people in charge of the archives and books. Wouldn't they know what sort of documents were stored here?"

Naia pushed down a twinge of doubt. What if Zolin was right? What if what she thought was an earth-shaking discovery actually turned out to be unimportant? Still, it hurt that Zolin didn't believe in her. And there was the most important thing...

"You didn't see where I found those boxes. It was so deep I wasn't even sure I was still in the library." She swallowed. "And you didn't see the Shroudling."

Zolin went still. "Shroudling?" He drew in a breath. "I *knew* you weren't telling me everything!"

Naia looked down, tucking her hair behind her ear. "I didn't want to complicate things. I thought we could just look at the boxes, and those would give me all the answers."

"Tell me about the Shroudling," Zolin insisted.

"I almost think it's actually a ghost," she hedged.

"Of a Shroudling." Zolin's gaze was flat. "Tell me about the Shroudling."

Naia sighed. "It was how I found the boxes. It was almost like I was being led, though I didn't realize it at the time." She closed her eyes, remembering the cool, wet mist on her skin, the odd way the lamps had flickered. She took a deep breath and related the story.

When she finished, Zolin was frowning. "You were deep, you said. Do you think you could find it again?"

"I hope so, since I didn't get all the boxes that were there." Naia wondered suddenly why it hadn't occurred to her to go back for more of the boxes. She'd been so wrapped up in the letters... all right, perhaps she *was* a little obsessed. But this was a mystery like nothing she'd encountered in the course of her studies. It was bound to keep her attention.

"I think you should take me there tomorrow," Zolin said. Naia opened her mouth and he held up a hand, "No, not tonight. It's very late, and if you don't need to sleep, *I* do. But tomorrow, after classes, let's go to the library and you can show me this trove of boxes. Maybe I'll even get to see this Shroudling spirit."

Naia was gratified that his tone, when he spoke of the Shroudling, had no patronizing tone. She wasn't sure what all he was thinking, but it seemed like the Shroudling *did* change things for him. She should have told him about the Shroudling from the start—perhaps they wouldn't have argued so much over it. She should have trusted him.

"All right. Sleep well, then." She rubbed her temple, which was just starting to tighten a little. "For that matter, maybe I'll brew some of your migraine tisane before I go to bed."

Zolin had been moving to the door, but at that, he stopped. "Do you want me to do it?"

That made her smile. "No, it's just the beginning aura of it. I don't think it'll get any worse, but I'd like to be sharp tomorrow when we explore."

Zolin grinned at her, "See you tomorrow, then."

Naia knew, somehow, that she was dreaming, but she also knew she wasn't quite Naia anymore.

She was wearing armor and her shoulder ached from an old injury. She had been up too late the night before, watching the enemy campfires. And here she was again, in the same guard tower, staring out into the bloody sea of mud outside the walls of Silverdene.

How many days had she bought for her daughter to get far from here? Surely the enemy would come again today. There were so few defenders left.

Vyx sighed and rubbed at her shoulder. They would fight to the bitter end, despite their numbers. It was part of the agreement they'd made with the queen, and part of the vow she had made privately to Zera. Besides, if Duergo and his advisors thought a sacrifice would please the spirits, then it must be a whole-hearted sacrifice.

What if sending Zera away has spoilt that? *She shook off the nasty thought. She had been faithful in her religious observance all her life, honoring the spirits and the gods, and she believed what she had done was right and necessary.*

The high king had witnessed the treaties ratified. His people had brokered their original peace with the Crelin. He must know it was the Crelin, not the Srelang, who had dishonored that peace.

"Please let her reach Ranarr," she whispered.

"Warleader?" It was the voice of one of the guards.

Vyx looked over at him and smiled. "Sending a prayer to the spirits," she told him. "We should all gather and send a prayer collectively before the sun gets higher."

"You think today will be our last?" the guard asked. His voice held no hesitation, though she sensed a little fear.

"I think it will," she said.

She didn't fear death by now. It felt almost like a relief, to know that her struggle was nearly at an end. She prayed it had been enough. She prayed Danae and their remaining people had reached the mountain fastnesses. She prayed the spirits and the gods would honor this sacrifice.

But even if none of it was enough, she could do little about it now.

"I'll have the corporal sound assembly, then," the guard told her.

"Very good."

She didn't leave the window. She wondered tiredly if she had one more rousing speech in her. Perhaps her captain would lead the prayer. He had been temple trained, chosen as an officer because of his ability to read and write several languages as well as his righteous character. Vyx nodded. It felt right. She would have him do the honors.

Thunder crashed across the valley. Was it natural weather, or were the gods answering them? She looked up, straining to find any glimpse of the moon that should still be setting in the west. When she looked to the front again, lightning blinded her and she went still.

Naia wiped her bracered arm across her forehead, trying to dispel the sweat and blood gathered there. It shoved her helmet askew, flipping the bedraggled raven plume into her eyes. With a curse she snatched at the feather, pulling it from its fitting. She raised her sword arm for another stroke and realized she was in the midst of battle, trying to topple a siege ladder. The soldier at her right was screaming, reeling back from the wall. The soldier to her left had fallen.

A Crelin warrior clung to the wall, trying to drag his lower half up over the edge. Vyx stepped back, maneuvering for room to slice at his head. She stepped on something that gave. She stumbled, and the man she'd stepped on moaned.

It was all the opening the Crelin needed. He surged over the wall, shouting in triumph. He advanced on Vyx, leaving the next man on the ladder to secure it in place. Vyx lifted her shield and shifted her feet again, trying to regain proper footing. But the walls were slick with blood and rain. Her head was spinning, her breath catching in her chest.

This is the sacrifice, *she thought, and cast aside her shield.* This is the moment.

She didn't try to dodge as the Crelin's blade slid home in her chest.

Naia woke, gasping, drenched in sweat and shivering. She stared blindly ahead of her as her heart pounded. Then lightning flashed, followed almost instantly by a crash of thunder. Wind swirled into the room, and she realized it was her own room at the University.

It was her own room, and the rain was lashing in through her open window.

Naia scrambled out of bed, rushing to shove it closed. She stared, bewildered, at the rain-pelted glass. Had there been thunder before bed? She couldn't remember. She was so tired.

Rubbing at her shoulder, Naia turned to go back to her bed and then froze in her tracks.

Lying on her pillow was the bedraggled feather of a raven.

CHAPTER EIGHTEEN

T HERE WAS A DRAGON in the Sanctuary Deep.

Zolin had, over the past few weeks, discovered many unexpected things in the Sanctuary, but a dragon was definitely the most unexpected.

The sinuous, gemstone-green creature was coiled in an open-air porch, surrounded by ravens. She opened her eyes when Zolin stopped walking with a scuff of his boots. She didn't move otherwise, though, and since he'd heard enough to know she had brought Dzornaea and Yar, he assumed she wouldn't eat him.

Well, he *hoped* she wouldn't.

He gave her the same bow he would use for one of the Masters. "Your pardon, lady. I didn't mean to intrude. I'm just on my way to the Sanctuary archive."

She still didn't move, but he felt a sort of pressure in his head, or around his head, or perhaps inside his chest. Something told him she was amused at him. He wondered if, with more practice, he would be able to use mindspeech with her, as he was learning to do with Master Bekir.

The ravens flapped into the air around the dragon, calling raucously, and then settled down again. Zolin bowed again and backed out of their space. He didn't turn his back on the dragon until he had a wall between them.

"Well, if I'd actually hoped to get some sleep, that impulse is gone," he muttered to himself. Not that he'd truly hoped for sleep any time soon. Naia's revelation about the Shroudling, along with the news Captain Dzornaea had given them, wouldn't stop spinning in his head.

He heard a soft chuckle just before Bekir came into sight, walking toward him along the passage. "I see you've met Lady Xellax." Bekir's eyes twinkled, though his mouth was set in grim lines.

"I wondered where the dragon had got to," Zolin admitted.

"Ravens and dragons make good companions for each other," Bekir said. He turned down the passage to his study, beckoning for Zolin to join him. "Historically, dragons have been fairly frequent visitors on the White Stone."

"I've never heard anything about that!"

"The Deep doesn't give up its secrets to just anyone, you know." Bekir glanced over at him. "You've never asked me what errand brought the dragon. I was pleased to see

Revalis had chosen you to serve Captain Dzornaea and the Voice of Dragons. Did you have a chance to eavesdrop?"

Voice of Dragons? Zolin felt his face growing hot. "Er. Was I supposed to?" he hedged. He thought he'd been less obvious than Shirin, but he should have known better.

Bekir snorted. "I would expect no less from my mentee," he said. "Tell me what you understand to be the issue." They reached Bekir's study and he gestured Zolin to a seat while he turned on his spirit burner.

"I know Captain Dzornaea was fighting on the prince's side in the civil war," Zolin said, wondering if he should admit that he'd spoken to her less than an hour ago. "And I heard her say her ship sank. I couldn't tell if it was because of a battle, or...did it happen during that bad storm?"

Bekir hummed an affirmative.

"I didn't really understand about Yarrax, though. I know he came to deliver a message, and it seemed like the message was from the dragons? Or from *his* dragon? But I wasn't certain, from your conversation with them, how that mattered to the war." Zolin threaded his fingers together in his lap. "But tonight we met them on the way back from the tavern, and she told us that Yarrax's message, whomever it came from, was maybe what *started* the war."

Bekir nodded. "If the Voice's message is correct—and I have no reason to think it is not—then the sleeping gods are waking, and storm magic, that has been the basis of Amethir's grip on this half of the world, is twisting in some way."

Zolin wondered if he was imagining the slight emphasis Bekir seemed to place on 'twisting', but he was afraid to ask. "Then did they come here to request Diplomatic intervention in the civil war?" There couldn't be any other reason, could there? The Ranarri certainly wouldn't interfere in the war through any other means.

Bekir poured the water into his teapot. "I think they came here because they hadn't anywhere else to go. Captain Dzornaea is not the sort of woman who is used to being grounded." He carried the tea tray over and sat in the other chair.

"Will the Diplomats intervene?"

"I believe so, although there are several different arguments to the matter. We have received an appeal from Princess Azmei, though some argue that because she is Tamnese, her request shouldn't count. Revalis Ingan is Amethirian, which you might not know. His brother, in fact, is the general of the king's army. He is reluctant to intervene, but because of that connection, he has recused himself from the decision." Bekir leaned back in his chair, tenting his fingers in front of him. "Inkeri Felazar is of the opinion that we should remain independent of the conflict unless the king himself invites us. Parvan Taclis is scolding loudly that we should have intervened as soon as we heard of the conflict, without waiting for an invitation."

"And what do you think, Master?"

Bekir sighed and looked at him, the twinkle entirely extinguished from his gaze. "I think we have made grave errors that might even now be too late to correct, Zolin." He shook his head. "There have been rumblings of unease ever since the attempted assassination of Tamnen's princess, and while we were thorough in addressing our mistakes at that time, we did little to be proactive about what those rumblings might mean."

Zolin waited, keeping his gaze on Bekir's face. What rumblings was Bekir talking about? What sort of errors could the Diplomats have made?

Even Diplomats make mistakes, Naia's voice said in his memory. He'd been so angry at her for provoking Master Inkeri, and even angrier when they realized Master Revalis was observing them. But now, it seemed, Bekir agreed with her.

"We've grown complacent." Bekir rose and poured two cups of tea, handing one to Zolin. "Over the centuries, we have taken it for granted that we are superior, even-handed arbiters of policy. We have come to believe we make no mistakes, and that is a dangerously false belief—which costly lesson Revalis learned firsthand when Harkai of Strid broke the peace negotiated with Tamnen." He blew across his teacup, his gaze fixed on the ceramic rim. "I don't fault Revalis, you understand. I've been as guilty as any of this complacency."

"But how?"

"Tanvel told me he had a bad feeling that the attack on Azmei was part of something larger than a rebel's grasping at power. When we discovered it was the princess' cousin who had betrayed her, we dismissed it as an internal affair, but Tanvel felt there were loose threads in that tapestry. He tugged at several of them, but the last one he tugged proved his downfall." Bekir shook his head. "And in my grief, I failed to remember his warnings that larger forces than mere kingdoms were at play."

"Then Master Tanvel knew the gods were waking?" Zolin jiggled his foot. Why wouldn't Bekir get to the point?

"I don't know," Bekir said heavily. "And that not knowing bothers me. We often discover records of the true missions of Servants of the Deep, but those discoveries often aren't until decades later. Tanvel left me nothing specific I can point to, nothing but hints and vague comments. I know of no place to seek anything more. But I'm left with a churning in my stomach that tells me there's something I have missed."

"Did he have a study or quarters here?" Zolin had met Tanvel once or twice, but the Shadow Diplomat had rarely spent long on Ranarr, and Zolin had never seen him once Princess Azmei became the man's apprentice.

Bekir waved his hand at the room around them. "This was his. I moved my things here after our last parting. We'd shared quarters above-Stone, of course, and I had my teaching office and classroom there. I had never kept quarters here, because I had never needed them." He sighed. "After he returned to the Deep, I wanted the comfort of living where he had lived."

Zolin blew across his tea and took a sip, grateful when it didn't burn him. That was a dead end, then; Bekir would have searched every inch of the study before moving in, and probably more than once since then. He pursed his lips, wondering if he should say anything about Naia's Shroudling vision. But it wasn't really his tale to tell, and he wasn't sure it was related to anything. Until they'd had a chance to go to the place where she'd seen it, he would keep it to himself.

"Bah. I didn't mean to sour the mood," Bekir said, straightening in his seat. "Did you come seeking me for a reason, or were you simply exploring the Deep and stumbling over dragons along the way?"

Zolin hitched a shoulder. "I couldn't get my thoughts to settle," he said, which was true. "I'd meant to come down and look at the mosaics to distract myself. But a dragon is an admirable distraction, and then you found me."

Bekir chuckled. "Indeed. I'm afraid I've done nothing to help settle your thoughts."

Zolin sipped his tea again. "No, that's true," he said thoughtfully, "but at least you've given me other thoughts to swirl around in my head for a while." He grinned. "I suppose I ought to try to sleep so I won't nod off during lessons tomorrow. I had no idea becoming a Diplomat involved so little sleep, Master."

"Ha! Wait until you're a full Diplomat, my lad." Bekir flapped a hand at him. "Go on, get you to bed. Your meditation instructor will not go easy on you if you fall asleep in class."

Zolin grinned, drained his cup, and left. He had more questions than he'd begun the evening with, but somehow confiding to Bekir made him feel better about it.

CHAPTER NINETEEN

W HEN NAIA ARRIVED IN the refectory the next morning, she was surprised to see an announcement posted on the doors.

"Classes and lectures are canceled this morning. All final-year trainees should report to the Council Chamber when the ninth hour bell rings."

The younger trainees were unbothered by the announcement; the chatter Naia overheard on her way to the food line was all about what they would do with their morning of freedom. After collecting her breakfast, Naia found her other yearmates at their usual table. Talaria and

Jousia had their heads together, whispering, while the others discussed openly what the announcement might mean.

"It has something to do with that Amethirian pirate the dragon brought," Shirin insisted. Evfra, arms folded across his chest, looked as though he disagreed, but he didn't openly argue with her.

"I don't know," Zolin said. His eyes were thoughtful, but his fingers were picking apart a piece of ginger dulse cake. "Did you hear anything that boy with her said?"

Shirin rolled her eyes. "He was a child. Probably a cabin boy."

Naia blinked. If they were talking about that Yarrax who had been with Captain Dzornaea last night, he was only three or four years younger than Shirin. He'd said something funny about dragons, hadn't he? But maybe he just meant the dragon had brought them to Ranarr.

"It's probably something about the Autumn Evener," Evfra said. "It's less than a month away."

"They wouldn't have canceled everything at the last minute for that," Shirin snapped. She caught herself, though, and when she spoke again, her voice was calm again. "If it's something routine, they would have announced it ahead of time."

"That's a good point," Naia said, reaching for the butter dish. She hated agreeing with Shirin, but the abrupt nature of the summons did seem odd. Besides, Shirin had been shooting nasty looks at Naia and Zolin more often lately; it couldn't hurt to stroke her pride a bit.

The agreement just made Shirin look as though she'd bitten into a sea-sour, though. "What would you know about it? You've been missing so much class lately, the masters probably decided they might as well cancel them."

Naia took a bite of her buttered kelp biscuit and ignored her, meeting Zolin's gaze. She thought he seemed guarded, and she wondered if he knew more than he was telling. If he did, though, why wouldn't he have told her?

"Well, whatever it is," Evfra put in, "there's no point in speculating until the meeting."

Talaria looked up from her consultation with Jousia. "And whatever it is," she added, "it won't do us any harm to turn out in our best. I suggest we all go back to our rooms to make sure we look smart and prepared before we meet at the Council Chamber."

Naia noted in amusement that Talaria carefully didn't look at Jousia when she said it, but it was true that Jousia looked a little more tousled even than usual this morning. Her hair sported a cowlick and her robe was fastened haphazardly in front.

"Good idea, Talaria," Naia agreed. She was feeling agreeable in general, she realized, because Zolin was finally taking the Shroudling letters seriously. Whatever this morning's meeting was, it couldn't be as important as showing Zolin to the place in the library where she'd found the letters and seen the Shroudling.

Shirin made a scoffing noise, but that was because Shirin was never less than perfectly turned out any time she was seen in public. Naia couldn't understand how the masters continually overlooked Shirin's vanity, but this morning she wasn't even annoyed by it. She saw Zolin eyeing her speculatively, but she just shrugged at him and ate another scone.

When they assembled again outside the Council Chamber, Naia expected to be kept waiting. Instead, an honor guard opened one of the huge double doors and stood aside for them to enter.

Her earlier calm was shaken by the sight of all the masters seated around the large council table. Master Revalis's expression was serene but kind. Master Inkeri's smooth face showed no emotion, but her gaze was sharp. Master Parvan conveyed patience and superiority, though she wasn't quite sure how—perhaps in the set of his shoulders.

There were other masters—Bekir, Dukara, Arlax, and others she knew only by sight—but Naia's gaze kept going back to Inkeri's face. She only just managed to not jump when Revalis spoke, instead.

"Senior trainees, welcome. We have left you seats at the table."

At his gesture, they all took their seats. Naia sat as far from Inkeri as she could, but unfortunately that put her next to Shirin. The other woman didn't look at her, though. She was fiddling with a gold-and-leather wrap bracelet on her left wrist. It was a surprising indication of nerves.

"We have summoned you here to tell you that, after long deliberation, we have decided to end your training early." He paused, but though Naia's heart jumped in her chest, neither she nor the other trainees made any reaction. She didn't even glance at Zolin. They were all suddenly on their best behavior, a defense against the sudden chaos being thrown at them.

"I know you were all in the city when the dragon arrived. That dragon carried with it a young man who has been called as the Voice of Dragons. If the message he bears is true, much will be needed from the Ranarri Diplomats.

We have ever risen to the demands of the other nations, and we will do so again." He folded his hands on the table.

Inkeri spoke next. "Final examinations will begin next week. You will have the rest of the weekend to complete your final projects to the best of your ability. We will, of course, take into account that your plans have been cut short by a month, but you would do well to remember that a Diplomat's plans are often cut short by events beyond their control. This will be a test of your resilience."

"When the examinations are completed," Master Parvan said, "Those of you who pass will be given assignments under the mentorship of a Master Diplomat. Some of you will likely be sent abroad immediately. By the end of the month, many of you, it is to be hoped, shall be Diplomat mentees."

Naia felt as if the words were skating off an icy surface in her mind. She heard them, but they didn't actually penetrate. They were expected to be prepared for final examinations *next week*?

Master Bekir sat forward, and it seemed like his gray eyes twinkled when he said, "I am sure you have questions. We will answer them to the best of our ability."

They were all silent for several heartbeats. It would be unseemly to begin blurting questions without giving them full consideration, after all. Naia wasn't even sure what question she would like answered first. For that matter, she wasn't even sure she knew enough to formulate the correct questions to ask. Beside her, she heard a faint clink as the beads on Shirin's bracelet hit the table.

"May we be permitted to know what message the dragons have sent?" Zolin asked finally.

If they had been alone, Naia would have narrowed her eyes at him. His tone was so carefully regulated that he must already have some inkling of what that message was. He'd learned more while serving with Shirin than he'd told her—or perhaps he *had* told her, and she'd forgotten. She'd been wretchedly miserable that night.

Master Inkeri opened her mouth, but to Naia's shock, Revalis cut her off. "The dragons tell us that the sleeping gods are waking, and forces stir to bring upheaval to our world."

The sleeping gods are waking. Naia blinked. What did that even mean? Would the gods interfere in mortal affairs? Were they involved in the Amethirians' war?

"What do the priests say about this message?" Evfra asked. His voice was calm, assured. It gave Naia a safe place to anchor her thoughts.

"The god of peace does not have much commerce with the others, but the priests do say there is less peace to be had in meditation." Parvan shifted in his seat, which shocked Naia. The masters must also be disturbed by this message, if he was showing any discomfort.

Talaria cleared her throat. "Does this underlie the wars in Tamnen and Strid and Amethir?"

"Perhaps—" Bekir began, and then *Inkeri* cut *him* off.

"Enough questions. You are dismissed. You have the weekend to prepare for your examinations. We have high expectations of you."

With that, she stood. The other masters stood as well, though more slowly. Naia got the feeling Inkeri had rushed them, but none of them would gainsay her once she had spoken. A rush of frustration pushed up in her chest. What good were Diplomats and their rules of etiquette and impartial discussion if the Diplomats didn't even *allow* discussion?

But she stood with the other trainees and followed them out of the Council Chamber. Her peaceful mood from breakfast was entirely vanished. She found herself glowering at the floor as she trailed down the stairs behind the others.

"Does this underlie the wars in Tamnen and Strid and Amethir?" Shirin's voice was whiny and pitched high, the barb aimed at Talaria. "What a stupid question."

Zolin saw Talaria flinch ever so slightly. He wanted to leap to her defense, but arguing in the hallway might bring unwanted attention from the council, who had stayed behind when the trainees left.

"Why is it a stupid question?" Naia countered, and Zolin swallowed a groan. God of peace, why couldn't she keep her mouth shut?

"The war between Tamnen and Strid has been going on for years," Shirin said. "If it were caused by the gods awakening, don't you suppose we'd have heard about them sooner than this?"

"Perhaps," Evfra mused. He was tapping his fingers against his chin. "And then again, perhaps the war is what woke the gods. Anyway, they might not tell us. We're just trainees; who are we to be told what the priests have been thinking?"

"Some of us are just trainees," said Jousia, an edge to the sweet tone of her voice. "But Shirin is someone *important*, Evfra. She ought to know, oughtn't she?"

Zolin blinked. What had taken Jousia, to speak such open hostility?

"You wouldn't know someone important if they bit you, Jousia Short-stance," Shirin snapped. "You can keep your opinions to yourself."

"You needn't be rude to her," Talaria protested, but so softly Zolin wasn't sure anyone heard her but him.

"Short stance, maybe," Jousia said, the edge growing sharper. "But at least I'm not short in intellect, Shirin Lack-wits."

"Stop it, both of you," Naia said, and her voice was firm. "We should all be pulling together on the nets. We'll all be in the soup together if we don't."

"Of course you'd say that, since you need so much help from your devoted pet Zolin."

Zolin felt his stomach flip at the poison in Shirin's voice. He wasn't sure it would help if he opened his mouth to argue with her, though, so he lowered his gaze, studying the hem of her robe instead of looking up at her face.

"Don't speak of him that way!" Naia flared, and Zolin's stomach flipped again. *Oh, god of peace, bind her tongue, won't you?* he thought. "Zolin's worth ten of you, Shirin, no matter how much your family may be worth in the banks. At least he's a decent person who actually cares what happens to others."

There was a sudden small silence. It was as if they were all trying to absorb what Naia had just said. Then Shirin chuckled nastily.

"Go on, talk sweet about him. If the only way you think you'll pass is to sleep with the competition—"

Her words were cut off by a sharp smack as Naia lunged at her. Shirin reeled back, one hand flying up to her mouth, which was trickling blood from a split lip. Naia shook out her fist but kept moving toward Shirin, her expression ablaze.

"You might as well go back to your rooms and hide," Naia spat. "You've always thought you were better than us, ever since we were children, and you've been an utter nightmare this past year. You'd better hope you don't need any help preparing for your final examinations or finishing your project, because not one of us will help you."

Zolin's heart was thudding in his chest, and he wasn't sure which thought made him feel sicker, that Shirin believed he and Naia were lovers, or that Naia had *assaulted* Shirin in an appalling display of violence.

"Stop it, both of—" Evfra rumbled, but he was interrupted by a cool, quiet voice speaking from behind them.

"Trainee Sedorr, you will attend me in my office."

There was no inflection in Master Revalis' voice, but it sent a chill down Zolin's spine. Why, oh *why* couldn't his best friend control her temper better?

The fire went out of Naia's expression, but Zolin fancied it was still smoldering underneath her sudden stiffness. "Of course, Master Revalis," she said, and she did a good job of matching his cool tone, but her voice shook anyway.

Zolin watched as the master strode down the hallway, Naia scrambling to keep up, and for one horrible instant he thought he might vomit. When he looked at the others, he saw they were all as openly horror-struck as he felt.

Talaria's mouth was hanging open, Evfra was shaking his head slowly, and Jousia had gone pale.

Shirin gave a nasty laugh and spun on her heel, walking in the opposite direction. "Best bid farewell to your lover, Zolin," she hissed as she passed him.

The hallway was suddenly quiet enough that Zolin could hear the cries of gulls on the breeze outside the arched windows. He took a ragged breath, trying to figure out where this had all gone so horribly wrong. As he stood there, staring, the others slipped away silently, leaving him only sympathetic looks.

Chapter Twenty

Naia's knuckles were throbbing as she followed Master Revalis's straight back. It was a very long three flights of stairs before they reached the level with his office. As Revalis stepped off the stairs, he stood aside, one arm gesturing gracefully yet economically for her to precede him. She felt heat rush through her. Did he think she was going to run?

But she squared her jaw and stepped past him, keeping her eyes straight ahead. She knew her steps were stilted. Every time her foot came down on the marble hall, it felt like it was jarring her every bone. There was a hot ache at the back of her throat, and she could feel her eyes stinging.

God of peace, don't let me cry, she prayed. It would be horrible if she cried out of fury and Master Revalis thought she was afraid.

By the time they reached his office and went inside, her heart felt as if it were trying to claw its way out of her chest. How had she managed to mess up so horribly? And why? She'd taken every barb Shirin threw at her for so long now, *why* did she have to lose her composure and snap—and worse, in a public place so close to the Council Chamber, where the masters probably all witnessed it!

Revalis walked around his desk and sat down. He did not gesture her to a chair. His posture was exact, shoulders squared over his hips, hands folded on the desk in front of him. Naia felt his gaze rake her features, though she didn't dare meet his eyes. She needed to blink, but she was afraid if she blinked, the stinging would become actual tears. Instead she unfocused her gaze, trying to keep her eyes open as long as possible.

Finally Revalis said, "That was unseemly, Trainee Sedorr."

Was she supposed to respond? Naia lowered her head, dropping her gaze to the front of his desk. What could she possibly say? It *had* been unseemly. It had been against every principle she had been taught. But it had felt so inevitable, like if she didn't hit Shirin, she would swell up and explode. What else could she have done?

Revalis sighed. "Your stubborn silence does you no credit."

Naia opened her mouth, choked on a breath, and then croaked, "I do not mean to be stubborn, Master. I do not know what to say."

"Well, that's a start." His inflection didn't change at all, but for some reason the room felt a little warmer than it had. "I cannot imagine what possessed you to physically assault a fellow trainee in a public hallway."

Naia swallowed. Should she defend herself? Grovel? But if she tried to grovel, he would know she didn't mean it.

"Shirin is never playing when she says appalling things, Master," she said finally.

"Mm." His stillness was beginning to make her want to twitch. "Nor is King Harkai, Trainee Sedorr. And yet I have met him and treated with him and have managed not to assault him."

She felt a horrible urge to laugh rising up in her throat, and she swallowed again to prevent it. He hadn't meant it as a joke; he'd meant it as a rebuke—not only for her temper now, but for her criticism of his negotiations with Harkai two weeks ago.

"I give you my deepest apologies, Master Revalis." She didn't choke on the words, which she thought was very big of her. She was already beginning to feel sorry, as well, which fact made her temper try to fan back into flames. Why should she apologize? Why shouldn't Shirin apologize?

Revalis was silent.

Naia's legs were beginning to hurt. She was standing too straight, her muscles too tense. She didn't know what he wanted from her. Why hadn't he dragged her in front of the other masters to be punished? Why was he studying her so closely? She swallowed again, trying to work moisture into her dry mouth.

"You are the most frustrating creature I have met in years," Revalis said finally. His tone was conversational now, though still chilly. "You possess a keen intellect, a fine mind for strategy, a passion for understanding, and a group of loyal friends. And yet you cannot overlook one spoiled brat of a child who pokes at your weak spots out of her own pain."

Naia gaped at him for a bare instant before snapping back to attention, but it was too late.

Revalis sighed and dropped his head into his hand. "What am I going to do with you, Naia Sedorr?" When she didn't answer, he huffed a silent breath. "Sit down before you fall over. You shouldn't lock your legs like that when you're standing on ceremony."

"Master Revalis?" she ventured, but she crept to the other chair and sat as ordered.

"By all rights, I ought to throw you out. I'll hear from Inkeri, at least, when she learns of this." He shook his head and looked up at her finally. His gaze seemed sad. "If we were anywhere but on the brink of a world at war, I would send you to the Deep for a year and see what they could do with you. They've certainly trained more willful minds than yours."

Naia gave up on trying to speak. It almost sounded as if he *didn't* plan to throw her out, but for some reason that didn't soothe her galloping heartbeat.

"But we *are* on the brink of a world at war." Revalis almost seemed to be talking to himself. "I believe we need you on our side. I have too much faith in Bekir to ignore his advice." He sighed again and pinched the bridge of his nose as if he had a headache. "And yet, if you aren't punished, I set myself against Inkeri, and possibly others. And I can ill afford that."

Oh. He *did* have a headache. *Naia* was his headache. She felt a sudden flush of shame.

"I know I struggle with emotional control, Master," she blurted. Then she wanted to kick herself, because blurting something out while he was talking, whether to her or to himself, was exactly what she shouldn't be doing. "I try to keep my temper. I do try. I failed very badly today, I know that."

Sweet gods, Naia, you're only making it worse. It was as if she could hear Zolin's voice in her head. It made her want to giggle, but it also made her want to cry.

"Tell me what I must do to get better. Please, Master."

Revalis met her gaze, and though it felt like it was rending her soul, Naia forced herself to hold it. She would not look away. She would let him see how sorry she was. She had to convince him to give her a second chance.

After what felt like a lifetime, he said, "I am staying judgment for now, Trainee Sedorr, but that does not mean you shall have no punishment. You are confined to your quarters or the library. You will take your meals in your room. Once your final examinations are over, we will revisit this matter."

He was going to let her sit for final examinations? Then that meant he was leaving open the possibility that she could still become a Diplomat! Naia bit back the hope, forcing her expression to remain solemn.

"Yes, Master Revalis. Thank you."

Revalis stood, his face unchanging, but his eyes suddenly grim. "Don't thank me yet, Trainee." He gestured at the door.

Naia, not daring any more, stood and fled.

CHAPTER TWENTY-ONE

"THAT WAS SORT OF your fault," Zolin told Jousia as they watched the others leave. What had made her speak to Shirin like that? They all knew that to engage her only made everything worse. And Naia always wanted to protect everyone she cared about, so of course she'd jump into the fray.

Jousia's expression was extremely blank. "I...didn't think Naia would...act like a sprung trap," she said slowly.

"But why did you even dig at Shirin?" Zolin caught himself frowning and smoothed the expression away. "Come on, let's get away from the Council Chamber."

They'd given the others enough of a head start that they shouldn't catch up.

Jousia grunted. "I'm just so tired of her. She can't stand that Talaria's better at languages than she is. So what? Talaria's better at languages than all of us, I think. And the way Shirin acts as if she's always so superior..."

She trailed off, then gripped Zolin's elbow and tugged him into an alcove halfway down the stairs. Too surprised to resist, he let himself be tugged. When they were hidden from the view of casual passersby, she folded her arms across her chest.

"Did you know Shirin's only here on sufferance this year? Her attitude was bad enough when she really was richer than the rest of us put together. But this past Midwinter, her parents were caught in some sort of financial scheme, and the Diplomats were getting ready to censure them. The only reason Shirin didn't get censured with them is that they took ship and left her behind, so everyone thought she must be innocent of their schemes."

Zolin's eyes widened. "What sort of financial scheme?" He lowered his voice instinctively, then glanced over his shoulder to make sure the stairs were empty.

Jousia shrugged. "Evfra's the financial genius, not me. He could explain it—he tried to explain it to me." She grinned briefly. "I understood less than half of it." Her expression sobered again, her dark eyes serious. "But it was something that cost a lot of people a lot of money. Someone did a good job of hushing most of it, but I know there were at least two families ruined because their daughters' dowries were suddenly gone."

Zolin's thoughts were swirling. This could explain so many things about Shirin's behavior this year. Not knowing which thought might be most important, he seized one. "Then why didn't the Diplomats throw Shirin out? She's never really seemed like Diplomat material. I thought they kept her because of the money."

"They aren't supposed to do that," Jousia pointed out dryly. "No, I don't know. I wish they had thrown her out. Becoming a sponsored student certainly hasn't done anything for her personality. You'd think she would be grateful, but instead she just—pick, pick, pick." She shook her head.

"How long have you known all this?" Zolin demanded.

"I overheard things back around the Spring Evener that made me curious, and then I started watching Shirin more closely, and I heard a few things that made me wonder." Jousia's eyes gleamed. "After a while I realized Evfra was watching her, too—they haven't been studying together as much this year, had you noticed? So a few weeks ago I asked him what he knew. We put everything together then."

Zolin was frowning again. He realized it when Jousia poked him in the forehead. He shook himself and sighed. "Who else knows?"

"Just Efvra and me, as far as I know. He didn't want to ruin things for her—you know he's always had a soft spot for her—and I wanted to keep it as leverage, in case she did something truly awful. I didn't mean to let it just slip out, but she just—ooh, she just made me so angry today. I thought a cutting remark might put her in her place." Jousia looked up at him, tucking one corner of her mouth in her anxious tell. "I didn't mean to set Naia off."

"Naia's been a powder keg ready to blow for a while now," Zolin said absently. He was putting things together now, things he'd observed in Shirin recently, things about why Master Revalis had chosen her to serve Captain Dzornaea with Zolin, things he'd wondered. "Don't tell anyone else, all right? Talaria would only feel sorry for Shirin, for one thing."

"Isn't that the truth." Jousia shrugged. "I won't tell anyone, but I will tell Naia I'm sorry, if I get a chance."

Zolin looked at her soberly. "I hope you get that chance."

When he and Jousia reached the main level of the University, Zolin turned his steps toward the library. He didn't suppose Naia would be free of Master Revalis' lecture yet, but he could at least look for her in her favorite study spot. And if she wasn't there, well, just across from that spot was one of the best ways down to the Sanctuary Deep.

Ten minutes later, Zolin was sitting at a table in the Sanctuary refectory, pen scratching as he scrawled his thoughts out onto a piece of paper.

Shirin's parents had defrauded people and then left their daughter behind. Did Shirin know what they were doing before they were caught? Whether she did or not, she'd been abandoned by them. She was probably furious at them. And they all knew she'd been hoping for an offer of marriage from Councilman Peligrin, but that wouldn't be forthcoming if she had no dowry. Perhaps she'd thrown herself on the mercy of the Diplomats in order to stay. It wasn't a change of heart, certainly, but she must know there was some security in being chosen as a mentee. More security than being the penniless daughter of fraudsters, anyway.

Did Bekir know all of this? Zolin felt certain Bekir knew a great deal about what went on in the Stone. But did he know what a pet Inkeri had made of Shirin? Did it matter?

Why am I having bad feelings about Inkeri? he wondered. *Is it just because she's horrid to Naia? Or is it something more?*

He cast back over the last several weeks, trying to figure out why his mind immediately connected Shirin's situation to Inkeri's criticism of Naia? It might be that he was just biased because Naia was his best friend. Or perhaps there was something to it—perhaps Inkeri was afraid Shirin wouldn't be eligible as a mentee unless Naia were disqualified. Certainly Naia stood a better chance of scoring high on final examinations than Shirin did.

Would any of the masters, even Inkeri, do something so underhanded? He didn't know. Master Bekir would probably know, but Zolin wasn't willing to ask any questions that would sound like he was accusing Inkeri of something. Not when he didn't even know if he believed it himself.

Worse, he didn't know what his next right thing was. There were so many things cramming into his head, and he knew he ought to be making a list of them, but it seemed so dreadfully overwhelming. His mind was becoming swamped like a fishing boat in a bad storm.

"Do the forms!" he murmured in realization.

He stood, shoved his messily-scratched paper into his pocket, and left everything on the table. He'd already seen that Servants of the Deep respected people's belongings and space. He would find one of the openings where he could look out on the sea, and he would do the forms.

The Deep might bring comfort when thinking couldn't.

Chapter Twenty-Two

S MOKE TICKLED ZERA'S NOSE as she approached the edge of the trees. It wasn't thick and clinging like the smoke of Glanyrafon. This smelled like a cookfire, or perhaps several of them. She crouched and scanned the sky, looking for the source of the smell. Could she finally have made it to Holywell?

"Spirits, please," she whispered.

There—a haze of smoke hung in the air to her left, but it wasn't thick enough for the whole town to have been burned.

She had seen what the Crelin invaders left of Glanyrafon. She had waded through the sludge of still-smoldering ashes, searching for any signs of life. Of course there had been none. The outlanders were thorough.

She'd felt sick ever since.

Reaching the riverbank, she crouched and splashed water on her face. She wasn't sure how many days had passed. She slept only in brief snatches when she felt secure enough to close her eyes for a while. She'd eaten the last of her food earlier today, but if she had truly reached Holywell, the priests would feed her. They'd probably even supply her with food and a boat for the rest of the trip downriver to the sea. Then it would be just a matter of finding someone in a coastal village who would sail her to Ranarr.

Zera shifted her pack, trying to find some position where her shoulders didn't ache. She was used to traveling and sleeping rough, but usually she was in a company with horses and packmules. When this was over, she would have to change the training regimen for the queen's soldiers.

Then it struck her. When this is over, you'll be alone. There won't be any soldiers left but you.

Swallowing against a tight throat, she sighed and headed upstream, where the smoke told her Holywell must be. She would find a bridge or ford sooner or later; wagons from the outlying farms had to have some way across the river.

She hadn't been to Holywell since her naming day twenty-seven years ago. It would have changed since then, especially with the arrival of the Crelin. The priests and spirit speakers had urged welcome for the outlanders—much good it had done them. Holywell, as the seat of the goddess' worship, probably encouraged intermarriage with the outlanders. She just hoped their appeasement stance wouldn't prevent them from aiding a queen's messenger.

She circled around much of the town. Her filthy clothes would attract attention she didn't want. Life went on as normal in Holywell, from what she could see. It would be foolish to lower her guard.

When she finally reached the temple hill, she trudged up the road, head lowered, hoping she looked like a pilgrim. She was halfway up the hill before she realized she should have removed her armor. Curse her for a fool! No pilgrim would travel like that. But it was too late. She tugged her cloak more closely around her.

The temple was empty of worshipers, which was odd, but the priest at the door welcomed her. He bustled her into a pleasant room with a fireplace and a table.

"We don't see many travelers these days," he told her. "What are the roads like?"

Zera shook her head. She'd stayed off the roads as much as possible. "I didn't encounter any other travelers myself," she hedged.

"Things are unsettled, for certain," he said. He placed a bowl of stew in front of her. "Do you know how things are with the rest of the kingdom?"

It was odd that he didn't even mention the evacuation orders the queen had sent out weeks ago. They had known there wouldn't be full compliance; too many Srelang folk had attempted to enfold the outlanders into their lives. But that the priest would know nothing about it? Zera frowned.

"The outlanders burned Glanyrafon," she told him. She began to eat. "Haven't you had any ravens from the queen?"

"Burned...Glanyrafon?" He stared at her. "Outlanders? That can't be true. You haven't walked all the way from there, have you?" He looked over his shoulder, as if making sure the door was closed behind them.

"I saw it myself," she told him. "And they burned Crag-mond before that."

"Cragmond? But there's leagues and leagues between the two towns. Why would anyone burn them?" The priest went to the fireplace, where he prodded it gently with a poker.

"The queen ordered evacuation to the mountains," Zera said bluntly. "You had to have received word. The Crelin broke the treaties. We've been fighting a holding action for weeks."

The priest sighed, his shoulders slumping. "I wish you'd pretended to be a normal pilgrim," he told her, without turning. "I could have let you go."

Hair prickled at the back of Zera's neck. She was on her feet, blade drawn, before the priest turned, but she wasn't fast enough. The door burst open and soldiers poured into the room.

"We were told no one survived Glanyrafon," one of the soldiers said. "Good thing we didn't believe the lying na-tives." She leveled her sword at Zera. "There's no point in resisting."

Zera turned an accusatory look at the priest. "A traitor priest."

He glared at her. "Traitor? Who's the traitor? The priest trying to keep the peace, or the queen who's chosen to abandon her people?"

Tingles ran down her back. "You did get the ravens. You're just revolting against the queen's edicts. Against the holy commands of the high priest and his conclave."

"We just want to live in peace!" the man said. His hands knotted together, knuckles white. "We don't care about Cre-lin coming in—the more people we have, the more hands to work in the fields. There's enough room for all of us."

Zera sneered at him. "If only the outlanders wanted to live in peace, as well," she said.

She dropped her blade onto the table. She could force them to kill her, perhaps, but that wouldn't achieve her mother's last command. She would allow them to take her captive and hope she could escape. She nudged her pack further under the table, hoping the others hadn't seen it.

"Wise choice," the soldier said. "You, get her pack. We'll take you to the commander and see what he wants to do with you." She gestured another soldier to tie Zera's arms behind her back.

"Your commander promised there would be no blood shed on temple grounds," the priest said.

"No blood shed!" Zera cried. "The blood of our whole people is on your head, priest! Curse you and curse your so-called holy well, that spreads only perversion and lies!"

She felt the spirits crowd close around her as she spoke. Then her knees weakened and her breath came short. Her curse had been heard.

Arama knew the Diplomats would have Amethirian food served if she requested it. They were unfailingly polite hosts, even if they were infuriatingly noncommittal. But she wasn't one for sitting in place for long—at least, not when that place didn't have waves under her feet. Going to the Chatty Raven was at least something to do with her time while she waited for the rest of her crew to arrive on Ranarr.

Yar seemed happy to trot along at her side, so they were heading out of the University grounds towards the Amethirian quarter. As they approached the gate, she saw Bekir, who still hadn't admitted to being a Diplomat, approaching them.

"Captain," he greeted, and his silver-gray eyes crinkled at the corners as he smiled. It was disconcerting to think of a Diplomat that wasn't a stone statue of a person. "I was just going to come looking for you."

Arama raised her eyebrows. "And why is that?"

"We've had word from the *Argenta*. They're less than a day from port. Your stormwitch has been speeding their passage, so they should arrive on the evening tide."

"That's some good news, finally," Arama said, breathing more easily. "Everyone's well?"

"I presume so; the *Argenta*'s captain would have mentioned if it were otherwise." Bekir tilted his head. "Where are you bound?"

"The Chatty Raven," Yar said. It startled Arama. He had such an odd way of jumping into a conversation after spending a quarter glass locked in his own head.

Arama grinned sheepishly. "It's a nice taste of home, and the bard there knows all the songs I grew up on," she admitted.

"Fine food, indeed, and Ellyl's singing is not to be missed," Bekir agreed. "I'll instruct the *Argenta* to send your crew there when they dock."

"My thanks," Arama said. It would be good to have Zek and Kinnet back with her. She felt a sudden pang of renewed loss—Carig wouldn't be with them. Her first mate was lost to the deeps, and though she knew it was the only death he would have wanted, it still cut her to lose him.

Bekir didn't seem to notice her sudden grief, or at least he kindly ignored it. He merely nodded and walked on into the University. Yar had noticed, though; his skinny hand slipped into Arama's and squeezed quickly, then tugged away again.

Arama gave him a faint sideways smile and started walking again.

The bard was playing to a nearly empty tavern, which seemed odd. Arama and Yar took a table near the front and center and ordered a fine big lunch. When the bard saw Arama, they tipped their head with a quick wink and shifted the song they were playing until it became a sea shanty about northeast winds and siren songs.

Arama couldn't help grinning and joining in with the "Heave her round, lads, into the weather, and let the sirens sing," that made up every other line in the song. Yar surprised her by picking it up after a couple of repetitions. His voice wasn't confident, but it warmed Arama's heart to be singing with a crewmate—of sorts—once again.

As the song ended, the serving girl and the tavernkeep brought two trays of food and drink to the table. The tavernkeep tossed a glance over his shoulder at the bard, who grinned, set their lute aside, and hopped down from the stage.

"Storm Petrel, I'll hope you'll allow me to join you." The bard's speaking voice was husky and warm.

Arama gave them a rueful grin. "As long as you promise not to sing about me while I'm here." She should have known the bard had recognized her. They'd probably spotted her the first time she came into the tavern, despite the crowds.

The bard laughed. "You can't begrudge me a professional interest in your exploits. They've paid for many a meal over my career." They stuck out a slender hand. "Ellyl."

"Arama." She grasped the hand briefly, surprised by the strength in that grip. "This is Yarrax."

"Yar is fine," the boy whispered, and to Arama's astonishment, he offered the bard a shy smile.

"Yar it is, then," Ellyl said. They answered the boy's smile with a brilliant one of their own. "You're not from Amethir, are you?"

He shook his head. "Tamnen. But I've been to Amethir. I liked Maron."

"Maron's just one city, my lad. Wait 'til you see Dalasan and Glimmerguard. They're as different from Maron as they are from each other." Ellyl helped themself to a fish roll and dipped it in the spicy green sauce before popping it into their mouth.

"Are you from one of those places?" Yar asked.

"I lived most of my life in Glimmerguard." Ellyl grinned. "But I was born in Stony Lonesome, inland. I like the sea better."

Arama was content to let them carry the conversation; she filled her plate with fried potatoes and fish rolls and sat back in her chair. It was nice to see Yar take to someone.

As they talked, Arama learned the bard had come to Ranarr ahead of the storm that wrecked the *Dawn Star.* They knew about Anderly's demise in a freak storm, but after a glance at Arama's expression, they changed the subject to Yar's home city of Meekin. That led Yar to explaining how he'd become friends with a woman called Aevver and traveling with her to the Valley of Voices, where he met a dragon.

"That's right, you both arrived on dragonback, didn't you?" Ellyl said slyly. "What's that like?"

Yar launched into an enthusiastic description of the journey. Arama found her lips twisting wryly. She hadn't found the experience quite as sublime as Yar. She'd nearly lost her stomach the first time Xellax sprang into the air, and she wasn't certain she'd got it back until they landed at Ranarr.

Ellyl was free until the evening crowd, so it seemed natural for them to join Arama and Yar when they left the tavern. As the three of them walked, Yar chattered about the market and all the Tamnese products that could be found there. Eventually, though, he got distracted, seemingly by something Xellax said in his head.

Arama glanced over at Ellyl and found the bard studying her. This close, she could see they had a blade-thin nose and purple irises. It was attractive, especially with the artfully touseled dark hair the bard sported. She wondered if Ellyl was trying to seduce Yar. She hoped Ellyl wasn't trying to seduce *her*; that would be awkward.

"What do you think caused the war?" Ellyl said.

Arama gaped at them for a moment before catching herself. "Think? Mm." Her lips curved in a rueful grin. "Well, the witchery's been fouled somehow. That was at the root of it."

"Fouled? How could that happen?"

"The gods," Yar said, attention jerked back to the conversation. "One of them is—breaking things."

Ellyl tilted their head, which was very appealing. "Just the one?"

Yar shrugged, apparently oblivious to the bard's attractiveness. "Well, they're *all* waking. Maybe it's more than one."

"We're certain of the one, anyhow," Arama said dryly. "The One we don't name is certainly involved."

Ellyl nodded, their dark brows drawing together. "What woke them do you think? Or is that backwards? Perhaps they're waking because of the witchery fouling?"

"Either way," Arama said, "the king wouldn't listen when he was advised to halt the witchery until it's sorted out."

"I advised him to REPENT," Yar said, and Arama couldn't help but shiver as she felt the dragon's voice in that last word. She glanced around, hoping no one else was near enough to overhear. The street was empty of anyone but the three of them. That was odd.

"Repent," Ellyl said. "That's not the sort of thing a king likes to be told." Their voice was wryly amused.

"King Rekel certainly didn't," Arama said. "That's why Vistaren broke with him. Vistaren and at least one brigade and about a third of the Stormwitch Academy, from the reports I've seen."

"That's why we need to get back to Amethir," Yar put in. "The prince needs to know what we learned from the stormsingers."

Ellyl's violet eyes widened. "What did you learn?"

Yar ignored the question. "The Diplomats sent a ship for the others." He scratched his ear. "We wrecked, but Xellax could only carry two of us here."

"Suddenly I'm sorry I sang 'The Wreck of the *Aglaia*' the other night." The bard actually looked sorry.

Arama opened her mouth to reassure them, but before the words got out of her mouth, she realized their conversation had distracted them from their surroundings. They had turned onto a narrow side street. The buildings were tall overhead, and a little further along the street, a several scruffy-looking men and women stood in a small knot. One of them was a tall, young woman with black hair gathered into a crown of tiny braids. Arama squinted, trying to recall where she'd seen that woman before.

"I think we took a wrong turn," she said, and changed directions in what she hoped was a casual manner.

Whether it was casual or not didn't really matter to the four men who had closed in behind them. One of them was leering at her, a missing tooth giving him a rakish look.

"This is th' Storm Petrel, lads," he said, and before she could react, another person had brought a cosh down on her temple.

Arama reeled, flashes of light blocking her vision. The last thing she heard before a second blow knocked her out was Ellyl shouting for Yar to run.

CHAPTER TWENTY-THREE

THE SOLDIERS DRAGGED ZERA to a large tavern in the river district of Holywell. The Crelin commander had reserved the largest room for himself, of course, and from the dish-stacked tray on his desk, he was living well in his stolen home.

His blue-black hair was swept back in a tail. He stood as his soldiers hustled Zera into the room, his blue eyes fixed on her face.

"One of the Srelang warriors, commander," the woman soldier said. "We caught her trying to coerce aid from the priests."

The commander raised one dark eyebrow. "What is a lone Srelang warrior doing in Holywell?" he asked. "Our reports have you all on the run."

"She mentioned Glanyrafon, sir," the woman said.

"A scout, then?" He cast his gaze up and down her form. "But not wearing a scout's armor. You look like someone important to your fellow savages."

"Savages?" Zera burst out. "When we offered you succor and land, and you took with one hand and struck with the other? Who is the true savage, outlander?"

The commander didn't rise to the bait. "We didn't have any choice. Our islands were sinking beneath the sea."

She glared at him. "And we took you in. We would have been glad of you, had you not started killing to take our land!"

"Ah, but there are so many of you," he said, his voice lilting with amusement. "And with your ignorant worship of spirits, with no thought to the seven gods who have given us all life, you would corrupt our people. Already some of ours have begun going to your native temples, even when our arkon has forbidden it."

Zera bit back the retort that sprung to her lips. Worshiping the spirits wasn't ignorant; they had been sent as companions by the gods. And if it were so ignorant to worship the spirits, why had she received such mighty aid on her long journey? Why had she felt her curse take effect the moment she uttered it, if the spirits were not worth worshiping?

He shook his head. "If your queen had simply accepted our arkon's offer of a marriage treaty, it wouldn't have come to this. Your women are comely enough, after all, in spite of your savage markings, and your men are strong. All you had to do was agree to adopt our ways and we could have lived in peace."

"Adopt your ways?" Zera snapped. "This is our land!"

He smirked at her. "Then perhaps your spirits should have protected it for you." He looked at the soldiers. "Lock her in the cellar. I'll deal with the priest first. Then we'll take this one back to Simiri. Arkon Bricot will have a use for her, I imagine."

Zera didn't bother struggling as they dragged her to the tavern's cellar. One of the soldiers got a tray of food and water on their way through the kitchen, so they must not intend to starve her. A pair of rough-built beds offered her a place to rest. She didn't know what was coming, but she would not turn down an opportunity to regain her strength.

She woke from a deep sleep to the sound of footsteps thumping down wooden stairs. A boy had been sent to retrieve the empty tray. He was so young he hadn't received even his nameday tattoos yet, the first of the valemal that would eventually depict his entire life on his face. Eight years, perhaps, or nine. He watched her with huge eyes, but he didn't look afraid.

He pointed to a corner when she asked about a chamberpot. He didn't seem inclined to leave, though. "What goes on in this town?" she asked. "Why are the outland soldiers here?"

"They came a week ago," the boy said. "Some people fought, but most didn't. They said they'd spare us if we cooperated."

"Why did they come here?" Zera asked.

The boy shrugged.

"What have they done since they came?"

"Mostly eaten our food and scolded people." He dug one dirty toe into the packed floor. "They're weird. They pray to gods that they say are asleep. They can't hear the spirits."

"They don't even believe in the spirits," Zera said bitterly. "How many soldiers are there?"

The boy shrugged. "More than I could count. More than the harvest parties we have in the fall."

Someone shouted from the stairway.

"You'd better go."

"One of the maids says we're cursed because we turned our backs on the spirits." He held out a water flask she hadn't noticed. "She sent you this. She told me to leave the door unlocked when I leave."

Zera stared at him. "Do you know where my weapons are?"

"She was going to steal them and put them in the pantry. I don't know if she's done it. I did what she told me, though."

Another shout came, followed by footsteps.

Zera gripped the boy's shoulder. "Keep your head down, lad. And whatever gift is left to me, I grant to you. Take my blessing and live through this."

The boy stared back at her for a moment, then turned and scampered for the stairs, the dishes rattling on his tray.

So not everyone in Holywell was a traitor. For a moment she felt a pang of guilt at her curse. But even if not everyone was a traitor, their priests were. They'd sold her to the Crelin without even asking who she was or what errand she was on.

At least the maid had sent her more water. Zera uncorked the flask and tipped a sip into her mouth—and then spat it back out into her palm.

The water was bitter and black.

CHAPTER TWENTY-FOUR

Z OLIN WAS AFRAID HE had not endured the past two days with as much grace as he would prefer. Master Inkeri had hauled him into her office, questioning him about Naia's behavior and accusing him of being an accomplice. Bekir had finally intervened, but he had immediately chivvied Zolin down into the Sanctuary Deep, where he'd set him to ever more complicated moving meditations. Whenever Zolin tried to ask about Naia, Bekir had hushed him and demonstrated yet another form for Zolin to master.

When Bekir finally released him, Zolin barely had the energy to trudge up the stairs on the most direct route to his rooms. He'd collapsed into his bed, only to jolt awake soon after dawn with Bekir's summons ringing in his head.

The Deep's magic was changing how he interacted with his master as well as the world around him, but a second day of movement had told him nothing about Naia's fate except that she had not yet been expelled. Master Bekir dismissed him before supper that night, and instead of heading to the refectory, Zolin returned to the stairway that would carry him to Naia's library nook.

Stomach rumbling, he slipped out of the door, pulling it closed softly behind him before ducking out from beneath the tapestry. To his relief, Naia was sitting in her chair, watching for him to appear.

"I heard you coming," she said, which Zolin knew was impossible. He'd been placing each step carefully. But he didn't bother contradicting her.

"I'm sorry I haven't been able to get away until now," he said. "Master Inkeri interrogated me, and Bekir's kept me close since he rescued me from her."

Naia snorted. "I'm glad he rescued you. She hasn't been at me, but only because I've been hiding up here."

Zolin lowered himself onto her footstool. He was going to have to find a chair to drag up here. His legs were too long for this. "What happened?"

Naia filled him in on her conversation with Master Revalis, relating her utter astonishment that she hadn't been summarily ejected from the University. "It had something to do with Master Bekir, but I don't understand why. I don't have a class with Bekir this year."

Zolin's stomach gave a guilty lurch that he couldn't attribute to hunger. Bekir must have done it for Zolin's sake. He must know how close they were. But how could he explain that to her?

At that moment, he felt the sharp tug of a summons in the region of his chest. Frowning, he rubbed at it. "I'm glad they didn't kick you out. Maybe they thought it wouldn't be fair, this close to being finished."

"Whatever their reasons, I'm grateful." She sighed. "I don't feel much better about it, though. I'm not at all convinced they won't throw me out once they're done with the rest of you getting mentors."

"I'm sure—"

Come.

The call was so urgent Zolin was halfway to his feet before he realized it. He paused awkwardly as Naia stared at him.

"Sorry," he gasped. "I need to—"

COME.

Naia's hand flashed out and circled his wrist. "You need to tell me what's wrong," she said.

"I need to go," he said, tugging against her grip.

"You just got here."

"I just—I just—" He gave up on trying to think of an excuse. She could see through him.

Her fingers tightened. "Nope."

He cast his mind back to those five rules he'd been given. He hadn't actually sworn not to tell anyone. Master Bekir hadn't said why he and Tanvel kept it from each other, but it had almost seemed it was part of their explicit instructions. But if it wasn't explicit in Zolin's instructions...

And Naia had seen the doorway, anyway. She knew it went somewhere.

He felt the *COME* a third time. He gulped. "All right. But you have to promise not to ask any questions." He stared hard at her, holding her gaze with his own, until she nodded. "Come on, then."

He led her back through the door and down the stairs, pausing first to call the handrail light so they could see. He heard surprised intake of breath, but she didn't speak. She trailed him all the way down to the Sanctuary level, her footsteps ringing a little louder than his. Zolin's heart felt like it was pounding in his throat, but what was he supposed to do? Bekir hadn't explained this part of the summons to him; he hadn't said how to mask it when Zolin was in company.

And it's Naia, anyway.

He followed the tug to the place where he'd encountered the dragon. He was almost unsurprised to find Master Bekir standing before the green dragon. It was more surprising to see Yar and that Amethirian bard from the Chatty Raven standing on either side of Bekir. His master wore a bemused expression, but it didn't shift much when he saw Naia following Zolin.

"Master Bekir!" she exclaimed. "You're why Revalis didn't expel me!"

"I am glad I could be of service," Bekir said dryly. He glanced at Zolin, who shrugged.

"Your call felt urgent, and I was with Naia. She could see something was wrong."

"Just as well, perhaps," Bekir murmured. He sighed.

"They stole Arama!" Yar blurted.

Startled, Zolin looked at Bekir, who indicated the Amethirian bard. They sketched out the rough details of what had happened, their husky voice sounding half bewildered. Their purple eyes were large and expressive in their brown face. Zolin watched their slender fingers tangle in each other as they spoke. It was strange to see how clearly distressed they were.

"If they'd been robbers they would have chased Yar and me," they finished. "I just keep thinking about the Strid bounty on the Storm Petrel's head."

"Is that who they were?" Naia asked.

"Their accent was Strid."

Yar went to lean against the green dragon. "I recognized that woman who was with them. With all the long braids."

Ellyl nodded. "I had taken her for one of you trainees. I've seen her at the Raven." They were tracing a thumb along their jaw. "She carries herself with importance, and she likes to flaunt her hair."

Zolin's stomach flipped. "Shirin? Shirin was with the Strid?"

"It was the woman who served us bland tea and pastries with you," Yar told Zolin.

Sleeping gods, it *was* Shirin. But what was she doing with the Strid? Zolin frowned. "What sort of bounty—" he began, but Naia cut him off.

"What do we do?"

Damn it, she'd promised not to ask questions!

Bekir's eyebrows had drawn together. "We were already quietly searching for the captain. She is a guest of the Diplomats. It is unthinkable that we should let anything happen to her. But that Shirin would be involved..." He shook his head. "That will keep. For now, I have sent word to Captain Dzornaea's stormwitch, whose ship should be docking any moment now. If the Strid *do* have the captain, they'll want to get away from Ranarr as quickly as possible."

The satisfaction in Bekir's voice didn't make any sense to Zolin, but it apparently meant something to Yar.

"Kinnet's going to stop them!" he said jubilantly.

Ah. "And they can't sail for Strid if a storm blows up and keeps them in port," Zolin said, and he thought he sounded just as satisfied as Bekir.

"And if the Strid kill her?" the bard asked quietly.

"If I know King Harkai, he'll want her alive," Bekir said grimly. "And any Strid crew will know that as well as I do. Better, perhaps."

"Do you think Strid is trying to impact the Amethirians' war?" Zolin asked.

"Harkai's hatred of the Storm Petrel goes back much further than this war," Ellyl said

"I am sure it won't grieve him to throw the Amethirians off balance any way he can, however," Bekir agreed.

"So what do we do *now*?" Naia asked again.

Bekir shook his head, but the look he gave Naia felt fond. "Now, my impatient Trainee Sedorr, we wait."

As Naia subsided, glowering, the bard huffed. "I am used to singing my nation's history," they said. "It feels very disconcerting to suddenly be playing an active role in it."

Naia's posture straightened and she looked sharply at Ellyl. "You know a lot about Amethir's history. I haven't found many references to Silverdene at all, but you sang *two* songs about it the other night."

Ellyl's smile was mysterious. "It's a bard's job to know the obscure bits as well as the bits everyone knows."

"How can I learn more about Silverdene?" Naia pressed. "It sounded like it fell, in that ballad."

Zolin remembered the melancholy that had hung over the room and settled into his spirit as the ballad ended. More than Silverdene falling, it had seemed almost as if the world were ending.

"It did," Ellyl said, their voice grave. "There's barely a stone left on stone, these days."

Zolin realized suddenly that Bekir's gaze on Naia was sharp and very focused. He turned to his master, hoping to distract him from the conversation. It couldn't do Naia any favors if her one advocate learned she was chasing what might be a figment of her imagination, rather than working on her final project.

"I was surprised at how strong I felt your call, Master," he said, shifting to stand a little between Bekir and Naia.

"Your control and perception are improving." Bekir smiled. "And you are more open than you were even two weeks ago."

"I find a comfort in the moving forms that I never felt in stillness," Zolin confessed. He wasn't even sure how to explain it. Something settled inside him when he moved through the deliberate forms. He knew where each movement was supposed to take him, and what his body would do at the end of each phrase of movements. The focus built into a comfortable weight inside him, making him feel both more grounded and more alive.

"Good." Bekir rested a hand on his shoulder. "You were well-chosen, Mentee."

Zolin couldn't help grinning at his master, and he felt a warmth in his belly when Bekir grinned back.

"I ought to leave soon," Ellyl said behind him.

"No, indeed," Bekir said. "You must stay with us tonight, Ellyl."

"I'm supposed to be on the stage in less than a glass, and I need to warm my voice before performing." Ellyl's expression was serious, but they didn't look as though they were arguing in earnest.

Yar spoke up from where he was curled into the green dragon's front leg. "You might be in danger. Those people, whether they were Strid or not, saw both of us."

Ellyl's shoulders slumped, but they nodded.

"I'll send a message to the Chatty Raven," Bekir said. "They can hardly argue if I keep you here for Diplomat business. We have enough room here in the Sanctuary for you all to stay together while we wait for news."

That made Ellyl perk up a bit, but the mood as Bekir showed them to a room that looked like a glorified dormitory was tense.

Arama woke in darkness to the smell of fish guts and piss. Her stomach roiled and she barely got her head turned to one side before she vomited. She wanted to swear, but another heave caught her off guard. She tried to roll onto her front and that was when she realized her hands were manacled behind her back.

Her head was throbbing, the beat of it matching her heartbeat and the churn of her stomach. A groan escaped her before she could help it. Then she held her breath, trying to listen to her surroundings. She couldn't see very far at all, though there were a few faint lines of light above her.

She was lying on her right side, arms twisted behind her. Her ankles were bound as well. She gulped hard several times, trying to quell her nausea.

Concussion, she thought sluggishly. How long had she been out?

"Ellyl? Yar?" she whispered. It didn't feel like anyone was in the immediate vicinity, but with her senses dulled by a blow to the head, she couldn't be sure.

Somewhere above her, muffled but not too far distant, someone laughed. They weren't too close, either, though. It sounded like there was a door or a wall between them.

Footsteps pounded across the floor above her and she realized it wasn't a floor at all—it was a deck. She was on a ship.

Hot-cold fear flashed through her, leaving her shivering in its wake. She hadn't just been kidnapped, she'd been impressed! Her heartbeat spiked and she had to swallow hard to keep from vomiting again.

Think, Arama! Think!

All right, she was in the hold of a ship. Had those men taken her to their ship? She cast back, trying to remember details—how many of them? Had Yar and the bard escaped?

They didn't kill me. That's no accident. She took a shaky breath and lifted her head from the deck. Dizziness seized her. She had to close her eyes and lower it back against the rough boards.

She couldn't move. No matter, she could still listen. Keeping her eyes closed, Arama worked to even out her breathing, attempting to gain some control over her body despite its infirmities.

The voices on deck weren't speaking Amethirian or Common. There were many voices. Too many. Then one voice rose above the others, shouting an order, which was echoed back to him by other voices.

Arama stiffened. *Cast off?* Then they were still in Ranarr! She struggled to lift her head again, and this time she forced the nausea down so she could wrestle herself into a sitting position.

Cast off. How had she known that's what the order was? It hadn't been spoken in her language, but she'd recognized it somehow. What language were they speaking?

Someone yelled again, and this time she recognized the word '*rannda.*' It meant Ranarri, so perhaps the Ranarri were searching for her even now? Then her laggard brain caught up with her memory and she groaned.

"Strid. It's the Strid."

She knew enough of their language to have a conversation about important things like surrender, loot, kill, and prize. She couldn't speak well enough to chat politely over coffee, but she'd always thought it was important to be able to understand your enemy as well as possible. The Strid had been her enemies for decades longer than the folks on the other side of the Amethirian war.

All right, you're prisoner of the Strid. Calm down. They won't do anything drastic. Her mental voice giggled a little. *There's that bounty, after all. You're worth a lot as a prize.*

She tried to quell the other part of her mind, which told her the bounty had said nothing about taking her alive.

Shouting overhead caught her attention again. The voices sounded startled now, perhaps even alarmed. A breath later, thunder cracked the world in two, bearing down on her with the weight of something physical. Arama winced, squeezing her eyes shut, but it didn't shut out the pain. She tried again to steady her breathing. She was going to throw up again if she wasn't careful, and that wouldn't do her any good.

The ship was rolling more than it ought to, if they were still at dock. She would have felt it if they'd left the slip, though. They had to still be in dock.

More shouting, louder thunder, and then a hatch overhead crashed open, blinding her with the lightning that flashed across the opening.

Footsteps thudded onto the deck next to her and then a toe drove itself into her ribs.

"Stop this!" The man ordered in coarse Amethirian.

Thunder rolled from one side of the world to the other. He hadn't closed the hatch behind him. Arama could see the almost constant flicker of lightning. She realized suddenly that she was grinning.

"Stop it!" Another kick.

Arama wheezed, but she couldn't help but laugh. "S'not me," she told him. Sleeping gods, her head hurt!

"You're doing this! Damned witch!" He drew his foot back again and this time Arama twisted out of the way of the blow. The metal shackles on her wrists and ankles bit into her flesh, and one shoulder protested the angle she landed at.

"I'm no fucking stormwitch!" she snapped. Then she couldn't help but laugh. "Don't you stupid Strid know stormwitches have silver hair?"

He snarled, lunging in to grab her shoulder, and this time she couldn't twist away. The man shoved his face close to hers, hot breath hitting her cheek. He was missing part of his ear. Arama wanted to bite the rest of it off. She snapped her teeth at him.

"I'll kill you!" He hit her in the mouth. Thunder all but drowned out his words, and Arama laughed again despite the pain.

"Oh, but I'm sure I'm worth more to King Harkai alive," she said, and grinned. "You know how excitable he is." She could feel blood trickling down her chin.

More footsteps thudded overhead. A man's head and shoulders were silhouetted against the lighting from the hatch. "Burr! Cap'n says to secure the prisoner."

"She's secure!" her captor shouted back.

Arama took that opportunity to kick out with both feet. It wasn't much of a kick, barely glancing off the side of his knee, but he swore and shook her by the shoulder he still gripped.

"Bloody sea siren!" he yelled, and wrenched her arms up further behind her. Something made a very unpleasant *pop* and white hot pain seared through her shoulder.

"The bounty doesn't say anything about undamaged." Burl's voice was ugly with amusement or worse.

Antos preserve, he's dislocated it.

She didn't pass out. She *wouldn't* pass out.

But she did let the world go gray and fuzzy around the edges for a while.

Naia paced the length of the dormitory again. Yar and El-lyl were watching her. Bekir had disappeared somewhere, promising to return as soon as there was word.

Zolin took a couple of slow breaths and moved his feet into the first position of The Seasons Change and Moun-tains Stand Still. He wasn't sure he would be able to chan-nel his own worry into the forms, but it was worth a try.

He sensed more than saw Ellyl's focus shift to him. He was curious about the bard, too. Why had they been drawn into this? Was it mere coincidence? But Bekir had taught him there were few coincidences. Everything was connect-ed somehow; it was merely a matter of finding the right threads that tied things together. Zolin shifted his hands, holding them apart from each other in imitation of a finger loom, envisioning the warp and weft of fate.

"You were going to tell me more," Naia said abruptly.

The bard leaned back in their chair. "Was I?"

"Silverdene." Naia spun and took several steps towards Ellyl. "Where was it? It *was* in Amethir, wasn't it?"

Zolin lowered his eyelids halfway, trying to look as though he were absorbed in his own movements rather than their conversation.

The bard was silent for so long Zolin didn't think they were going to answer. Finally they said softly, "It was in part of that place now known as Amethir. It was not called that then, though."

"What *was* it called?" Naia asked.

Zolin realized he was frowning and tried to smooth out his expression. "How long ago was that?" he asked, moving his hands slowly apart.

"Hundreds of years." Ellyl sounded sad. "It was called Srelang, that part of the world."

"I have never heard of Srelang." Zolin heard the uncertainty in his own voice as he spoke.

"Not so many records still exist." Ellyl's hair had fallen in disarray around their lowered face. "I made a study of the ones we still have at the Bard's Collective."

Zolin swept his hands back together, then moved them in the same direction, as if pushing something away from himself.

"Were there maps?" Naia asked eagerly, making Zolin smile. "Where *was* Silverdene?"

"It's right in the song," Ellyl said, lifting their head. They fixed their purple eyes on Naia's face, the lines in their face making them look older. "It's called Stony Lonesome these days. In the foothills north of the Gehb River."

At the edge of the Shroudling kingdom. Naia sucked in an audible breath. Zolin glanced over at her, losing his place in the form. Before either of them could speak, however, the dormitory door flew open so hard it crashed against the wall and rebounded.

They all jumped. A tall, lithe woman strode into the room, her silver hair floating around her face in a cloud. She had olive skin and was scattering what looked like dust onto the floor. "That is the last of the seaglass," she said in a loud, atonal voice. It was somehow musical despite the strange quality.

Bekir followed her in, scooting around her to look her in the face. He pressed something into her hand. "I have a few more pieces, stormwitch."

She snorted. "Time is short, Diplomat." But she clenched one white-knuckled hand around what he'd given her.

"Yarrax, Zolin, you are needed. Quickly." Bekir gestured at Zolin. "We must go *now.*"

"Go?" Zolin was already moving.

"Captain Dzornaea must be rescued before the storm abates."

"How? We couldn't stop them before." Yar was standing, but his jaw had a stubborn tilt to it.

"You didn't have me before," Bekir said. He gave them a grim smile. "Or the assistance of a Shadow. This time you will have both."

"And me," said a man lingering just outside the doorway. He had fair skin that was sunburned, and wore his reddish-blond hair in a long tail. "I'll not abandon the captain."

"Yes, and Mr. Zek," Bekir agreed.

Zolin darted a glance at Naia, but he could already tell she was eager for the rest of them to be gone so she could quiz Ellyl more about Silverdene. She didn't meet his gaze as she said, "Be safe."

Bekir was already striding out of the room. Zolin jerked his head at Yar and they fell into step behind the Diplomat and the sailor.

"Xellax wants to help, but I think she's too big," Yar said.

Bekir chuckled. "A dragon might be overkill, in this instance. But her offer is certainly appreciated. I hope you will convey that for us."

Zolin blinked, impressed that Bekir had remembered to his politesse even now. Zolin had forgotten Yar was more than a scrawny teenager who had kept the captain company. He wanted to ask how they knew where to go, but it seemed a foolish question. Bekir wouldn't be leading them down hallways between Sanctuary storerooms if he didn't know where he was leading them. Why waste time asking questions?

As they neared the end of a hallway, a woman with dark hair and eyes peeled away from the shadows and fell in beside Bekir.

"We've located the Strid ship," she said. "At one of the lower slips, clean enough to not be taken for smugglers, but too shady to be anything honest. They were planning to depart on the tide before the storm blew up." Her eyes glittered in the semi-darkness of the passageway.

"Good. And you can get inside quietly? We don't want a bloodbath."

Zolin could only see one corner of her mouth, but it quirked as if she wanted to smile. "Certainly. It will be a very peaceful rescue."

CHAPTER TWENTY-FIVE

ZERA COCKED HER HEAD, *counting. The priests were still ringing the temple bell at each hour; it was nearing midnight. She crouched by the cellar door, almost afraid to try the handle. The boy had said it would be unlocked, but there was no guarantee the maid had succeeded. There was no guarantee the soldiers hadn't caught the boy at it and punished him.*

But the spirits were still with her. She felt their eyes on her as she stood, reaching out for the handle. The spirits wouldn't have heeded her curse just to abandon her now, would they? Zera took a deep breath and turned the handle.

The door swung open. Zera froze, listening for any signs of life stirring in the tavern beyond. Hearing nothing, she whispered a plea to the spirits to muffle her footsteps, then slipped out into the passage that led to the kitchen.

They'd taken her weapons and armor, but at least she still had her boots. Even if the maid had managed to steal her pack and weapons, there wouldn't be time to dress for battle. She had to be swift and silent.

What will happen to these folk if you abandon them here and flee to save your life? *The thought rankled. But what could she do? They wouldn't be able to travel as she intended to travel—as she* hoped *to travel.*

The boy was waiting for her at the pantry.

"Vanda drugged the wine for the soldiers," he told her in a hushed whisper. "But not everyone drank it."

Zera nodded and strapped her swordbelt around her waist. "You and Vanda, and any who helped you, should go hide in the forest," she told him. "I can't stay and protect you."

The boy nodded. "Are you really our queen in disguise?" he asked, eyes shining.

Zera couldn't hold in a snort. "I'm not Queen Danae, lad." Then she thought, What's the harm? Give this boy and his people some hope. *"I'm the warleader's daughter. I'm carrying a message from the queen to the high king at Ranarr."*

"Spirits guide you, then," the boy said, and pointed down the hall. "That's the back door."

She was forced to kill two guards just outside the stables. She hesitated, then stole a horse. She wouldn't be able to feed it, but it would get her away from Holywell faster than if she were on her own feet.

By dawn she was leagues outside of the city, but she knew they would be pursuing her. And worse, they knew her object—she hadn't been cautious enough with the priest. She should have told him she was on her way to Simiri. At least then they would look for her in the opposite direction.

She abandoned the horse when she judged herself halfway to the coast. She had seen gulls on the wing overhead. She was near enough that she could feel the pull of the sea, and she knew she would be able to draw on that strength.

She waded into the river until she stood waist deep, then she took out her dagger and drew it across the back of her off hand. "Spirits, receive my sacrifice," she whispered, letting her blood drip into the water. "Let it be enough."

She had never attempted anything so ambitious before. She hadn't even completed her training. Her audacity might prompt the spirits to smite her at worst, or abandon her at best. But they had accompanied her so far. And nothing but audacity would be enough to complete her mother's assignment to her.

"Help me walk in your mists to the shores of Ranarr."

The pain in Arama's dislocated shoulder was bad enough that she didn't notice, at first, that the storm was getting weaker. It wasn't until her captor sent his crewmates back upstairs that she realized the rolling of the deck was lessening.

Burl grinned at her. "The pain makes you lose your grip on the witchery, does it?"

"I'm no stormwitch," Arama said again, but to her dismay she sounded more tired than angry.

"Doesn't matter. We'll be able to cast off soon. And then we'll take you to our king and collect the bounty on your head." He wagged his head. "Hate to be in your boots then."

Something thumped overhead. Arama squinted upward, but between the pain in her head, the roiling of her belly, and the throbbing in her shoulder, she wasn't tracking very well.

Burl was still rambling on, another thump overhead going unnoticed by him. Arama began counting in her head. Every ten seconds or so another thump sounded, and by her reckoning the noises were moving.

Finally something thudded directly overhead, making enough noise that Burl stopped talking to himself and frowned.

"What's going on up there?" he shouted. When no answer came, he swore and stomped over to the ladder. As he reached the foot of it, the hatch opened. Wind and rain poured in through the opening, and lightning flashed overhead, but Arama couldn't see anything—or any*one*—else through the hatch.

Another thump overhead, further away from the hatch.

Arama hauled herself into a sitting position, nearly fainting from the pain as her shoulder bones ground together in ways that were never intended. Sweat trickled down her temples. Burl swore again and began climbing the ladder. Just as he reached the top, something rustled behind Arama. She looked around dizzily, seeing nothing but shadows and lightning. By the time she'd turned back to look at the hatch, she was just in time to see Burl's feet disappearing as if he'd been jerked through it.

Sea Lord Antos, Arama thought, *I don't care if it's more pirates, as long as they're not* Strid *pirates.*

A dark form dropped through the hatch, landing lightly on the deck. The figure crouched there at the base of the ladder, and Arama thought she caught the glint of steel.

"Captain Dzornaea, is it?" The language was Amethirian, spoken with a Ranarri accent.

Arama breathed out slowly. "If you're here to kill me, do it without jolting my shoulder. And if you're not here to kill me, I'm going to presume you're here to rescue me."

The woman chuckled softly. "That shoulder does look bad. I can give you something to dull the pain."

"And my wits with it? No thanks. Just push it back in place." Arama struggled to her feet, swaying slightly.

"Stubborn as I always imaged you'd be," the woman said. She took several swift steps closer and then pain lanced through Arama as the shoulder jolted back into place. Then the tide of pain ebbed, letting Arama draw in a slow breath.

"Don't suppose you'd tell me your name." Arama groaned and swayed again, allowing the woman to brace her.

"Carassa." White teeth flashed dimly in the darkness. "My friend Tanvel was a great admirer of yours."

Arama sighed and nodded. "My thanks, Carassa. I think I can climb now."

She could, but she had to use her good arm to tuck her bad one into her belt first, and then climb one-handed to the top of the ladder. When she got there, she paused, trying to see around her.

The lightning was retreating, the sound of thunder still loud but not overpowering. The deck seemed oddly untidy. She wondered if they'd had cargo come loose in the storm.

"Captain." She recognized Bekir's voice and looked up to see him extending a hand to her. He'd already noticed that she was favoring the bad arm. He waited for her to reach up and clasp his wrist with her good hand.

As soon as she had the deck under her feet, she braced herself against Bekir and looked around. "Sleeping gods, did you kill them all?"

Bekir chuckled. "Carassa's efficient, but not so bloodthirsty as all that. She incapacitated them, and I daresay the Strid pirates will be astonished to wake up in custody of the Ranarri Guard."

"I don't suppose you have a weapon for me," Arama said, counting the crumpled forms she could see.

"I found your sirenstooth, Captain," Zek said from behind her. "Their captain had it in his quarters."

Arama grinned. "Good man, Zek." She turned to look at him. "I'm glad to see you in one piece still."

"Aye, thanks to you and Yar, mum. The Ranarri ship as picked us up had a peacehealer on board. Did you know they can fix sun poisoning?"

"I think they can fix damn near anything," Arama said. "I'm certainly hoping they can do something about concussions."

"Bekir will get you back to the Sanctuary and see about that very thing," said Carassa, climbing up the ladder behind her. "I'll stay here to see that the rest of this mess is cleaned up."

Chapter Twenty-Six

Z OLIN LEANED AGAINST THE infirmary wall in the
Sanctuary, watching the peacehealers examine Captain Dzornaea. They were intent on their work, and he had
no wish to interrupt, but Master Bekir hadn't given him
any instructions on what to do when they returned from
their rescue mission. He glanced over to where Naia sat on
the floor, her arms drawn up around her knees. She gave
him a tiny smile.

Zolin's task during the rescue had been to use the magic
of the Deep to create an aura of harmony around the Strid
ship. It had kept them from notice as Cassara and Bekir

worked their way around the deck in opposite directions. Cassara had used blackout powder against her opponents, but Zolin wasn't certain what Bekir had done to cause the Strid crewman to sleep. He hoped an explanation would be forthcoming at some point.

Finally Bekir turned from where the healers were talking to the captain. He glanced around the room, found Zolin, and came over to him.

"You did well, Zolin. You have come a long way in a short time. We will discuss tonight's events, but first I must consult with the other masters. I need to know if Inkeri was aware of Shirin's perfidy. Things could have gone very badly as a result of her actions."

Zolin thought things had gone badly enough, considering the injuries Arama had sustained. Then again, they had been able to rescue her and prevent the Strid from carrying her off to their kingdom. Zolin remembered how much trouble the Diplomats had suffered when Princess Azmei of Tamnen was believed to have been assassinated right under their noses. This might not be quite as bad as that, but with the news of the gods waking and dark forces at work, it might prove to be worse.

"I'm glad I was able to be of use, Master," Zolin said. "What would you have me do now?"

"For now, stay in the Sanctuary." Bekir rubbed the bridge of his nose. "And be sure Naia, Yarrax, and Ellyl stay in the Sanctuary with you. I don't want any of them out of our protection just yet. Here, I know we can keep them safe."

Zolin watched his mentor leave the room and then he crouched next to Naia. She looked at him sidelong. He found himself wondering how much she had learned from

Ellyl while they were invading the Strid ship. For that matter, where was the bard, anyway?

"Where are Ellyl and Yarrax?" he asked her.

"With Xellax. Ellyl was fascinated to meet a dragon up close, and they wanted to ask about some of the lore they were taught." Naia shook her head. "We are living in strange times, Zolin. I always wanted to be a part of something bigger than me, but this is..." She tucked her hair behind her ear. "This is bigger than I can comprehend."

Zolin draped an arm around her shoulders. "I suppose we should consider ourselves lucky to have an Amethirian bard who knows some dragon lore. Come on, let's seek them out. Master Bekir wants us to stay in the Sanctuary for now."

As they stood up, Naia frowned. "Does he think there's danger even in the University?"

"With Shirin involved?"

Naia paled. "I'd forgotten about her in all this mess. She'd love to have a chance to push me off the Stone, I don't doubt."

"She might not know anyone recognized her. If she doesn't realize we're onto her—"

"But they won't be able to keep Captain Dzornaea's capture quiet forever," Naia said.

"Perhaps not. For now, let's leave that to the masters to worry about. I thought you might like to see the mosaics down here. They're ancient, and utterly beautiful." Zolin led the way out of the infirmary.

They found Yarrax and Ellyl in the rookery with the dragon. Ellyl was playing an idle tune on their lute while Yarrax teased one of the ravens with a morsel of food.

"Their beaks are strong. It probably hurts if they bite you," Zolin said as they approached.

Yarrax jumped and dropped the food. "Xellax says you came back with Arama and the others," he told Zolin. "Is she all right?"

"She's angry, I'd say, and injured, but not too seriously for the healers." Zolin folded his arms across his chest. "I was going to show Naia the mosaics. Do either of you want to come?"

"I've never been this far into the White Stone," Ellyl said. "I confess, I've been itching to look around."

Zolin nodded. "I don't know if I'm supposed to, normally, but I think we're ignoring what's normal right now." He glanced at Yarrax. "I didn't think about how your bondmate couldn't join us, though. I apologize."

The green dragon yawned, displaying long, sharp teeth. She lowered her nose to touch Yarrax's forehead and the boy laughed. "She says she doesn't mind waiting. She can smell secrets upon secrets down here."

Zolin wasn't sure what to say in response to that, so he just nodded and led the way out of the rookery.

The Sanctuary seemed emptier than usual. When they passed through the refectory, there was no one sitting at the tables. Zolin didn't even hear the clatter of dishes. The lamps were turned low, and only every other lamp was lit. How late was it? He'd lost all track of time while they'd been recovering Captain Dzornaea.

When they reached the mosaics, Zolin was gratified to see Ellyl's mouth drop open in surprise. Naia's expression was carefully blank, but as she tilted her head back to take it all in, her eyes sparked with curiosity.

Yarrax crouched in front of one section. "There are dragons in the mosaic. Xellax said they've been here before, but this must have been a long time ago."

"I don't know how old they are," Zolin admitted. "Some are older than others, and you can see a different hand in some of them."

"Some of these stones are precious," Ellyl murmured. They traced a finger down blue inlay that made a waterfall spilling down the face of a huge white cliff. "I can feel power in these images."

Zolin nodded. "I can tell what some of them are. The Northern Cascade, for instance." He gestured at the waterfall. "But there are others with mountains and battles, and there are ships in one of the earliest ones. I don't even think I've seen all of them. Every time I think I have, I find something new."

"Look at this," Naia breathed. "This fortress, with the mountains behind it...and what is that rising up to surround it? Is it—is it *mist?*"

"The Shroud," Ellyl whispered. "This might be the raising of the Shroud."

Zolin looked at where Naia's attention was focused. "But why would the Sanctuary have anything about the Shroud?"

"I think this is all connected," Naia said. Her voice was quiet, as if she were afraid to speak it aloud. "I think I found those letters and saw that—that spirit—and *you* ended up in the Sanctuary—" She nodded to Zolin— "and the dragons came here with Arama and Yar—and it's all connected."

Zolin wanted to ask how that could be possible, but he didn't want to argue. He cleared his throat. "Naia, there are ways from the Sanctuary into the library. I think...I wonder if you somehow found your own way into the Sanctuary, when you were seeking. Why don't you show us where you found those letters?"

Naia found it disorienting to try to find her library trove from this direction. She had lost all track of time and distance when she wandered through the library that first time. She only knew it felt like she was deep, deep in the library. But coming down into the Sanctuary from her favorite spot, then lingering overnight in parts of the Stone she had never even known existed, had taken her sense of direction entirely.

Zolin walked at her side without speaking. She had sensed a distance growing between them, the past few days. She'd disappointed him when she attacked Shirin, but he'd sought her out again, anyway. But then when Master Bekir had summoned Zolin and Zolin had brought her with him into the Sanctuary, it had driven home that Zolin's path was not going to be the same as hers.

You knew you'd probably be parted from your friends, even Zolin. Why do you feel so lost? She felt as if the ground under her feet was composed of sand and sliding shale.

She tripped suddenly on the threshold of a room. Flailing to catch herself, she scraped her knuckles against rough stone. She managed to keep from falling, though she did bump into Zolin and rebound into the wall.

"Ouch." She stuck her stinging knuckles in her mouth, widening her eyes to look around her. It was so dim here, the shadows lurching up around them in weird dances. "Do you feel that?"

"Feel what?" Zolin asked.

"The damp air." Naia peered around, straining to make out more detail than stone walls and shelving. "There shouldn't be damp, it's bad for the scrolls and books."

"It isn't damp," Ellyl whispered. "It's mist."

Naia sucked in a breath. It *was* mist. She'd found her way to the room with weather in it. The Shroudling trove!

"Are you there?" she breathed, taking several steps away from the others. There should be lanterns here. Her exploring fingers encountered a spiderweb and she recoiled. "I came back."

She heard someone moving behind her, and then light flared in Zolin's cupped hand. "Maybe you were being called by the Deep when you found this place." He sounded tentative. "I think we're still in the Sanctuary."

Naia looked over at him and realized he hadn't struck a flint—he was actually *holding* fire. She gasped. "Zo—"

"It's fine," he said, and gave her a blinding grin. "This is the magic of the Deep. It's what I've been learning."

"Diplomats don't do magic," Naia whispered.

"Obviously they do," Ellyl said. They sounded amused. "But why are you so surprised, Trainee Sedorr? If you've been seeing spirits and finding things you shouldn't, haven't you also been doing magic somehow?"

Naia shivered. "I don't think *I've* been doing magic. It was more like the spirits were calling me."

Ellyl held their hand over Zolin's, slender fingers curving over the light. "How long ago did you find these documents?"

Naia had to count. "Three weeks? Or maybe four."

"Closer to four, I think," Zolin said.

"And what happened?" Ellyl pulled their hand back, tucking it into their belt. "You said it was like being called?"

"I couldn't stop looking. I had to keep going, deeper and deeper, and then I found the room with weather—*this* room."

"And then—"

"And then it got so, so cold. I could see my breath." Naia shivered again, remembering. "And then I saw her. I thought she was a spirit at first, because she vanished and then came back. But then I could feel her magic, and I could feel her *sorrow*." She sucked in a breath, feeling that soul-rending grief again.

Yar coughed. "Xellax says something is stirring."

Naia thought back to the dream she'd had, of the outlanders attacking the tall stone walls, the Shroudlings fighting back, the mist rising around them. "I've dreamed about her, but I haven't seen her since. If it weren't for the scrolls and letters, I would think I'd imagined it all."

"You didn't imagine it."

The light in the room dimmed, except for that cupped in Zolin's hand. The room filled with mist, obscuring the walls and blurring her friend's face. "Zolin—" Naia began, and then gasped.

The Shroudling was with them.

Ellyl dropped to their knees, staring open-mouthed at the figure. Zolin was staring, too, one hand creeping to his dagger. Naia licked her lips and took a single step closer to the Shroudling.

The figure was more definite today than it had been the first time. Long hair was braided away from the face and tumbled down over thin shoulders. Those huge violet eyes seemed almost liquid. The Shroudling had its face turned toward Naia. It stretched out its hand, only pausing when it was so close Naia could feel the cold radiating off it.

"I've read your letters," Naia whispered. "I've dreamed about Silverdene. I don't know what happened, though." Her heart was racing in her chest. "Can you show me?"

Chapter Twenty-Seven

WATER SLAPPED AGAINST SOMETHING, *a strangely muted sound. Zera looked up, but all she could see was the mist, thick and swirling around her. She had to be close, though, unless she was hearing things. There were no shoals between Ranarr and the mouth of the river.*

Zera stumbled. One foot broke through, splashing into the ocean. She sucked in a breath and sent a silent plea to the spirits.

The mist had carried her this far, far across the surface of the bay, past the point of turning back—but she was reaching the end of her strength. Perhaps the spirits were, as well. They were powerful, but not omnipotent.

She heard it again, the slap of water. Zera dragged in a breath, straining to hear beyond the muffling thickness. There! The sound was waves breaking against rock! She had reached Ranarr!

Dragging in another, sobbing breath, Zera forced herself to take several more halting steps. Her footing pitched suddenly, throwing her off balance. She stumbled several more steps, felt her balance going. She threw her arms out to catch herself. She was so close! She couldn't fall now!

But she couldn't regain her footing. The mist was thinning into wisps that slipped through her fingers. Her toes were wet. Water splashed rudely against her face, so different from the gentle pat of the mist on her cheeks.

"Please!" she gasped, and pitched forward.

She was caught by strong human arms. Arms that closed around her, keeping her from falling. But were they friend or foe?

Zera struggled, too weak to break the hold on her. The arms loosened a little, holding her more gently, as if their owner wanted to soothe her terror.

"Lady Mistwalker, you are safe," rumbled a man's voice. "I welcome you to the Sanctuary Deep and extend our grace to you. You are safe."

Zera's eyelids fluttered closed. She wanted so badly to rest. But even if she was safe, she still hadn't completed her mission. "I am not a mistwalker," she rasped.

The man lifted her easily, though his hold was still gentle. "I make bold to contradict you, lady, but I have just seen you walk in the mist across the bay."

He was carrying her somewhere. She tried to resist snuggling against his chest, but he was so warm. The mist, though it had shrouded and protected her, clung to her with a bone-penetrating chill. Her clothes were soaked through, and she could feel her teeth chattering.

"I am..." She struggled to find her voice. "I am Zera nas Vyx, mistwarrior and warleader's daughter."

The man's stride never faltered, but she thought she heard his heart speed up under her ear. "Then I welcome you, Mistwarrior Zera nas Vyx. Allow this servant of the Deep to shelter you in the Sanctuary. I will give you food and dry clothes and a place to rest, and you will apprise me of your purpose here."

Zera lost track of time. She felt hands undressing her, drying her, and wrapping her in clean clothes. She was able to swallow hot broth when it was held to her lips. But her eyes felt as if they were sealed shut. She could pry them open for brief glimpses of her attendant, enough to see his chalky-gray skin and dark beard. But each time she opened them for a shorter and shorter length of time.

At some point, he must have left her. At some point, she slept.

Naia reeled back, bumping into the bard. Ellyl's fingers gripped Naia's elbow, holding her up.

"It was your kingdom first," Naia gasped. "The outlanders invaded and took your land from you, and then they called your land Amethir and kept it for themselves!"

She could feel the rightness of it as she spoke. The Shroudlings—the *Srelang*—had been the native inhabitants, the Crelin the aggressors. That invasion had sown the seeds of the Shroudling war all those years ago, whenever the invaders had come.

"The last war was just you trying to take your land back, wasn't it?" she whispered. "The warleader's sacrifice *did* raise the Shroud, bringing it up to protect your people. And then something happened, twenty years ago, and the Shroud began to fail. That was why no one knew where you'd even come from—because you'd never really been gone, just hidden!"

"The Srelang dwelt in the mists, biding time until the gods and spirits called them forth," Ellyl said. They were almost singing rather than speaking. "The sleepers awoke and the singers returned, and now the very world is twisted on its foundation."

The Shroudling still stood, head bowed, in front of them. Her hair had tumbled around her shoulders, both hands raised to cover her face. Her shoulders moved as if she were weeping.

"You aren't the warleader," Naia realized. "You're the warleader's daughter. You're Zera."

The Shroudling lifted her face, and Naia knew she'd guessed right.

"Your mother sent you away before the siege," Naia whispered. "She gave you the treaties and letters to carry for her. Were those—your shoes I found?" But they had been so small! "Your daughter's?"

Those huge violet eyes fixed on Naia's face. What did the tracery on her face mean? Was it a signifier of her position?

Did it indicate whether she was a magic user or a warrior? Was it her family lineage?

"There's so much we still don't know."

Ellyl's hand rested on Naia's shoulder. "But you know so much more than you did," they said. "Well done, Naia Sedorr."

Naia turned her head to look at the hand, then followed the arm up to Ellyl's shoulder, to the dark hair and blade-thin nose. "You know more than you're saying," she accused. She could almost imagine the tattooed tracery across Ellyl's fine cheekbones and sharp chin. "You're a Shroudling too, aren't you?"

There was a long silence as amethyst eyes met darker ones.

Ellyl's thin lips twisted, but Naia couldn't read the emotion there. "I am descended from the Srelang people, yes. We—my people—keep the lore, and after the Shroud began to fail, we deemed it time to wander the world outside again."

"But you didn't tell me any of this before!"

"I couldn't." Ellyl huffed a sad laugh. "I knew you were asking about Silverdene, yes, but how could I know what you intended to do with that knowledge? We have not had good luck sharing our secrets with others."

Zolin stared at Ellyl, a sinking feeling in his stomach. How could he feel betrayed by someone he knew so little? And yet somehow, their failure to share every detail of their life before coming to Ranarr felt like a complete betrayal.

He shook his head slightly, trying to clear it of undue emotion. If he were calm, if he channeled his energy properly, he could make Ellyl tell them what they knew.

"Ellyl, do you mean to say that you know more of the lore we have uncovered than you had shared with us?" he asked, curving his hands to form a cup for the energy of the Deep. He was quite certain he sounded reasonable.

He wasn't sure why the bard drew back from him.

"Zolin, *stop*," Naia said, and something in her voice made him pause and look at her.

Naia gazed back at him severely, her eyes steady on his. "Whatever this strange magic is that you are learning, it is unfair to use it against someone who has only ever shown themself to be our ally." She folded her arms across her chest. "I have *never* known you to be so rude."

It hit him like a slap across the face. They had been friends for years, and yet she called him *rude*? How could she think—But he had *made* her think it, hadn't he?

Zolin bowed slightly, one palm pressed hard against his chest. "I apologize most deeply," he said. "I should not have reacted with such emotion. Clearly I am not yet fit to become a mentee to one of our great Diplomatic masters."

He heard Naia's slow exhale, which told him that she believed him, that she trusted in his repentance. He did not hear a similar reaction from Ellyl.

He met the bard's violet eyes. "I promise you, Ellyl, bard of Amethir, bard of Srelang, that I wish you nothing but good." His voice was husky, but he hoped it conveyed his genuine intent. "I pledge to you, Ellyl, that I bear no ill will toward the Srelang kingdom or people," he murmured, "and that I wish more than anything to broker peace for your people within the current political world."

He wasn't sure what Naia's snort indicated. Did she think he was being overly dramatic? But this moment felt important. It felt as if this might be exactly why Zolin had been called to the Deep. He waited.

Ellyl's chest rose in a deep inhalation. The bard pushed their dark hair back behind one slender, slightly pointed ear.

"I accept your pledge, Zolin Leite of the Ranarri Diplomats," they said in their own husky voice. "I accept that you intend no ill to me or my lords or mine own people. I pledge to you yourself that I intend no ill will to you or your lords or your own people." Those violet eyes darted to Naia's and pierced her with a lancing gaze. "I pledge that I intend no ill will to Naia or Zolin, partners in diplomacy and discovery, or to their teachers and mentors."

Zolin wanted to snap for Ellyl to leave Naia out of it, but he recognized in himself both a strange possessiveness and a strange resistance. He had no right to try to protect Naia from her own discoveries. He glanced at Naia, whose mouth had dropped open in pure astonishment. Beside her, Yar was grinning in delight. Zolin wondered how much Yar had known, or guessed, based on things his dragon had told him in private.

"Secrets upon secrets," he murmured. He let his gaze rest speculatively on the younger man for another moment, then turned back to Ellyl.

"What would you have of us, Ellyl?"

The bard, for the first time, seemed almost at a loss. They looked down at a stone shelf that glistened from the mist condensing on its lip. Finally Ellyl shook their head.

"I am no mistwalker. I don't possess any of the magic of my kindred. I knew there was a chance the warleader's daughter had escaped the Great Sacrifice, but there was never any evidence. So I and some few of my folk set out into the wider world, to pursue any whisper we might hear." They chuckled, an oddly bitter sound. "I don't think any of us believed we would ever find anything."

Yar reached out and put a hand on Ellyl's shoulder, just for a moment. "I set out into the wider world myself, not so long ago," he told them. "The Voices in my head drove me mad, and I wasn't sure I'd find them, but I did. You've met Xellax."

Ellyl's drawn expression cleared a little and they smiled at Yar. "Do you think there's a dragon waiting at the end of my quest, young prophet?"

"I'm no prophet," Yar muttered. "So whatever I say doesn't matter. But I think there's *something* waiting. And I think we ought to meet it."

"Well spoken," Naia murmured. "I think maybe it's time for us to approach Masters Bekir and Revalis. Tell them what we know and what we think, and see if they will pursue justice for the Srelang people."

"Justice for the Srelang?" Ellyl pursed their lips. "Do you truly believe it is so easy?"

Naia laughed sharply. "Easy? Not at all. There's already one war in Amethir, or had you forgotten? Justice for the Srelang might well provoke another. But..." She shook her head. "But this knowledge coming to light, of what happened before, of how the current king is only the descendant of invaders... That might give the Diplomats cause to intervene."

"Zera said she was going to the high king at Ranarr," Zolin remembered suddenly. The vision clung to him as thick as the mist that surrounded them. "Why did she think there was a high king here?"

"Ranarr has ever been the arbiter of justice," Yar said unexpectedly. "But the high king's authority toppled when he failed to defend the Srelang from their invaders." His eyes flashed silver in the dim light. "Xellax says that was when the dragons withdrew from Ranarr. But now she thinks perhaps this is why the sleeping gods awake. The time for justice is due."

Chapter Twenty-Eight

ARAMA FELT DISORIENTED WHEN she woke in the infirmary of the Sanctuary Deep. The peacehealer had soothed the swelling where she'd been hit, and whatever he'd done had soaked into her brain, easing the spinning and unsteadiness. It wasn't gone, but when she sat up in her bed, she didn't feel like heaving her guts up.

What had woken her? She frowned through the darkened room. She was the only patient, so she had the ward to herself, but the door at the far end of the room stood half-open. The peacehealer had told her he would be close enough to call out. The warm, steady light of a lantern shone in the next room, but didn't spill far into the ward.

Arama took an experimental deep breath, pleased to find that it didn't make her shoulder twinge at all. She'd never been tended by a peacehealer before, but she thought Amethir should send folk for training at Ranarr. Clearly they had superior skills here, and perhaps it was something that could be trained.

Voices caught her attention. A woman and man arguing, it sounded like. No, a woman and two men. Was that Bekir's voice? The woman's voice had the cold, even quality of the Diplomat. Had Yar and the trainees come back?

"I don't wish to wake the captain until she wakes on her own." That was the peacehealer, the first clear words she could make out.

The woman said something she couldn't hear, and then there was a lower rumble that must be the other man.

Arama sighed. Obviously they wanted her, and since she *had* woken on her own, the peacehealer could hardly complain.

She swung her legs over the side, wincing at the cold stone floor under her bare feet. She was wearing only an oversized tunic, so she tugged until the blanket came off her bed. She wrapped it around herself as she walked to the doorway.

Antos preserve, she always took her sound body for granted until something took that away. She must learn to appreciate every moment she was able to walk without effort.

She leaned against the doorframe, feeling weak and headachy but not dizzy.

"She has woken on her own," Arama announced. It would have been much more dramatic if her voice hadn't cracked on the second word.

She grinned ruefully as the people assembled in the room turned to face her.

The peacehealer was seated at a work table, remedies of some sort spread out in front of him. Bekir lounged against the wall opposite Arama; he flashed a grin at her when their eyes met. Revalis stood with folded arms, tall and resembling nothing so much as the great herons said to carry the ghosts of drowned ship captains. The last person in the room, leaning over the work table, was a short, muscular woman with close-cropped brown hair. As she realized Arama's gaze was on her, she wiped the anger from her expression and straightened.

"Very well, Inkeri. You wished to see Captain Dzornaea." Bekir's voice was acerbic. Arama still had trouble believing he was a Diplomat, but she was coming to realize there were Diplomats and then there were *Diplomats*.

Inkeri was obviously one of the former. She gave Arama a straight-backed bow, her gaze apparently on Arama's shoulder. Her face betrayed no emotion as she said, "Captain Dzornaea, I have come to extend my deepest regrets for the actions of one of my students."

Arama blinked. "All right."

Bekir snorted. "Arama's met a fair few students recently, Inkeri. Would you like to be more specific?"

The woman darted a look at him, and for a moment Arama almost thought she could detect irritation. "If you would let me continue, Bekir?"

He made a generous gesture as if he were conceding.

Inkeri clasped her hands in front of her. "Captain, the injury and indignity that have befallen you are my fault. I have foolishly allowed myself to be guided by sentiment in my dealings with Shirin Terezein. Because of this sentiment, I overlooked signs that she was...faltering in her training."

Revalis coughed.

Inkeri huffed what almost sounded like an actual sigh. Arama found herself both feeling sorry for and amused by the woman's struggle. "Her family lost its status and fortune earlier this spring, and we believed—we hoped—she would accept her lot and settle into her training." She pursed her lips and said, "*I* hoped she would. Revalis and Bekir have never been of the same mind."

"In a point of fairness, several other training masters did agree with you," Revalis said.

Arama decided it was time to take pity on the woman. "I understand it was Shirin Terezein who informed the Strid I was here. As I recall, the bounty was quite a large one." She let her pride about that show in her grin. "If I'm being honest, it's on me as much as anyone. I knew there was a bounty on my head, and I'd allowed myself to forget about it."

"In a point of fairness," Bekir said, glancing slyly at Revalis, "you did have a civil war and shipwreck to deal with." Revalis coughed again.

Arama chuckled. "It still isn't a good idea to forget that Harkai of Strid wants you dead or alive." She looked over at the peacehealer. "If we're going to be discussing all this, could I have something to eat?"

"You aren't feeling nauseous at all?" he inquired. When Arama shook her head, he stood and went to the door.

"If I had been more vigilant, Shirin wouldn't have felt at liberty to betray you," Inkeri said.

Arama sat in an available chair, pulling the blanket tighter around herself as she folded her arms. "Very well, I accept your regrets. Please stop apologizing now." When it came right down to it, it wouldn't hurt to have a Ranarri Diplomat in her debt. Perhaps something good would still come of losing the *Dawn Star*.

"Thank you." Inkeri didn't relax.

The peacehealer came back into the room, followed by a young woman carrying a tray. She held it patiently as he gathered his remedies out of the way. When they unloaded the tray, it had not only broth and bread for Arama, but a pot of tea and several cups.

"We did fail in our duty to safeguard you, Captain Dzornaea," Revalis said. "That the Strid would even attempt to collect on a bounty while they were berthed in our neutral city is a sign that King Harkai has grown too bold. I, too, bear some of the blame, for I brokered a peace that Harkai betrayed. In so doing, he showed the world that Ranarri Diplomats can be defied. It was my greatest failure."

Arama blinked as realization stole through her. She didn't just have *one* Diplomat in her debt. She had the whole bloody lot of them. She fought a sudden urge to grin fiercely at them. Though Bekir didn't seem to mind outward expressions of emotion, the other two would obviously respect her more if she could keep her exultation to herself.

"It is possible that Ranarri intercession in the civil war in Amethir might restore some of your standing," she suggested, keeping her voice as neutral as she could.

"That is a conclusion we have also reached," Revalis said. "Although it was not our intention to approach you with it in the middle of the night, Inkeri felt her honor could not withstand another moment's delay."

Arama was shocked to see a line of pink burn along Inkeri's chalk-colored cheeks. So Diplomats did *have* emotions, after all! To keep herself from commenting on it, she took a bite of her bread.

"I believe our best course of action will be to outfit you with a ship," Bekir said. "One large enough, obviously, to accommodate your dragon companion, as well as a contingent of Ranarri Diplomats...and Diplomat mentees, I think." He exchanged a glance with Revalis. "We recently determined that the current class of trainees should be graduated ahead of schedule. Due in part, I must confess, to the fact that your people seem intent on killing one another and spreading your unruly weather to all corners of the world."

Arama snorted. "Believe me, the prince is doing his best to put a stop to that."

"Indeed." Bekir sipped his tea and then made a face. "What is Amethir, without her stormwitchery?"

Arama took a sip, too, and understood his expression. The tea was barely tepid. These Ranarri and their strange habits! "Well, Diplomat Bekir, I think it's past time for us to discover just that."

Naia looked at her companions, seeking in their faces the anger that was twisting her gut. Yar leaned against an archive shelf, frowning at his laced fingers. Ellyl looked more sad than angry, their gaze on one of the flickering lamps. Zolin, though… She met his gaze and a chill rushed through her.

Zolin's gaze was hot, his jaw clenched. His fingers were still curved to cup light, but the tendons stood out on the backs of his hands, and the light they cupped was faint.

Zolin was angry.

She didn't know whether to be satisfied or nervous. This new path he had chosen—or had been chosen by—had no strictures against expressing emotion, it seemed, and her best friend suddenly looked like a stranger. He didn't look away from her, unflinching in his anger. She wondered if he'd always been angry, and just better at hiding it. But then he spoke, and she changed her mind.

"Everything we believe in," he said, his voice low. Ellyl lifted their head and turned to look at him, but Zolin still held Naia's gaze. "Everything they *made us* believe in. Justice. Objectivity. Evenhanded judgment." His eyes glittered, and Naia realized they held unshed tears. "Everything they molded us to be, Naia. It was all a *lie!*"

Naia blinked several times, trying to catch up to him. "Zolin, what—"

"They told us we were superior because we were Diplomats," he said. "They said we were fair, unbiased observers.

They said we preserved peace, we protected the undefended. They said we were the only ones who could do so because we were *Diplomats*." He shook his head, a tear streaking down his cheek. "But it's all built on a lie. The Ranarri and their so-called 'arbiter of justice' abandoned an entire people to annihilation!"

Naia opened her mouth, but she was still unsure what she should say when the silvery light in the room brightened until she had to squint. It washed out the flickering light from Zolin's cupped hands as well as the light from their lamps. It drew all of their attention to the Shroudling, who stood alone in the middle of the room.

"I think she has more to show us," Ellyl whispered.

The Shroudling spread her hands in an invitation. Her expression held sorrow and anger, but it also held an emotion Naia couldn't name. She was looking at Naia and Zolin, her lips curving in a strange smile.

"Lady, you showed us some of what happened," Naia said. "Can you show us the rest?"

Beside her, Zolin made a noise in his throat. The Shroudling stretched one hand out to him, as if inviting him to clasp it.

"Let me lend you strength, lady," Zolin said. He stretched his own hands out toward her. As Naia watched, he took a deep breath and then blew it out. With it he seemed to blow out his anger, because his next movements were almost fluid with grace. He moved his arms in an arc, describing a huge, invisible sphere. He must be summoning power somehow, because his next movement lifted and held it out to the Shroudling. Her smile widened as she gestured her acceptance of his offering.

The room washed in a flash of silver so bright Naia squeezed her eyes shut.

When she opened them again, they were no longer in the archive.

Zera didn't wake until the servant of the Deep returned. The light of his lantern pressed against her closed eyelids like sunshine. She wondered if the sun had risen, if the sacrifice had been offered.

Had it been accepted?

The servant of the Deep was accompanied by a great ox of a man wearing a golden circlet. The big man stood straight and tall, gazing down at Zera. She stared back at him unabashed. She was too tired for courtesy.

His hair was grizzled and he bore a day's worth of whiskers. His skin was pocked and lined. His jaw was firm, his lips unsmiling. There were shadows under his eyes.

"You are the high king," she rasped.

He twitched, though he couldn't be surprised at her recognition, not when he was wearing that circlet. "I am." His voice was deep. It seemed the voice of a storyteller. The high king was said to love song, she remembered.

"I am Zera nas Vyx, mistwarrior and warleader's daughter." She was too weak to sit up; her muscles wouldn't obey her. She did her best to sound authoritative. "I come on behalf of Danae, queen of the Srelang, and our people. The outlanders have broken the treaties. They have slaughtered

my people, stealing our land and driving us into the mountains."

The high king's expression didn't change. "What do you expect me to do?"

Her eyes flew open wide. "Hold the Crelin to their sworn word!" She tried again to sit up, and this time she managed to pull away from the bed a little, until her stomach muscles screamed and she collapsed back. "Give my people justice!"

His eyes were the color of stone. "What justice do you think there is to be had, Zera nas Vyx?" He shook his head. "You may stay here safe from the destruction your people face. But there is nothing I can do for you."

Her chest was tight. She clutched at it. "The treaties—" she began.

"—are only worth as much as I can enforce them," he snapped. "The Vedick and the Crelin together are too great for any army I could field, and they are leagues away. If they come at Ranarr, we can sink and burn their ships and keep them at bay. But we cannot cross the ocean and half of your land to fight them in defense of a kingdom that has fallen."

The servant of the Deep had been silent, but now he said, "Eminence, we witnessed those treaties. Send the Shadows and the Deep against the Crelin, and we could join the remainder of the Srelang to defeat them."

Barely even looking at him, the high king drew his blade and thrust it into the man's side. "I will not sacrifice my kingdom for one that has failed," he said, and let the man slide, gasping, to the floor.

"Then you are also forsworn." Zera's panicked desperation fell away with that realization. She had failed. There was nothing more she could do. She had cursed Holywell. Would the spirits listen to one more curse?

"Who is going to know?" the high king hissed, and his blade opened her throat.

He stood for what seemed like a long time, watching as she and the servant of the Deep bled. It couldn't really have taken her long to die, but at last the high king turned on his heel and left the room. He didn't even spare a glance for the fallen man he left behind.

The servant of the Deep was still breathing, the shuddering, shallow gasps of someone whose lungs were filling with his own blood. But after the high king left, he dragged himself to Zera's bedside.

"I cannot save you, lady," he whispered. "I cannot even save myself. But I swear to you that your mission will not fail."

His hands were moving in a strange, graceful pattern, touching only the air. She thought she could see golden tracery following his fingers, but her eyes were dimming.

"I feared treachery. I hid your pack." The man's head drooped. Blood drooled from his lower lip. But he smiled. "Your story will be told."

CHAPTER TWENTY-NINE

T HE LIVING TABLEAU FADED. Zera's ghost stood silently, head bowed. Her form was dimmer, as if completing her tale had taken too much energy. Or perhaps now that her story was told, she would be able to rest.

Zolin blinked at his companions. The others looked as stunned as he felt. They all had wet cheeks. Ellyl's face was buried in their hands. Yar had his eyes closed tightly, and he looked like his entire body was tensed. Naia looked at Zolin, and their gazes met.

"She went all that way, only to be betrayed," she said brokenly.

Zolin tried to go to Naia and was surprised by his knees refusing to hold him. He sank to the ground, light-headed. Oh, yes, he had given Zera his power, hadn't he?

Naia's hands clasped around his. "This is why you were called," she said. "This is why I was called. We have to tell the others."

"Xellax says the others will come." Yar sighed. "They didn't know the extent of the betrayal. The dragons will bear witness."

Ellyl's voice was hollow. "What good is bearing witness now?"

Naia's hands squeezed Zolin's. "I don't know," she said. "But it is never too late to bear witness."

At Naia's words, Zera lifted her head. She was still solemn, but Zolin thought her expression was satisfied. She began to fade, the mist dispersing, until she had vanished from sight. Zolin wondered if any of them would ever see Zera again.

They couldn't go straight to Masters Bekir and Revalis, of course. Zolin had drained himself by helping Zera show her fate. He couldn't have walked all the steps to the Sanctuary infirmary even with assistance. He couldn't help but wish fiercely for his master, thinking of the unashamed tears Bekir had shed before. It seemed suddenly as if nothing would be better than for Bekir to wrap him in strong arms and let him cry.

He hadn't cried in so long. He was afraid of what might happen if he let that dam burst.

Naia exhaled softly. Her fingers squeezed his again. "Master Bekir," she said.

Then Bekir was kneeling beside Zolin, his gaze concerned and somehow also proud. "I felt your summons," he said, giving Zolin a crooked smile. "Thank the god I thought to bring the healer with me."

"You overstretched yourself," the peacehealer said, handing him a vial of pure trynen. "It isn't uncommon with newly called Servants of the Deep. You'll mend and find yourself stronger next time. Down that," he added, nodding to the vial. "It'll help, though it won't taste good."

There was a flurry of activity as Zolin was bundled onto a stretcher, wrapped in blankets, and borne back to the Sanctuary infirmary. Naia walked beside him. She had to; he couldn't pry his fingers loose from hers. She didn't seem to mind.

When they were finally ensconced in the infirmary once more, Zolin was tucked into a cot next to Captain Dzornaea. She sat propped up against the headboard. Zolin had to content himself with being raised into a half-sitting position by a wall of pillows.

Refreshments were brought, and Zolin was dosed with more trynen and a stimulating tea. Then finally the story could be told.

Naia started with her first encounter with the Shroudling and discovery of the documents. When she reached the part where Zolin stumbled out of the Sanctuary stairs and into her library nook, Bekir and Revalis both laughed. Zolin found himself staring at Revalis, whose expression slowly faded back to solemnity. The master lowered one eyelid in a slow blink.

The story seemed to take a long time to tell. At one point, Zolin drifted off, though he was still aware of Naia's voice talking, and then Ellyl's. Finally they came to the end, when they saw Zera's fate—and that of the servant of the

Deep who had aided her. Zolin sat up in bed to tell that part.

When they finished, Bekir released a deep sigh. "The Sanctuary's records go back a long time, but there is no mention of a high king anywhere that I have seen."

Revalis shook his head. "I always knew there were secrets buried in our past. Perhaps dangerous ones, yes, but I never imagined anything like this."

"What will you do, Master Diplomats?" Ellyl asked. Their voice was husky and deceptively low. From where he sat, Zolin could see their graceful fingers twined tightly together.

Revalis and Bekir exchanged a long look. Zolin couldn't read everything in that look, but it almost seemed as if they were having a silent conversation. At last Revalis sighed.

"We will make copies of the documents and take ship for Amethir. I don't know how the king will react, but it must be made known."

"Prince Vistaren would listen to you," Yar said.

"Prince Vistaren is a rebel," Revalis pointed out gently.

"But he's on the right side!" Yar's expression was mulish.

"I said nothing about right and wrong, lad. I speak of the power to take action on this revelation."

"And what makes you think King Rekel will respect this revelation any more than he did the one brought by Voice of Dragons?" Ellyl asked.

A brief look of annoyance crossed Revalis' face before he smoothed it out again. Zolin could hardly believe it. Revalis had always seemed so stoic!

"We will have to build contingency plans, of course," Revalis told Ellyl. "I do not have all the answers for you at this moment, bard of Srelang. But I swear to you, we won't let this be swept away again."

Zolin was surprised by a yawn that felt like it would split his face. Bekir saw it and chuckled. "I think we all need some sleep. In the morning, Revalis and I will convene the inner council. Whatever actions we take, we must take them in unity."

Zolin thought Bekir might have said something more, but he was burrowing back into his blankets and not listening. Sleep beckoned.

Naia knew she ought to be sleeping. Everyone else was—Master Bekir in his study, Arama and Zolin in the infirmary, Yar curled up with his dragon, and everyone else in the dormitory they'd used earlier. Even Master Revalis was sleeping.

Naia had tried to sleep, but there was so much in her mind she couldn't settle. After half an hour of trying not to wake the others with her tossing and turning, she slipped out of the dormitory in her bare feet. Outside the chamber, she felt less suffocated, though the air was still warm. She made her way along the passage, wishing she could conjure light in her hands the way Zolin could.

At the next intersection of hallways, she took the lantern hanging there. Leaving a pool of darkness behind her would help her find her way back, when she was ready to sleep. The Sanctuary Deep was still a fathomless mystery to her, though she could easily see Zolin was entirely in his element down here.

She felt a cool breeze kiss her cheeks and turned instinctively toward it. The large windows that opened over the ocean would provide some relief. After two more turnings, she realized she was in the rookery, where the dragon had chosen to bunk down with the ravens. She could hear the slow, deep breathing of a great creature in slumber. She wondered what it was like to sleep against those elegantly scaled sides. Yar was tucked against Xellax's foreleg, a dim shape in the darkness.

Naia turned down the wick of the lantern, not wanting to wake either of them. She skirted around the edge of the room until she reached the wide window ledge that looked out over the water. The pounding of surf against the White Stone added a sleepy susurrus to the sound of the dragon's breathing.

She settled the lantern on the ledge and then lifted herself up to sit on it, leaning her back against the stone. Outside, the moon was nearly full; its glow was bright enough that, had she been above stone, she wouldn't need a lantern.

"What now?" she whispered, staring at the white foam of the waves. Justice for the Srelang, but would Naia get to play any part in that? She'd discovered the documents; she ought to have a right to be part of that. She could visit Amethir, just as she'd always wanted. And better yet, perhaps she could help bring peace back to Amethir.

Something rustled deeper in the room, and Naia turned to look. Yar was approaching, hair tousled and mouth open in a yawn.

"I didn't mean to wake you," Naia whispered.

Yar grinned. "Xellax says you're the loudest mouse she's ever seen."

Naia cast a glance through the dimness to where the dragon was still lying, chin resting on the stone. "I'm sorry."

Yar shook his head. "It's all right. My thoughts have been bouncing around. I think the peacehealer gave Zolin something to help him sleep. He should have given that to all of us."

Naia smiled a little. "I'm glad it's not just me."

"I think this is all as it was meant to be." Yar came to stand next to her, propping his elbows on the stone ledge. "Xellax says we have an opportunity to mend two wrongs with this." He glanced over at Naia. "But she doesn't think there's any point in going to the Amethirian king."

"You've met him, haven't you?" Naia asked. "What's he like?"

"Proud. Kind, but in a thoughtless way. I wanted to like him." Yar fidgeted.

"Wanted to. But you didn't?"

"He was too proud. He wouldn't listen to Xellax. I don't mind him not listening to me, I'm just a boy. But he should have given more weight to what Xellax and the other dragons sent me to say." He frowned. "Will you and Zolin and Ellyl come back with us?"

Naia raised her eyebrows. "I hope so. But I may not have any say in it. I was in disgrace with Master Revalis before all this." Her cheeks burned at the memory. "I can't believe I hit Shirin."

"She deserved it."

Naia giggled and then sighed. "I didn't know that at the time. I was just at the end of my patience. I'm glad I did it, but the masters might decide not to let me graduate. If they fail me out of the training, I won't have anything left."

"If they fail you out of the training, they'll have to fail me out, too," said Zolin's voice from the darkness.

Naia straightened. "You ought to be in bed," she told him.

"So should you ought to be," Zolin countered. He was smiling. Naia must be getting used to seeing him smile, because his expression sent a hum of contentment through her. "But I wanted to check on you, and I saw you slip out of the dormitory, so I followed you here."

"So many loud little mice," Yar said, and laughed.

"I beg your pardon, Lady Xellax," Zolin said, looking in her direction. "But I had to know if Naia was all right."

Naia blinked. "Why wouldn't I be? We solved the mystery. We answered the questions and found out what happened to the writers of all those letters."

Zolin's smile went a little crooked. "Yes. I imagine finishing your final project will seem dull compared to all this."

She shrugged. "I just wish I'd been able to tell Zera goodbye. How long had she been waiting there for someone to find her? Was she trapped in that place? Or did she just appear because I was searching?"

"I don't know a lot about the magic of the Deep yet," Zolin said. "I'm not even sure what that servant of the Deep did to make sure her story was preserved. Did he make her a ghost?"

"Does it matter?" Yar asked, surprising her.

"I suppose not." Naia looked out across the water again. "I hope she can rest now. Now that her mission is accomplished."

No one answered. Something about the quality of their silence made her turn.

"Oh," she breathed. "It's you."

The Shroudling stood a few paces away, her liquid gaze on Naia's face. Her hands were clasped loosely in front of her. Tendrils of mist curled up around her, glowing a faint silver.

"I'm glad we met," Naia said. "I'm sorry it's taken this long for someone to find your story."

The Shroudling—Zera—smiled. It was a surprisingly sweet smile, unfettered with grief or rage. It made Naia wonder what Zera's life would have been like, if the Crelin had never invaded. She was training as a mistwalker. Naia wasn't certain what that entailed, but it seemed more peaceful than the path Zera eventually took.

"I hope you can rest now."

Zera bowed her head momentarily. She was still smiling. Naia reached out, her fingers stopping before they entered the glow that surrounded Zera.

"I think she will," Zolin murmured.

As they watched, Zera's glow brightened until they had to squint. And then, with a last flare of light, she was gone.

CHAPTER THIRTY

IT HAD BEEN YEARS since Arama Dzornaea sailed any ship but her own *Dawn Star*. She knew it would take time to settle into a new ship. The Ranarri Diplomats had spent the past week outfitting for her the *Aurora*, an Amethirian-built merchant vessel. It had heavier guns than she was used to, having been converted in Corrone City some years back. The double-masted schooner was larger than she was used to, as well—but it would have to be, to have room for a dragon on deck. On the whole, although she would rather have never wrecked the *Dawn Star*, *Aurora* was a step up.

She heard footsteps behind her, and glanced over to see Mister Zek.

"She won't be as nimble," he said.

She had promoted him to first mate, as he was the most senior of the sailors who had survived the storm. It still twisted her gut a little to realize she would never sail with Mister Carig again, but she had high hopes for Zek.

"She'll handle the weather better, I'll warrant," Arama said. "And with the strange group we'll have sailing with us, I'll be glad of the bigger guns."

Zek scratched his head. "We're still short of a full crew."

"Not for long. If we were flying my own flag, it might make folk think twice before signing on." Arama grinned. "But since the Ranarri Diplomats have graciously allowed me to fly *their* flag, on the way to Maron, at least, I imagine we'll be crewed before sunset."

"Just so long as you don't get the itch to go a-pirating before we get there," Zek said, and grinned back at her.

"I wouldn't dare, with Bard Ellyl on board. If I'm going to be immortalized in song, I'd rather it be for my honor and bravery." She looked over to where several of their passengers were climbing the gangway.

Masters Revalis and Bekir led the way, followed by Zolin, Naia, and Ellyl. The bard was laughing at something, glancing over their shoulder to where Yar followed. Kinnet brought up the rear, the stormwitch still looking a little haggard.

"You've got enough of both, mum," Zek said. "I knew when I signed on that crewing your boat would never be boring."

"Stormsingers, sirens, Diplomats, and now dragons and Shroudlings to boot." Arama shook her head. "I think, just to be safe, we'll make an offering to Sea Lord Antos before we cast off. After all, boring isn't always a bad thing."

"Mister Carig would be proud."

Arama touched her forehead in a gesture of remembrance. "I hope so." She glanced up at the sun, judging the time. "The outbound tide'll be on us before we know it. Let's get the last of our cargo stowed below and make certain our passengers are well settled. Another week will see us in Maron."

"Captain Dzornaea, the Diplomat contingent is aboard." Revalis hesitated, then said, "Have you heard anything about Balahar Ingan?"

Bless me, that's *why he looks so familiar,* Arama thought. "General Balahar sided with the king." She studied Revalis' face, which was carefully expressionless. He and Balahar shared their height, though Balahar was blocky where Revalis was more slender. "Your older brother, is it?"

"Seven years. I'm afraid we have never seen eye-to-eye. I will let Bekir take the lead, if we encounter him."

Arama shook her head. "I don't doubt we'll encounter him, Master Diplomat. And here I thought I was in for a quiet cruise under Diplomatic immunity. But since we're already in the middle of one family quarrel between the king and the prince, we might as well add your family quarrel to the mix." She grinned. "Just as well. We wouldn't want to get bored."

Zolin leaned against the ship's rail, tilting his head back to let the breeze blow his hair from his face. The *Aurora* was outbound from Ranarr's harbor, the chanting of the crew hoisting the sails a pleasant backdrop to the sinking sun. He drew in a long, slow breath, his shoulders relaxing for what felt like the first time in weeks.

"I've never been on a ship so large," came Naia's voice, her footsteps soft on the deck as she joined him at the rail.

He opened his eyes and turned his head to her, not bothering to fight the wide grin that slipped across his face. "You're going to love it," he predicted.

"Have you?" She gripped the rail and leaned on it, her gaze toward the open sea.

He shook his head. "I've spent plenty of time on the water. Never out of sight of Ranarr, though." He hadn't really missed the life of a fisher family, but he'd never lost his love of the sea.

Someone shouted behind them, and the ship lurched as the sails caught the wind and snapped full. Naia gasped. When Zolin looked at her, her face shone with delight.

"You feel it, too, don't you?" he blurted.

"The freedom. No more trying to hide," she said, and relief washed over him as he realized they hadn't lost whatever understanding they'd always had between them.

So much had changed, and he was certain many more changes were ahead of them. But he and Naia would always have their friendship, and the events of the past few months had proven nothing could break that.

"Did Revalis actually say you're his mentee?" he asked Naia.

Their departure from Ranarr had been hastily arranged. The special trynen tea Master Bekir gave Zolin had helped rebuild his magical and spiritual strength, but Zolin had been forced to spend much of the intervening time in meditation and movement practices. Whatever Naia's status, she wasn't a Servant of the Deep, and her preparations had kept her busy quite apart from Zolin.

It hadn't bothered him the way it would have just a few weeks ago, but he was still curious.

Naia snorted. "I'm a probationary mentee. He said he believes strongly in my gifts, but that he also isn't entirely certain my gifts were given me to serve Ranarr alone. I have no idea what *that* means, and he won't explain, of course."

Zolin glanced sidelong at her. He could think of a lot of things that might mean. Perhaps she was destined not to be a Diplomat at all, but Revalis wanted to keep her talents at their disposal until she found her true calling. Perhaps there was yet another secret sect of Diplomats that Revalis had in mind for her, as Bekir had chosen for Zolin.

And perhaps she would become a great adventurer discovering lost archives and ancient civilizations, instead of brokering peace deals and struggling to hide her quick temper and sharp wit.

It didn't much matter either way to Zolin. Bekir had told him, that first evening when Zolin was recovering his strength, that he would know when his own calling had settled on him. Bekir was right.

Zolin knew now, in this moment, he had been called to be Naia's partner and protector. Wherever her path led, the Deep would carry him at her side.

"Well," he said, when he realized how long the silence had stretched, with only the crash of waves against the hull to break it, "whatever your gifts are meant for, we'll find out when we get to Amethir."

From the grin she flashed him, he knew she'd heard that "we" for what it meant. She straightened and tucked her hair behind her ear. "We will indeed."

Acknowledgements

A LOT OF PEOPLE think writing is a solitary endeavor. The act of getting words on paper can be solitary, that's for sure, but writing is definitely a team sport, as Rhonda Parrish often says. This book absolutely would not exist without the help of a lot of people. Inevitably, I'll forget to thank someone important, but I'm going to do my best.

Lauran, Stephanie D., Lisa, and Alena S. are among some of the most important people I need to thank. These women were a crucial physical and mental health support network for me during approximately three years of serious burnout, writer's block, chronic depression, and anxiety. Words can't express how much they helped me get back on my feet and back in the writer's chair. I don't think it's an exaggeration to say they saved my life as a writer.

Thank you to Clarie Taylor, Becca Syme, Susan Bischoff, Kelly O'Dell Stanley, and everyone else at the October 2023 Liberated Author Workshop. The twin tools of the Enneagram and CliftonStrengths have been invaluable as I worked to finish this novel and plot the final book in the Storms in Amethir series. Thanks also go to Sarra Cannon, whose HB90 quarterly planning system has fanned the flames of my authorly productivity this year—and will hopefully help me finish the first draft of *Witchery's End* before 2024 is out!

Thank you to my local critique group, who critiqued this story in its first incarnation as a novelette of around 10,000 words. Chelsea, Garrett, Holly, Jim[2], Laura, and Peggy—thank you for letting me spend the past decade sharing words and growing in craft with you all.

Thank you to Russell Nohelty, who has been an ongoing encouragement over the course of our acquaintance.

Thank you to Grace Bridges for a phenomenal editing job. I'm also extremely grateful to LVAB for introducing us!

My family has always believed in me. I'm fortunate enough to have had a grandmother who spent her life researching and writing a local history/memoir of the small town her ancestors founded. Between her example of long hours at the typewriter and my parents' love of reading, passed on to me with nightly read-aloud sessions, I'm not sure I could have escaped being a writer if I'd wanted to. Fortunately, I didn't want to.

Most of all, thank you to every single reader who has written to me in the past several years, asking if this series would ever be finished. Thank you to each and every person who preordered this book from the day it became available. Your questions, curiosity, interest, and encouragement has kept me going.

About the Author

Stephanie A. Cain writes epic and urban fantasy. She lives in Indiana, where she works at a small liberal arts college and is writing the next book in the Storms in Amethir series. She enjoys hiking, reading, birdwatching, and general geekery. She has three cats, which she is well aware puts her firmly in crazy cat lady territory, and owns way more dice and painted miniatures than she needs. She can be found online at StephanieCainOnline.com.

www.ingramcontent.com/pod-product-compliance
Lightning Source LLC
Chambersburg PA
CBHW071222210726
48293CB00002B/540